THI

Books by Janet Maile

Second Genesis

Final Illusion

The Pretzel Affair

Saving Grace

CHAPTER 1

Esther was confused. She had woken up in strange surroundings, covered in bruises. Her head hurt and she remembered nothing but her name. People came and went, sometimes prodding at her and other times just asking questions. On the eighth day, they came to her with clothes and told her to get dressed, then put her in a vehicle and drove her a long way away to a place she didn't know. Driving through narrow, tree-lined roads, they eventually reached a half-hidden sign, 'Concealed entrance' and the driver said, "We're here." He turned into a gap between the hedgerows onto a long gravel drive which led to a large, red-brick house with two tall chimneys symmetrically placed, one on the left and one on the right.

"Where is this?" Esther asked, but the driver did not reply. She stared at the white, double glazed front door with its decorative glass panel. It seemed as much a stranger here among the sash windows, wooden barge boards and terracotta chimneys as she was. She shielded her eyes from the sun and looked up at the front of the house. A Juliet balcony on the first floor faced a distant ridge of hills, the undulating form broken by a mobile telephone mast.

The man framed in the open doorway was about Esther's height, with dark hair cut short at the top and shaved at the sides. His smile was more of a grimace and it revealed a gap between his front teeth.

"Welcome," he said. "I've been waiting for you."

She hung back, but the driver took her arm and walked her to the house. "Don't leave me here," she said as the man in the doorway grabbed her arm and pulled her inside.

"This is where you live now," he said. "I'm Ray."

He kept hold of her arm and pushed her into a large room, locking the front door behind him. Chairs of different styles were ranged around the walls like a reception area. The only sound was the steady ticking of a round schoolroom clock that hung above the brick fireplace. She sat down and waited.

"I expect you'll be wanting a hot drink after the journey," Ray said. She had not heard him leave, but he was now standing in the doorway with a steaming mug. He took a coaster from a set on the mantelpiece and placed the cup down carefully on the glass topped coffee table. Esther took a sip. It was hot and sweet. "What is this?" she asked.

"It's coffee – the way you like it," he said. Coffee. She repeated the word, rolling it around her tongue. Did she drink coffee? She didn't know.

Ray left her alone. When she had finished the drink, she went into the hallway and stood, listening. A door opened and shut, and suddenly Ray was beside her, pointing upstairs. In the upper hallway, a door was open. "In there," Ray said.

Esther hung back. She did not like the look of the grey walls, the lime green duvet cover and curtains and black furniture. "Dinner in ten minutes," Ray said, going back downstairs.

Esther opened the wardrobe. Empty. It was the same with the chest of drawers. If this was her room, where were her clothes, her make-up, her brush and comb?

She opened the plastic bag they had given her before she left. Inside were a pack of five pairs of knickers, two bras and a blouse with a price tag of £6.99. Underneath was an envelope containing five crumpled £10 notes.

She went downstairs and sat on the bottom step, listening to the clatter of pans somewhere at the back of the house. After a while, Ray appeared with a pile of plates. "In here," he said, entering a room further along the hall that looked out onto a large garden. There were signs that it had once been loved, but brambles and nettles had been allowed a free rein, strangling the roses, geraniums and dahlias. In contrast, the lawn had been recently cut and sported neat stripes.

Four girls sat at an old refectory table that took up most of the space: a short brunette reading a magazine, a dark girl with her hands in her lap and her eyes downcast, a tall, skinny blonde listening to music on headphones and a plain girl with a square jaw who was staring at a blackbird pulling a worm out of the ground. They looked up as Esther entered the room but did not speak.

Ray put the plates on the table and said, "Fiona, Yasmeen, Leanne and Rachel." He pointed his thumb at Esther. "Esther."

The sun came through the small panes of stained glass at the top of the windows at an angle, making a pattern on the end of the table. Esther sat down on the bench and traced her fingers around the patches of sunlight, wondering if she should offer to help Ray carry the food from the kitchen.

She ate mechanically, chewing pieces of lamb and carrot, listening to snatches of conversation for clues that would tell her where she was and why she was here, but the only talk was about bus timetables and work.

She spent the evening watching the television with Ray. The girls were upstairs somewhere. She could hear muted snatches of music and the hum of the refrigerator, but otherwise the house was silent. When she asked Ray a question about the television programme, he ignored her. After a while, she went to her room and got ready for bed.

Suddenly, she was awake in a sweat, her heart pounding. She had been in a dark, damp room with no windows and walls that were grimy with black dust. The only way out was up steep wooden steps. As she started to climb, the staircase grew longer until she was too weary and turned back. She moved around wildly, trying to find a way out, knocking against objects scattered on the floor. Something landed on her head, a spider on a sticky thread. When she tried to brush it away, it stuck to her fingers, swaying backwards and forwards, staring at her with eyes that were two evil pinpricks of light. She opened her mouth to scream but no sound came out.

She shoved the crumpled covers aside and swung her legs onto the floor, moving shakily to the window where she took in great gulps of air and waited for her heart to return to normal. She would not sleep now. Leaving the bedroom door open to illuminate the corridor, she went to the top of the stairs and listened. The house was in darkness and the only sound was a gentle snoring coming from one of the rooms.

Suddenly, Ray was padding up the hall in his bare feet. "If you're going to wander about at night, I'll have to lock you in your bedroom," he said, pushing her back to her room.

In the morning, she awoke to the smell of bacon cooking, the terrors of the night forgotten. Downstairs, nobody was around, and there was only one place setting on the dining table. Esther sat down and waited. After a while, Ray appeared with a plate of bacon and eggs and a mug of coffee. "I let you sleep late," he said, "seeing as it's your first day."

As she ate, Ray pulled a piece of paper from his pocket and pushed it across the table to her. "You're to go here," he said. "I've programmed the Satnav. Just follow the directions."

"Where am I going?"

"They'll explain when you arrive." He handed her a key. "The blue Fiesta," he said. "You're only to use it when I say, otherwise you don't go beyond the drive. Do you understand?"

She nodded. It was just one of many things she didn't understand. Who was Ray, for example. Was he her husband or her brother? Who were the girls?

She didn't even know if she could drive, but when she was sitting behind the wheel, her hands took over and she was soon speeding along the road, following the mechanical voice. Shortly after passing a sign for Pilbury, she drew up at a small, terraced property with decorative olive trees in white pots spiralling up the wall. As she reached up to the knocker, the door opened a middle-aged woman stood framed in the doorway, severe and unsmiling.

"Come in, we've been expecting you," she said and Esther stepped gingerly into the dark hall. Reaching out to the wall to guide her, she made her way towards a room at the end of the corridor, followed so closely by the woman that she could feel her breath on the back of her neck.

"There's nothing to be worried about," the woman said. "Just go in and lay down on the couch."

A sense of dread washed over Esther as she entered the room. A thick blind shut out all daylight and she could see nothing until the woman turned on a small lamp on a side table. The room was small, no more than a cupboard really. Following instructions, Esther lay on the couch and allowed the woman to fix something to her head.

The woman left as a voice came through the headphones, a calm, confident, hypnotic voice. Esther closed her eyes and allowed the voice to take away her worries and lull her into a semiconscious state. It led her into a dark passage, the gloom broken only by a sliver of light which entered through a small, dusty window in the wall high above. It felt as if the curved ceiling was pushing down on her and she was being slowly compressed, like flowers in a flower press.

"Find the talisman," the voice said.

Esther could just make out a table placed against the wall, covered in a black cloth, which would have been invisible except for the shaft of moonlight reflecting off the silky surface. She ran her hand over the top of the table, searching.

"There's nothing here."

"Look again. Find the talisman."

She knelt down and moved her hands slowly over the cold flagstones beneath the table: nothing. She continued moving, crawling on the hard stone, sweeping her hands in front of her. Nothing. She stood up and ran her hands over the walls, looking for a crevice or a ledge. Nothing. As she reached the table again, a wisp of fog descended, swirling into a tiny tornado and settling on the table. As she reached out to touch it, it disappeared and there, in the centre of the table, was a rough orange and brown stone which glowed with an inner light.

"I have it," she said. She expected it to be light, ethereal, weightless, but it was solid and firm in her palm. The inner light faded until she was left in darkness once again.

"Go through the door."

She had not come across a door when she had searched for the talisman.

"There will be a door. Find the door."

Esther put the stone carefully in the pocket of her jacket and made her way around the room again, feeling for a door. When she reached the far corner, her finger caught on a splinter. A heavy wooden door encrusted with raised iron ornaments had appeared where there had been none before. As she searched the rough surface for a handle, iron nails caught her skin and a sharp pain shot along her hand.

"Go through the door."

Esther hesitated.

"Go through the door."

Esther moved forward cautiously, feeling for the edge of the door frame and moving into the space beyond. The door swung shut behind her with a clang, leaving her in complete darkness, for there was no window here.

She turned back, but the door had gone, cutting off her retreat. "I must go back," she cried, her voice echoing in the empty space.

The voice was unmoving, unmoved. "You cannot go back."

She scratched at the wall where the door had been, but it was now a solid wall. Her fingers traced several scratches low down as if someone – or something - had tried to break the door down with their fingernails. "Let me out. I must go home."

"You are safe. No harm can come to you. Put your arms out, see if you can feel anything."

"There's nothing here, I want to come back." There was no response. "Are you there?" she called.

"I am here." The voice sounded far away.

Esther sank to the ground. "Where are you going? Don't leave me here alone."

The voice was gone. She heard footsteps, loud footsteps that resonated on a stone floor on the other side of the door. Shrinking back into the wall, she forced herself to be still and silent. The door opened and in the faint light which struggled to illuminate the darkness, she saw the silhouette of a short, stocky man framed in the doorway, blocking the only way out. He wore a long, blue tunic fastened at the waist with a wide leather belt. His black cloak was held in place by a gold fastener in a delicate filigree pattern, studded with dark red rubies like droplets of blood.

He took a torch from the wall and thrust it inside the room. Esther shrank back as the heat from the flames reached her. "There's nobody here, it must have been rats," the man said, speaking to someone in the room beyond.

"I sometimes lock my daughter in here for her own good," came the response, "but she would not have got in by herself!" Both men laughed raucously and the door began to close.

CHAPTER 2

Rolf had been working for Sebastian Dayton for two years, since he had come to England from Poland. Seb had put him up in one of the houses he owned, renting him a room at a discount price. The former lounge/diner had been divided into three and Rolf's room, the middle one, had no window. He didn't mind. There were six other people in the house and it was noisy and crowded if they were all there, but Rolf hardly ever saw them. He spent most of his time out working so that he could send his wages back home to Anna in Poland. Things were hard for her: there was much she needed to buy for herself and their daughter, Lidia.

Seb was good at getting the work in. With his dark, brooding good looks, the ladies seemed to melt when he appeared. He oozed charm and authority and they trusted him. At first, Seb priced the job up and gave Rolf anything he didn't want to do, taking a commission, but now he hardly ever got his hands dirty, preferring to employ others to do the work. Rolf was careful and meticulous, and most of the time he was happy enough, but he didn't like it when Seb gave him second-hand parts to install and charged the customer the new price.

Rolf got back from work one evening to find Seb waiting for him. "I've got a special job for you," he said. "Let's go inside and I'll explain."

Rolf went to the kitchen, about to offer a coffee, but changed his mind when he saw the dirty dishes piled up in the sink, the grubby tea towel hanging from the top of the fridge and the bowl of mouldy fruit on the worktop. He led the way to his bedroom, which contained a narrow bed which was too short for him and a small metal rail, on which hung Rolf's best shirt and trousers. Rolf took off the blue, padded jacket that he'd got from the charity shop, and sat on the bed while Seb leaned against the wall.

"I want you to go and see this man," Seb began, handing Rolf a piece of paper on which he had written a name and address. "He's a private detective. My wife's gone."

Rolf wondered at the word "gone." He knew the word was used when someone died as well as when someone left. What did Seb mean? As he was wondering whether to ask, Seb went on, "I've known for some time that she's having an affair. She left a note – she's gone to live with him. I wouldn't care – we haven't exactly been getting on lately, but she's taken the child, *my* child. I don't want another man looking after her."

Rolf could understand that. He loved his daughter and missed her and would hate to think he would never see her again. "You go to police?" he asked.

"They're not interested. She's an adult, she hasn't broken any laws. She's left of her own accord, so there's nothing they can do. I want you to go to this Jonathan Whicher. He's a private detective. Ask him to find her. But my wife mustn't know I'm looking for them."

"OK, what do I tell Mr Whicher?"

"It's got to be *your* story. Just tell him your girlfriend's disappeared and you're worried. Give Whicher this address so nobody can trace it back to me. Have you got that?"

Rolf nodded. "I understand."

"There's £500 in it for you," Seb said.

£500 for half an hour with a private detective! Seb must want to find his wife badly. Rolf could not hide his delight. It brought him one step nearer to bringing Anna and Lidia over here to live.

"I tell my lady customer I will be there early tomorrow to finish her conservatory. You want I go there first?"

"No, go to Whicher first thing. I'll take care of the customer."

After two years, Rolf was pretty good at finding his way around London. He left his car at home and went by the Tube, coming out in a shabby, run down part of London. The address Seb had given him was a tall Victorian building that had recently had a facelift and now boasted new double glazed windows and shining new paint. A solid glass door led to various offices on the ground and first floors, but Seb had said to go round the side and enter through a slightly dilapidated wooden door. It opened onto a steep staircase which rose directly to the third floor, at the top of which was a door with a glass panel, etched with the words, Jonathan Whicher, Private Investigator.

The door stuck on the carpet. He squeezed through the gap and stood before a middle-aged woman with dyed blonde hair who was talking on the phone. A man of about the same age came out of the inner office, holding out his hand.

"Come in, come in. I must get that door fixed." He had been saying that for the past ten years, since he first set himself up in this office. "Jonathan Whicher. How can I help you?"

The inner office was untidy. Files stood or lay on the shelves without any obvious order. The desk was littered with telephone books, maps, a magnifying glass and a cup half full of some indeterminate liquid. A half dead plant stood on the window ledge behind heavy velvet curtains whose weight had pulled the curtain rail down at one end.

Jonathan removed a pile of files from the chair and Rolf sat down. "I'm looking for my girlfriend," he began. "She live with me but a few days ago, she not come home. She not answer her phone, and I worry about her."

"What's the girl's name?"

"Angela. Angela Connors."

Jonathan took down the details and explained his charges. "Don't worry," he said. "Most missing people turn up within a week, safe and sound. Keep your phone on you in case she contacts you."

Jonathan had been a detective for thirty years and knew the drill. He would start with the hospital. He knew a nurse who owed him a favour.

Cynthia was tired. She had just finished her shift at the hospital and was on her way back to the Nurses' Home, crossing the small hospital garden where patients sometimes sat. Stopping to look at the fish in the pond, she heard a familiar voice behind her. Smiling, she turned. Her old friend Jonathan. The first time they had met, she was just coming off shift at five in the morning on a cold, frosty winter's day and had slipped on a patch of ice and gone down hard. Jonathan had come to her rescue, lending her his arm to lean on and helping her to an all-night café where he had bought her a latte. She'd often seen him after that as she was coming off shift. Five in the morning was apparently a good time for catching people who weren't where they were supposed to be.

"Buy you a coffee?" he asked, as he always did whenever they met.

When they were settled in the café, Cynthia asked, "Have you come to see me about the present?" Every year since they had met, Jonathan asked her to help him pick out a birthday present for his wife. Over the years, she felt she knew Silvia quite well, although she had never met her.

"No, not this time. It's something else. A man came to my office today looking for his girlfriend, Angela Connors."

"And you want me to check whether she's been admitted?" She picked up her cup and blew on it. "Anything for you," she said.

He leaned over and kissed her hand, bringing a smile to her face. He was a gentleman.

A few miles away, Detective Inspector Archie Bell was just waking up. He drew the curtains and looked out onto the houses opposite. The move to Camden six months ago had been a welcome promotion, but he missed the Yorkshire Dales where he had lived all his life. He had taken it for granted: the stone-built cottages, the heather moors, the dry-stone walls and the flower-filled meadows. It was, he thought, the most magnificent scenery anywhere, from the tip of its rocky crags to the depths of its caves.

Now, instead of a broad sweep of green from his office, all he could see was a low brick wall, a scrubby piece of untended land and an iron fire escape at the back of the antiques shop whose white painted frontage with Georgian style windows spoke of an elegance which was not matched by the back view. Instead of bird song, all he could hear was the squawking of parakeets that bred so prolifically in London. He was still struggling to adapt to the change but his wife, Mary, had immersed herself in all that London had to offer: museums, theatres and art galleries, as if she had been missing them all her life.

Archie preferred a stroll along the Thames or a walk up Primrose Hill, a welcome bit of green set among the miles and miles of houses which went right out to Surrey, Kent, Essex and what used to be Middlesex. There was a magnificent view from the top of the hill of central London's tall, modern buildings: the Shard, the Gherkin and the Cheese Grater. The York stone edging and quote from William Blake had been a surprise: *I have conversed with the spiritual sun. I saw him on Primrose Hill.* At the weekend, he and Mary sometimes combined their interests with a visit to Camden Lock, with its busy market, before strolling along the river to the more peaceful Little Venice where they would have lunch somewhere overlooking the river and maybe take in a boat trip.

A week earlier, he had been called to an address in Camden where the narrow houses were all identical except for the colour of the outside walls. In an attempt to infuse the houses with their own identity, the owners had painted them in different pastel shades: yellow, green, lilac, pink.

Someone had rung 999 and a constable had gone round, knocked at the pale purple house, announced his presence and, receiving no reply, looked through the lounge window, before taking a battering ram to the door.

Archie had taken PC Jessica Watts with him. She was a bright, intelligent, girl, with a mind of her own, not afraid to disagree with her superiors, and he had recently recommended her for training as a Detective Constable. When they arrived at the pale purple house, a man lay on the floor of the front room, dead, blood oozing from a gash on his head. The front door had been firmly shut when the constable arrived and there were no open windows or broken locks. Apart from the kitchen, there was one other room on the ground floor, furnished as a dining room, with a large oak dining table and four elegant chairs with seats of red and grey stripes. Through the French windows, he saw a small garden with a shed, a recently mown square of lawn and a narrow strip of weedy earth in which a solitary buddleia grew. It had probably seeded itself. The gardens to either side were mostly covered in decking or paving. If someone had come in the back way, he would have climbed over several garden fences to get in.

The forensics team had dusted for fingerprints, searched for splashes of blood, taking swabs and photographs. When they had finished in the house, they went to investigate the shed. It was old and shabby, with a door that hung off its hinges, revealing a lawnmower, a rotary airer, two deck chairs, a number of rusty tools and various gardening chemicals: weed killer, slug killer, rose pellets, bone meal … Some of the boxes had disintegrated and were leaking onto the shelf and they were all covered in spiders' webs. It seemed unlikely anything in here had been used for a very long time.

Archie had inspected the house. There were three bedrooms upstairs, two doubles and a small box room which contained just one item, a treadmill. In the front bedroom, an antique mahogany desk dominated the room, looking out of place among sleek grey cupboards. The computer had been bagged up and was waiting to be taken away. There was a whole team of analysts back at the station who would be able to get in and sift through it, looking for evidence.

The dead man had slept in the bedroom at the back. Archie slid open the wardrobe doors and noticed that there were no female clothes. There was only one toothbrush in the bathroom and only one hairbrush. The man clearly lived alone.

Among the documents in a folder, he found a driving licence, which gave him the man's name and date of birth. Fergus Cormac, age forty-two.

CHAPTER 3

Thinking only of escape, Esther sprang away from the wall and propelled herself through the narrow doorway into the room beyond before it disappeared for good. Bright sunlight streamed through the large windows at one end and the walls were covered in wooden panelling, richly decorated with strange mythical beasts – a dog with three heads, a woman with a serpent for a lower half, a creature with a lion's body and eagle wings, and a naked, wild-looking man wielding a staff. The room was warm from the heat of a fire burning in the large, carved stone fireplace. The man who had opened the door placed the burning torch back in its metal holder and threw a log onto the fire, releasing fiery beads which glowed and then died.

Esther saw her reflection in a polished metal chest that stood on the floor. She was no longer wearing jeans but a dress of green silk, lavishly embroidered with a golden fleur-de-lys pattern, with long, flowing sleeves. On her wrist was a silver bracelet decorated with a black and orange stone. Her talisman stone.

The second man stepped out of the shadows and strode over to the fire. He was a little taller than the other man, younger and more muscular. His red buttoned tunic, white undershirt and black stockings gave him a flamboyant appearance.

"The king has gone too far this time," he said. He spoke in a soft, urgent voice. "He demands more taxes to fund his war with the French. He would have my daughter too. We must take action. If we act together, we may defeat him yet, Robert."

"How many barons do we have on our side, William?"

"Not many support the king, but – "

William stopped speaking at the sound of a gentle tapping on the door.

"We will speak of this later," Robert said.

Into the room came a young lady, with high forehead, plucked eyebrows, small even teeth, a long neck and long dark hair visible beneath a barbette held in place with a long piece of white cloth which hung down to her shoulders. She glanced momentarily at Esther, revealing the colour of her eyes. Devoid of make-up, the violet eyes seemed to glow in the pale face. The girl turned away, standing before her father with her hips and belly protruding as if she were pregnant.

She kept her eyes downcast, her head turned away from her father's guest. "You wanted to see me, father?"

"Come, daughter, here is William Marshall come to pay us a visit."

The girl turned and curtsied, keeping her eyes downcast.

"Good morrow, my lady, I trust you are in good health," William said, giving the girl a lingering look.

The girl kept her eyes downcast. Two red spots appeared on her cheeks and she shifted her feet. "Yes, thank you sir."

"I have some news for you," her father said. "I have come to an agreement with Lord Goran of Wessex. Lady Goran died six months ago and he is looking for a new wife. You will be married within the month."

The girl stiffened and her lips trembled. "Thank you, father," she said.

"I have business with Sir William, but we will speak more of this later," Robert said. The girl curtsied and turned to go, followed by William's devouring eyes.

Confident that the two men could not see her, Esther left the shadows and slipped out behind the girl. As she did so, she heard Robert say, "I had to pay the man a handsome dowry, but the matter is settled at last. I have tried many times to arrange the girl's marriage, but her reputation has gone before her in these parts."

Esther followed the girl down a stone staircase, through the Great Hall and out of a large wooden door into daylight, where a foul smell of raw sewage stopped her in her tracks. Covering her nose with her sleeve, she hurried across the wooden slatted bridge, over the moat, across a wide cart track and up a gentle slope to a wood.

The path was rough. Rain from a recent shower dripped from the trees and made the way slippery. Esther's progress was slowed by a tall, elaborate head-dress she was wearing which snagged on the low branches of the oak and beech trees. As they entered a clearing, woodcocks rose from the trees with a mighty swish of wings, zigzagging over the tree canopy before dropping to cover again.

The girl made her way to a fallen log, picking a few small blackberries from the brambles which grew abundantly in this spot. Esther sat down beside her and the girl said, "I have been waiting for you." She held out the fruits.

Esther took a berry and put it in her mouth. It was sweet, without the sharpness of the fruit she had picked in the hedgerows as a child in her own time. "You can see me?" she asked. The wood rustled with the noise of creatures moving around under cover. A red squirrel climbed a nearby oak tree.

"Only I can see you," the girl said, "not my father or Sir William or the servants."

Esther held out her hand. "My name is Esther," she said.

The girl took her hand briefly, bowed her head and said, "I am Lady Estrila, fourth daughter of Sir Robert."

"What did you mean, you have been waiting for me?"

"I am very lonely," Estrila said. "I longed for a companion and hoped that one day someone would come."

"You have no friends, no sisters who would keep you company?"

"My mother died when I was born. My older sisters have been married many years and live some distance away. My younger sister was married six months ago on her 12th birthday and has told me that she does not wish me to visit her. Are you married?"

"I think so," Esther said.

"You do not know?"

Esther shook her head. "I can't remember anything, but let's talk about you. I heard your father say that you are to be married within the month."

"Yes, it was a source of much shame that no man would take me as his wife. I am pleased that Lord Goran has accepted the dowry, although – "

"Although?"

"He is as old as my father and news of his cruelty travels far and wide. A travelling minstrel came to the castle a little while ago and told a story. He did not mention Lord Goran by name, but all present knew it was he. A young boy stole an egg from his land. Lord Goran issued an order that he be pinned to a tree with his arms and legs outstretched. He commanded his best archers to release their arrows at the boy's legs, arms and neck so that he would not die immediately but slowly bleed to death. When the archers returned to the castle, the peasants wished to help the boy, but Lord Goran had left a guard there who blocked their path. The boy's father pleaded with the guard; he was seen on his knees begging the man to show mercy. The guard wavered, then set his face firm and said, 'I cannot disobey my master.' The guard was afraid for himself. His punishment for letting him help the boy would be death."

"You cannot marry a man like that. You will have nothing but unhappiness."

"I must do as my father commands."

Esther closed her eyes and wondered how she came to be in this strange place. The girl believed she had summoned her into her life but that was not possible. She wanted to go back, but she had wandered far from the passageway and did not know the way.

"I must return to the castle," she said, jumping up from the log. "Which path do I take?"

Estrila bowed her head. "I have offended you, my lady?"

"No, it's just that I do not know how get back to my time." Esther stared around, but none of the paths looked familiar.

"I will show you, my lady," Estrila said. Esther followed her, stopping to untangle her dress, which caught on the brambles. Eventually they came out onto a hillside with a view of the castle ahead. It was an impressive stone building with towers on two corners and turrets along the length of the wall. It was surrounded by a wide moat, not the pretty moat with an edging of pond plants and ducks on the surface that belonged to castles in Esther's time, but a dull and dirty moat that reflected no light.

To one side of the castle was a square maze formed of yew hedges making nine concentric circles. On the other side was a village consisting of a number of wattle and daub houses along a central path. A river meandered through the valley and nearby a man was bent over, cleaning cow skins. Beyond the village were wood lined trenches or tanning pits where the skins of the cattle were soaked in urine and dog dung to soften them. The area behind the castle was marshy and dangerous. An enemy approaching from this direction would risk being sucked into the wet mud. In the far distance, a steep hill rose majestically, seemingly ascending out of the water.

Esther descended the path that led to the footbridge over the moat. As she placed one foot on the swaying bridge, a loud, buzzing noise sounded in her ears. Clinging tightly to the rail, she lifted the other foot and placed it carefully on the next slat but she slipped and tumbled down towards the water.

When she opened her eyes, she was in a short but steep alleyway, sitting in the doorway of a butcher's shop. Raw slabs of meat hung from hooks in the window and two pheasants dripped blood on to the marble counter below. A faint clip-clop of hooves on the cobbled street increased in volume until a horse came into view, a magnificent white beast that almost filled the width of the narrow passage. A sudden breeze lifted the red and yellow blanket on its back.

The rider wore a long, loose dress gathered above the waist and a cloak that stretched out over the horse's back. Esther followed her to the top of the alleyway where the lady turned right onto a road, joining a noisy procession of men and women, some on foot, some on horseback. A man at the front with shaved head, red and yellow breeches and a hat with ass's ears kept up a steady beat on a drum suspended from his leather belt.

Esther watched for a moment then turned the other way, heading for a large tavern with mullioned windows further down the street. The heavy wooden door was bedecked with leaves and branches and stood invitingly open. Inside, men dressed in leather tunics and breeches stood at the bar swigging ale. A few women wearing long dresses sat at the tables. There was something wrong, something did not fit.

As a large man with a tunic pulled tight over his beer belly pushed roughly past her and into the tavern, Esther realised where she was. There were road signs, shop signs – Poundland and McDonalds' glaring livery were unmistakably of the 21st century. Yet nobody around her was wearing clothes from this time, nobody except her. The dress she had been wearing in the castle had been replaced with the jeans and T-shirt she had put on this morning. Instead of the pointed leather shoes, she had on her maroon trainers with white stripes along the side. She did not understand it. She closed her eyes and leaned against the tavern wall.

"Steady on there, are you all right?" The voice was unmistakably male, as was the earthy, musky smell that reminded her of the castle. As a firm hand slipped under her elbow, she opened her eyes, and found herself staring at

23

a man about her age in an open necked shirt and jeans. She looked round. There were cars in the High Street, neon shop signs glowed, and yet the inn, the procession were not of this time.

"Can I buy you a coffee?" the man said. "You look as if you need one. My name's Tom by the way."

Esther felt as limp as a rag doll. Her legs would hardly support her and she was grateful for the strong arm under her elbow. Tom led her to a nearby café which had striking blue pillars along the front framing large windows. Inside, all the plain wooden tables were occupied.

"It doesn't look much," Tom said, "but it serves the best vegetarian food for fifty miles."

Distracted, she asked, "Where is that smell coming from?"

Tom held up a paper bag. "Patchouli oil. Quite strong, isn't it. But are you all right? I thought you were going to faint."

A large, middle aged woman took her shopping bags off the chair next to her and Esther sank down gratefully. When Tom went off to join the queue for food and drink, she noticed a man peering through the window dressed in black jeans and black leather jacket. He was unkempt and unshaved, his long straggling hair blowing in the breeze, but there was something of Estrila's father about him. She blinked and when she opened her eyes, he was gone.

Tom returned with two coffees and drew up an empty chair. "Are you OK? You look as if you've seen a ghost."

"Oh, it's nothing," Esther said. "That man just reminded me of someone." She took a sip of coffee and went on, "What year is it?"

24

Tom stared at her, frowning. "2012. Are you all right? I can take you to the hospital if you're not feeling well. I've got my car nearby."

Esther shook her head. She understood now. She must have fallen asleep on the couch while listening to the soporific voice that came through the headphones. The meeting with Estrila, the castle, the village, had felt so real, but it was just a dream.

As she reached out to take her drink, she noticed that her fingertips were stained purple. She paused, hand mid-air. She had spent hours as a child foraging in the hedgerows and knew that there was only one explanation: the blackberries she had eaten with Estrila. She took a small mirror from her handbag and inspected her mouth. Her lips were purple too. Her head span and she slumped onto the table.

"Let's go outside for some fresh air."

Esther stared around at the people dressed in ordinary clothes. There was no sign of the long dresses and tunics.

"Where have they gone – the others?" she cried. "There was a man with a drum and a lady on a horse…"

"You mean the procession," Tom said. "It's the annual festival of St Collen, named after a hermit who lived on the hill. They make their way to the top of the Tor and hold some sort of service there. Did you come for the festival?"

"I don't think so, I didn't know anything about it." Or did she? Perhaps she had, and that was why she had dreamed of Estrila.

"It goes back to medieval times. They built a church at the top of the hill but all that's left is the tower. I came here to buy a book but forgot the festival was on."

Esther looked at her wrist and saw that her watch had reappeared. "I will have to go soon. I should have been back by now."

"Someone's expecting you?"

She nodded and Tom looked disappointed.

"That's a shame, I was hoping we could take a walk up the hill together and see what's going on.

"I'm sorry, I can't."

"OK, but here, take my card. Ring if you want to get in touch again."

Esther glanced at it. Tom Drew, folk musician. On the way back to the car she tore it into little pieces and put it in a bin. She knew instinctively that there would be trouble if Ray found it.

She knew she was driving too fast as she swung around a blind corner on the narrow country road. A car was coming the other way, and she yanked at the steering wheel, desperate to avoid a crash. The car swerved, scraping along the hedge, the wing mirrors collided and the horrified driver sped by just inches away. Esther braked, came to a halt, and waited for her heart to beat normally. It wasn't worth risking her life, however angry Ray would be that she was late.

She drove on slowly, braking carefully on the bends. She was nearly home when a tractor pulled out of a field ahead of her and she was stuck behind it, unable to pass. They crawled along until they reached the outskirts of a village, where the tractor turned down a side road. Esther increased her speed, bouncing over the hump-backed bridge. A little further on, she jumped as the Satnav spoke and announced that she should turn off the road.

Ray was pacing around at the end of the drive. "Where have you been?" he almost spat out.

"To my appointment."

He looked pointedly at his watch. "It doesn't take this long. What have you been doing?"

"I – er – got caught up in a procession. The Festival of St Cullen."

"I see." He glared at her. "Don't be late again."

She hung her jacket on a blue, plastic hook in the hall and went through to the dining room where the girls were sitting at the table, talking about their day. She sat quietly, listening, trying to understand where she was and who these girls were. This was a big house for just her and Ray. Had they decided to rent out the spare bedrooms, to help pay the mortgage, perhaps?

"What about you, Ray?" she asked as he came in carrying a tray of cutlery. "Where do you work?"

"My work is here," he said gruffly, putting the tray down on the table. "Here, set this out and I'll bring in the food."

Yesterday he had served up lamb stew and dumplings. Today it was liver and onions. Leanne said, "Whoever eats liver these days?" and refused to touch it. Esther ate mechanically. As the chatter went on around her, she thought about that afternoon and the mystery of the blackberry juice on her fingers. Had she stopped somewhere on the way and picked a few fruits and forgotten about it? It was possible and the only thing that made any sense.

The final words spoken by Estrila's father span round and round her head: "*No-one else will have her*". The words drilled down into the place where forgotten memories lay.

27

Unbidden, an angry face suddenly appeared before her. Go away, she told it, not realising that she had spoken aloud.

"Who are you telling to go away?" Ray asked menacingly and Leanne tittered.

"Oh, nobody," Esther said. "I thought I felt something on my face, an insect." She shuddered as she remembered the spider in her dream.

"She's lying," Leanne said. "She didn't mean that at all."

CHAPTER 4

On coming to London and finding himself in the soulless office he now inhabited in his working day, Archie had surrounded himself with plants: the mother in law's tongue, Dragon Tree and Flamingo Flower were his favourites. Colleagues smiled at him indulgently, a Yorkshireman who had not yet learnt sophisticated London ways. But the plants held a secret, one that if the hardened police officers ever discovered, they would no doubt drum him out of the force, or at least make his life so difficult he would have to move on.

Archie sat at his desk looking through the forensics report of the murder case. The blow on Fergus' head was a minor one that had not killed him. It had been the kick to his left side that had ruptured the spleen, leaving him to bleed to death internally. Nothing had been found in the house that matched the gash on the head. Whatever the murderer had used, he had taken it with him.

Fergus worked for himself as a maths and English tutor. The team had begun working through the list of his clients, but nobody so far had anything but praise for him. A set of golfing irons in the wardrobe had led them to the local golf clubs. A number of people claimed to have played with Fergus from time to time, but the enquiries had thrown up nothing useful. Nobody could suggest any reason why Fergus had been murdered. The bar steward remembered Fergus turning up with a girl last Christmas when the club held a dance, but he hadn't seen the girl again and had no idea who she was.

Archie read on and learned that Fergus had a brother, Kiernan, up north. The local police had already been in touch with him to tell him the devastating news. He could not offer any suggestions as to why his brother had been murdered but was able to tell them that his father had recently died and his mother was in a nursing home.

The team had visited the pubs in the area and learnt that Fergus usually frequented the Bull's Head, where he would join in with a game of darts or snooker. They had spoken to his friends, but nobody had any suggestion as to who had killed him or why anyone would want to.

Archie moved his stiff neck from side to side, stretched his arms and looked out of the window. A blackbird hopped off the wall into the antique shop garden and pecked at something on the ground. Archie had never fancied playing golf. Walking from hole to hole across manicured grass would be a poor substitute for the long walks he had taken over the Yorkshire moors, but maybe he should consider it now he was in London. The exercise would be welcome after sitting in a stuffy office all week. Mary might enjoy it too.

He turned to the second case, that of a young woman who had arrived at Accident and Emergency saying she had fallen and hit her head and could remember nothing but her name. She had no handbag with her, or anything that could identify who she was.

She had been left in the care of Mrs Underhill, a qualified hypnotherapist, and she had started talking – not anything useful so far, just stories of medieval life. His colleague, Kenneth Edwards, the police psychologist, would know whether there was anything in these stories that would help trace who she was and he could do with a break. He got up, stretched, and went along the corridor.

With a first class degree in psychology under his belt, Kenneth had a choice of plum jobs, but nearly forty years ago, he had chosen a career with the police force. The peak of his career so far had been helping the police in a difficult negotiation with a dangerous criminal who had taken several people hostage. He had managed to get everyone out alive and the criminal was now serving a long sentence.

Kenneth had invited Archie and Mary over for dinner when they first arrived in London and a few weeks later, Archie had returned the invitation. The dinners were now a regular thing.

Kenneth looked up from his computer as Archie sat down. After a few pleasantries, he said, "It was Freud who first used the term hysterical amnesia to explain the patient who can't remember anything, but there is no medical reason for it. In this case, Esther's mind is releasing those memories as a story of Estrila and her life in the castle and as such, they might provide valuable clues." He tapped at the report in front of him. "Here we have a young woman, Estrila, who is to be married to a cruel man."

"Esther isn't wearing an engagement ring," Archie said.

"There could be many reasons for that. We should not rule out the possibility of her being engaged, or married, or perhaps living with someone."

"Nobody's come forward looking for her."

"The man is described as cruel. What did the doctors say?"

"They said that Esther's injuries were consistent with her having fallen and banged her head, like she said. But

31

I'll check it out, see if there have been any admissions to hospital with unexplained injuries in the past."

"Is Esther a particularly beautiful young woman?" Kenneth asked. "In this story, Estrila is described as being extremely attractive to men.

Archie handed him a photograph. "I wouldn't have thought so, would you?"

"No, not the sort to have every man in the room after her," Kenneth agreed, "pleasant though she is."

"What are you thinking?"

Kenneth put his hands together, pointing his fingers to the ceiling. "This story suggests that Esther had a husband or partner who saw her in that light, imagined that every man was after her, or that she encouraged them. I realise that doesn't get us any nearer identifying her just yet though. Are you going to put her picture out to the press?"

"We will do, if we don't make any progress, but you know what will happen, we'll be inundated with calls from all sorts of people saying they know her."

"She will go to see Mrs Underhill again?"

"Yes, the doctors suggested six sessions initially, perhaps more. You don't think they're a waste of time, do you? It couldn't just be an overactive imagination?"

"Hypnotism has proved very effective in the past in such cases, but it's important not to suggest what might have happened to her. But Mrs Underhill is an experienced therapist and I don't imagine she would make such a mistake."

Back in his office, Archie asked Jessica to make enquiries at the hospital then turned his attention to the murder. The team had been doing house-to-house investigations and in the street of multi-coloured houses, one of Fergus' neighbours said she had been putting out the rubbish when she noticed a car parked in one of the Residents Only spots.

"They're not supposed to park there," the neighbour had said (as if they didn't know that!). There had been nobody at the wheel, she felt sure, or she would probably have gone and spoken to the driver. Later, when she looked out the window, it was no longer there. No, she hadn't got the registration number – it hadn't occurred to her it might be needed. What sort of car was it? A silver one, possibly a Ford. That was too vague to be of any use at all.

Archie issued instructions to the team to "speak to the neighbours again, see if anyone can tell us anything more about this car. And show the neighbour a few pictures of Fords, see if she can narrow it down. It's a long shot, I know."

Archie put away the file. It was time to forget about Fergus, Esther and medieval castles and go home. Over the years, he had learnt not to take his work with him. When he and Mary had first been married, the cases had got right into his head, they had been all he could think about. Back then, he had thought his work so much more important than Mary's day bringing up the children. Now he knew better. His own children had flown the nest years ago, but now Mary was needed again, to help with the grandchildren, Laurena, two years old and Filipe five. His daughter had explained that these were Spanish names and Archie supposed they had been conceived in the couple's Spanish timeshare villa, but he didn't want to be reminded of *that!* Archie looked at his watch. If he hurried, he would just be in time to see the grandchildren before their mother came and collected them.

Archie bought a bunch of flowers at the entrance to the tube station, as he had every Friday night since they came to London. It helped cheer the place up. He hadn't quite got used to sitting in a train underground, travelling through the darkness until it was time to push his way into the light, like a bulb in Spring. It was crowded tonight and he had to stand all the way, holding his bouquet up high so the flowers didn't get squashed.

**

Jonathan made his way to the hospital, timing his visit to coincide with Cynthia's break. He took with him two tickets for Showboat as she loved musicals and had been talking about the show last time he'd seen her. Silvie had dragged him along to see it in the seventies. It had been outdated even then, but it had made a comeback and received some excellent revues. It would help keep Cynthia sweet.

He was well known in the hospital now, and nobody challenged him as he walked into the staff room. He had been cultivating the nurses here for years. Cynthia was alone, sitting with her feet up, clutching her favourite cat mug.

"Hello, Cynthia," Archie said. "I wonder if you could use these tickets? A grateful client gave them to me, but we're seeing the family that day." Cynthia would hate to think it was a sweetener or a reward for her help.

"Are you sure?" she asked, beaming. "I've been wanting to see the show ever since it came to London." She took the tickets and tucked them in her pocket. "I was going to give you a ring when I've finished my shift. I might have found the woman you were looking for. I couldn't get hold of the file, but one of the nurses said there was a woman here she thinks might be the one you're looking for. She was discharged and went somewhere by ambulance. She didn't know where, so I went to talk to the ambulance crew. There's one ambulance man there who fancies me."

"More than one, surely," Jonathan said, right on cue.

Cynthia beamed again and said, "He told me she's gone to the Somerset Levels."

"That's helpful. Did he say where, on the Levels? It's quite a big place."

"No, unfortunately, I couldn't get anything more out of him."

"You're an angel, Cynthia. A miracle worker."

"So they say."

"I owe you one."

"These tickets are reward enough."

"Enjoy the show!"

Jonathan went outside and rang Rolf with the news. "What do you want me to do? Shall I continue the search down there?"

"I will phone you back," Rolf said.

***

Seb picked up the phone straight away. "Yes? Do you have any news?"

"Jonathan say my girlfriend is in Somerset Levels."

"Good. Where is she now? Did he get her address?"

"No, he only know that she is in Somerset Levels."

"Ring Whicher back and tell him you'll take it from here," Seb said. "And pack a few clothes. We're going to Somerset."

35

"What about the lady's conservatory? I say I will be finished Friday."

"I'll deal with her."

"I don't like letting customers down."

"Stop worrying. I'll tell her your mother is sick and you had to go home to see her. She'll be falling over herself to help you. It works every time."

"How long will we be away?"

"I don't know, however long it takes to find her. I'll pay you £200 a day. You'll have to pay for your lodgings and food, but you should still make a packet. Bring a few clothes and come and collect me. We're taking your car."

"Not your car?" Seb's car would get there twice as fast as his battered Skoda, even supposing they didn't break down on the way, and would be far more comfortable.

"It's in the garage. It will be a week or two before I can drive it," Seb said. "I'll expect you in half an hour."

Later that day, Rolf and Seb arrived at the outskirts of Yeovil. It had been a slow, tedious journey down the A303, with the engine complaining loudly and sending out foul fumes from the exhaust. Rolf wasn't happy. He could see himself spending his wages on the garage bill when he got home.

"It doesn't sound too good to me," he said. "You have to coax it along like a woman." It had begun to rain, too, and the wipers weren't working very well. He'd managed all right when he was making small journeys to customers, but he would definitely have to get a new pair now.

They were nearly at the Premier Inn. Seb took a wodge of money from his pocket, peeled off several hundred pounds and handed them to Rolf. "You're going to pay cash for everything we need," he said.

Seb had chosen the Premier Inn because they could remain invisible there. Nobody ever looked at the guests properly in those places. If anyone came snooping around, all they would remember was the Pole with a big pile of cash.

CHAPTER 5

Esther drove slowly to her next appointment, feeling jaded. She had woken up early, feeling uneasy, and worried all the way to Pilbury. The last time had been confusing and she still did not understand what was going on.

The same unsmiling woman took her into the back room and fixed the headphones to her head. Esther was determined to stay awake this time, but as the voice came through the headphones, her eyelids fluttered shut and the room dissolved. As before, she was in the passageway and the voice was telling her to pick up the talisman. It was not on the table, but she knew if she waited, it would appear. Sure enough, a little wisp of cloud materialised above her, twisting into a mini tornado and descending to the table where it evaporated, revealing the orange and black stone.

The wooden door was open this time. Picking up the stone and stepping through, she was in a long, vaulted corridor with large stone pillars supporting the ceiling. Through the small, mullioned windows ranged along one side came the unpleasant smell of sewage drifting in from the dark and sluggish moat in the distance. Directly below her was an inner courtyard where knights on horseback, dressed in padded coats and holding swords and shields, were giving instruction to a number of young boys, some only six or seven, on the art of warfare.

Today, Esther was dressed in a plain, yellow silk gown gathered above the waist and, she saw from her reflection in the window, an attractive matching headdress consisting of a long piece of material elaborately woven into two horns. She recognised the voices that drifted through a nearby open door as those she had heard before.

"We have the support of the northern barons," said Robert, "and soldiers of John's own household have sworn allegiance. They are positioned throughout the country."

"How soon can we march on London?" asked William.

"A few more weeks yet. Some say John will be ex-communicated by the Pope, which will support our cause. We are also hoping to get the Welsh barons on our side."

As she waited, listening, Estrila entered the corridor from the far end, with her father's seneschal close behind her. Pretending to be occupied with something outside the window, she gave a slight decline of the head to the man and he moved away. Before Esther could join Estrila, William came out of the room and sauntered along the corridor. Although she knew he could not see her, Esther pushed herself back into a slight recess.

At the sight of William, Estrila hung further out of the window, as if engrossed in the scene below. William came up behind her and put his arms either side of her, pressing his body against her back. He spoke quickly, his voice echoing along the corridor to where Esther stood.

"I will have you," he said. "Come to my chambers tonight." Estrila shook her head and tried to move away. The man leered. "Come to my chambers tonight or I will tell your father of the spell you have put on me. Then even Lord Goran will not want you."

When he had gone, Esther moved from the recess and hurried to where Estrila stood. Her eyes were glazed and her face pinched. She shook herself as if to shake off the memory of the encounter with William and said, "The others do not see you but the dogs will know you are here. Follow me. We will go to a safe place."

They went along the corridor, up a wide, stone staircase, through a doorway into another corridor and up a narrow staircase with a door at the top, moving silently on their soft leather soles. When they were both inside, Estrila locked the door. From the window was a clear view of the village beyond the moat, surrounded by fields and in the distance loomed a steep hill. People were dotted among the narrow strips of land, digging or harvesting the crop; a man in charge of a plough pulled by four oxen came into view, while another urged them forwards with a whip.

The room was much smaller and cosier than the room downstairs. A large bed dominated the room with its elaborately carved, wooden canopy from which hung rich, thick red curtains embroidered with flowers. Tapestries, mainly of hunting scenes, hung on the wall. The bed itself was thick with covers, and the linen sheets had been turned backed, revealing a large bolster covered with a protective cloth. Estrila gestured to one of the two carved wooden chairs with curved sides and velvet cushions that were either side of the fireplace.

Esther sat down. "I am grateful that you have returned," Estrila said, taking the other chair. "I feared that you would not come again."

"When are you to be married?" Esther asked. It was only a couple of days since she had last been here, but she had no way of knowing how much time had passed in Estrila's world.

"The marriage will be in one week's time."

"That man I saw in the corridor – I saw him here before."

"Yes, that is William Marshall. He is working with my father to lead a plot against King John. My father thinks I do not know, but I have heard them talking."

"He behaved badly towards you. You will not go to him?"

A shadow passed across Estrila's face. "It is not his fault. It is because I am bad. My father has locked me in the cupboard many times, but still I am bad. It is my eyes, the colour of my eyes. It is a sign that wickedness lies within me," Estrila said.

"Who told you that?" Esther asked.

"My father has explained things to me. My mother died when I was born. My father said it was my wickedness that killed her. He says that he is glad she did not live to see how wicked I have become."

"But that's terrible," Esther said.

"Yes, you are right, I am terrible."

Esther leant forward in the chair. "No, I did not mean that."

"I have tried so hard to be good," Estrila said, tears in her eyes, "but there was no-one to tell me that when a woman's first blood leaves the body, she must protect herself with a sprig of Lady's Mantle tied to the end of the bed, or the devil enters her at night."

"You think the devil has entered you?"

"Yes, it is the devil that makes me put a spell on men. They look at me and desire me. This is why my sister does not wish me to visit her; she is afraid her husband will be caught in my spell. All the ladies are angry with me and their husbands want my father to ban me from the castle so that there will be no trouble. My father is a good man. He told me he would not desert me, but would find a husband for me. Oh, what can I do? I do not look at them, I keep my eyes downcast but they force me to look at them, and then … "

Esther felt overwhelmed, powerless. This poor girl believed herself to be so wicked, she was even grateful for a marriage to an old, cruel man. Estrila was beautiful. It was not surprising that many men desired her – but to punish her for this instead of them was unforgiveable.

"When men approach me, I cover my face with my veil and yet the wickedness is still there," Estrila continued.

Esther moved to kneel down beside Estrila's chair. "But you are not wicked, don't you understand, it is the men. If a man is unfaithful to his wife, it is he who must be punished."

"Oh no, Lady Esther, that is not correct. The woman must be punished for making herself desirable to him."

It was on the tip of Esther's tongue to say, it's like living in the Middle Ages, when she realised that she *was* in the Middle Ages. She was sure now that she was not dreaming. She would never think that it was a woman's fault if she was beautiful, even in a dream, but this was how they thought back then.

"I know it is I who am wicked," Estrila continued. "I must go to William tonight, or he will tell my father that I put a spell on him while I am betrothed and Lord Goran will not have me."

"This is not right. You do not want to marry him anyway."

Estrila's shoulders trembled. "My father has arranged the marriage to try to purge the wickedness from my body. It is a source of much shame that I am not yet married and I am already sixteen."

Esther did not know what to do. The girl was being forced to hand out sexual favours to an old man in return for the saving of her reputation. It was like that time when …. She pummelled her head with her fists and ordered the memory to get back where it came from. She did not want to think of it, she did not want to remember any of it.

Estrila suddenly jumped up. "I hear the dogs," she cried. "They have detected you. Oh, you must not be found here."

Esther listened. The low growling was distant but growing nearer. Estrila ran to the door, turning back with horror on her face. "They are too near, you cannot escape, there is no way out. Oh, they will burn me at the stake." She fell to her knees, sobbing. The noise of claws on the stone floor in the passageway below echoed along the corridor. The dogs would soon be at the bottom of the narrow staircase. Esther ran to the window, but a smooth stone wall dropped straight down to the ground. There was no escape in this direction.

"Help me," she called out.

Suddenly the voice was there. "Place the talisman in your open palm," it said. The talisman. Esther patted her skirt, feeling for a pocket. There were yards and yards of material in her long skirt, but no pocket. Estrila crawled over to her and pulled at a tanned leather drawstring bag hanging from the belt. She reached inside and handed the talisman to Esther as a guard banged on the door.

"Lady Estrila, are you all right in there?" The dogs were sniffing and scratching at the door. The room began to turn. A loud buzzing noise filled Esther's head. When it stopped, she opened her eyes and saw that the room had disappeared.

"Are you all right?"

Esther blinked. She was sitting on a hard pavement and a lady who looked vaguely familiar bent over her with a concerned expression.

"Are you OK? Did you fall?" the lady asked.

Esther considered her arms, her legs, her body. Nothing hurt. Carefully, she began to stand. "I must have fainted," she said vaguely.

"Let me help you up."

"Before you go – do I know you?"

The woman shook her head. "I don't think so. I was just passing when you slipped to the ground."

The scene was comfortingly ordinary. There was no castle, no lady on a horse, just a market town on a dull Wednesday afternoon with people hurrying along the road, or dawdling, looking in the shop windows. It can't have been more than an hour since she had left home, but it seemed a whole lifetime away. As it started to rain, she dodged into a shop doorway for shelter.

"Hello."

"Tom!"

"Room for a little one?" he asked, squeezing next to her out of the rain. "You looked miles away. I thought I might bump into you if I came here at the same time." Esther smiled. How nice to meet a man who did not feel the need to pretend they had met by accident.

"Have you time for a coffee, or do you have to dash away again?"

Ray would be waiting, but maybe one coffee would be all right. She would tell him she had had to shelter from the rain. It was true, after all.

They waited until the traffic had stopped at the lights and made a mad dash across the road to the café on the other side. It was small, with only room for a couple of tables and chairs and a long bench under the window. It was crowded with shoppers, their umbrellas dripping by the sides of the tables and their bags blocking the way. Esther scanned the menu as the coffee machine bubbled away: vanilla latte, gingerbread latte, cinnamon latte, bubble tea, chai latte…She had never had anything like this – at least, she didn't think she had – and had no idea what she might like. She settled for a mocha and hot chocolate while Tom ordered a double espresso for himself.

"So, do you work or are you a lady of leisure?" Tom asked, when they were perched on the high stools by the window, watching the rain dripping down the glass. Esther felt afraid. She could not remember whether she had ever worked, or anything about her life before she was taken to the house where she now lived. She settled for, "I'm not working at the moment." To prevent him asking any more questions, she quickly asked, "What about you? I saw from your card that you're a musician."

"Yes, I play the guitar in a folk band, but you can't make a living from that. During the day, I'm an accountant. Boring, I know. I've been visiting a client, trying to get his VAT returns sorted out."

It had been a mistake to agree to sit in the café with Tom. It only led to more questions which she could not answer. The thought of telling Tom that she could remember nothing made her feel vulnerable. She drank quickly, sneaking a quick look at her watch.

"I know," Tom said, "You've got to go. But before you do, I was thinking - if you'd like to hear the band, we're playing at the inn just up the road tomorrow. It would be great to see you there." As an afterthought, he added, "Bring your husband along too."

"Oh, I'm not married, that is …."

Tom waited, but no explanation came. Esther was thinking. She knew enough about Ray to know he would not allow her to go by herself and she did not think he would come with her. Maybe he would agree if one or more of the girls went too. "Can I bring some friends?" she asked.

"Yes, the more the merrier," he said.

"I'll see what I can do," she said, picking up the pink leather handbag that Leanne had given her when she had learnt Esther didn't have one. Through the window, she thought she saw a glimpse of a man with long, unkempt hair, wearing black jeans and a black jacket.

Driving home, she reflected on the afternoon's events. She wanted to help Estrila, but what could she do? She had been propelled into a little snapshot of something that had happened hundreds of years ago and in all probability, was a dream. Her attempts to explain things to Estrila had not helped. She thought about the meeting with Tom. He was a nice man, straightforward, didn't play games and didn't pry, either; but it was Estrila's face that kept coming into her mind's eye.

She drove home carefully, afraid she might skid on the wet roads. As she turned into the drive, Ray was waiting for her in the porch.

"Another festival?" he asked sarcastically.

Esther shook her head. "Not this time."

"What then?"

Esther shook her head and pushed past him. Grabbing her elbow, he said. "Not so fast. You're going to tell me where you've been."

"It was raining," she said. "I had to take cover, I didn't have my umbrella with me." She looked him straight in the eye, challenging him to call her a liar. "Before that, I was listening to a busker," she said. "He was good. He told me he plays with a folk band. He says he's playing tomorrow and has invited us all along."

"All of us or just you?"

"No, all of us."

"You told him where you lived? I've told you you're not to give out the address to *anyone*." Ray's voice had a gritty edge to it.

Esther didn't even know the address. She knew the house was a couple of miles out of town, but that was all. The house had no name or number on display and the road was just an unnamed route through the countryside. "No, he suggested I brought some friends along." she said.

He stared at her hard, as if trying to draw the truth out of her. Finally, he let go of her arm. "I'll think about it and let you know."

Esther rubbed her elbow where he had gripped it too tightly. Back in her room, she took off her T-shirt and put on a long-sleeved top. There would be a bruise later.

She went downstairs to the kitchen. It had been extended at some point and now stretched most of the way along the back of the house. The cupboards looked as if they had been there for years, with their heavy wood panelling and hinges coming loose. Someone had fitted out the kitchen with labour-saving devices, some of which had never been used: a bread maker, a food processor, an ice cream maker, an electric mixer, a toaster and a microwave oven, but not the most useful thing of all, a dishwasher. An old portable radio stood on the window tuned to Radio 4 but it had been a long time since anyone had switched it on.

Ray was at the cooker, stirring a saucepan. "Can I help?" Esther asked.

"No, but you can lay the table."

Esther wondered if she could cook. She had no idea, she couldn't remember.

She went in the dining room and glanced at the bookshelves. Ray had been angry yesterday because she had rearranged the collection of books. They had been in strict alphabetical order of author, but she had put them into subject order for non-fiction and style for fiction. Ray had ranted at her as he moved the books back, pushing her out of the way when she tried to help.

The girls came in and sat at the table. The arrangements regarding these four girls were a mystery. Ray had never discussed their presence in this house. They hardly ever did any of the household jobs, cleaning, washing, cooking or ironing, which made her think that they were paid guests. She knew nothing about the financial arrangements. She had no access to any money except the weekly allowance Ray gave her which he allowed her to spend when they went to the supermarket. Ray did the odd maintenance job around the house – cleaning the gutter, mending fences, as well as the cooking, but he spent most of the day in his office, a small room off of the kitchen. She had no idea what he did in there.

It was confusing, but perhaps this was how people lived. She had no way of knowing as she could remember nothing, not even what society's expectations were of women. That's what made it so difficult to talk to Ray and the girls. She had no point of reference, no past. It was like being in a foreign country, not knowing the language or the customs but being expected to obey the rules, even though you had no way of knowing what they were.

The girls were like shadows behind a glass wall: she had nothing she could tell them and they had almost given up speaking to her. Ray, though – Ray was always there, always watching her, ready to tell her if she did something wrong, which was most of the time, not because she wanted to defy him, but because she could not remember how she was supposed to behave, or the myriad of rules he had for every occasion.

If she could get her memory back, she would understand her life here, but until then, she must live in a world she could make no sense of. Why, for instance, did Ray allow Leanne to listen to music on her headphones when they were eating, even though he had a rule that it wasn't allowed? Most of the time, Leanne did what she wanted, but Esther always got into trouble if she ignored what Ray told her.

Halfway through the meal, the phone rang in Ray's office. When he came back, carrying bowls of peaches and cream, he said, "Tomorrow, we're all going to a folk club."

Esther was surprised, and did not know how it had happened that he had agreed. She never knew how he would react to things.

Leanne pulled a face. "Not a folk club," she protested. "I can't be seen there!"

"You can thank Esther for that," Ray said. It wasn't his sort of thing either, but he had been given his orders. The voice on the end of the phone had told him, *"Go to the folk club, Ray, we need to know who this Tom is. Find out as much as you can about him."*

When Ray left the room to get the drinks, Leanne pinched Esther beneath the table. "It's all your fault," she said. "I'll pay you back for this."

Esther wondered why Leanne seemed to hate her so much. Had she done something in the past to her?

Ray didn't like this job. At the age of twenty-eight, he had been manager of a sports accessories shop, selling everything from golf clubs to swimming caps. Within the next five years, he was expecting to own his own shop. Then the big sports store had moved in down the road and taken most of their trade. The financial crisis of 2008 finished the business off. It had been difficult to get another job and he had finally taken the only thing he'd been offered, working for a security firm, accompanying prisoners to and from court or other prisons. He didn't like it, but he had a mortgage to pay.

One day, an email had come round about this job, and Ray had leapt at the chance to live in a spacious home and get paid for it. He had rented out his own house, using the rent money to pay the mortgage. It had seemed a good deal, but it wasn't as easy as he thought it would be. There was the cooking for a start. He thought he'd be able to get takeaways or frozen stuff but the supermarket was ten miles away and there were no takeaway restaurants nearby. Anyway, the one time he'd tried serving up a supermarket ready meal, Leanne had refused to eat it.

As he entered the dining room with the drinks, Leanne glared at him. "I'll only go if I can take my Walkman," she said.

"OK," Ray agreed. He knew the other girls resented what they thought was his leniency regarding Leanne, but he'd been told not to upset her. She was OK anyway, always good for a laugh. This morning she had been particularly flirtatious with him. He knew it was a game, but he didn't mind, it put him in a good mood. He wasn't fooled. Yesterday she wanted to get out of her chores because she "had an important letter to write". He wasn't stupid, he knew she never wrote letters. Who did these days? Everything was done by text. He had played along, giving the extra tasks to Esther, who was easy to control and never complained.

Esther looked from one to the other. What was it about these two? Were they having an affair? It seemed unlikely, but anyway, was that any of her business if they were? She had no idea. Ray, with his eyes too close together, his thick wayward eyebrows and a large gap in his teeth, and slim, attractive Leanne, who could get any man she wanted. It didn't seem very likely but she knew how to get round him, that was sure.

Yasmeen said in her quiet voice, "Lovely, thank you."

CHAPTER 6

Archie preferred the incident room to his own office. It was lighter, faced the front and had a view of the gardens of the houses opposite. They were just a foot or two deep, but the owners had packed them with plants and hung colourful baskets on the walls. It was all quite jolly.

Jessica was looking through a report on her computer and two other members of the team were talking quietly together. "Have you been back to the woman who saw the car in a residents' bay on the day of the murder?" Archie asked. "Did you show her pictures of the range of Fords?"

"I did, but she wasn't very helpful. She seemed to think it was either a Fiesta or a Focus but she wasn't sure at all. But we have found something else, an article in the local paper." She switched screens to reveal the story of a girl who was run over by a car about a month ago and was in hospital suffering from brain damage. "Fergus Cormac was a witness to the accident," Jessica said. "He told the police that the driver didn't stand a chance, the girl ran out from between parked cars. Her mother, Amy Tindall, wanted the driver prosecuted. She said he was driving too fast, but Fergus disagreed. He said the driver was being careful and he could not avoid the accident: the girl just ran out between parked cars. The skid marks showed that the driver was within the speed limit but Mrs Tindall continued to blame Fergus. There's a picture of her and her husband."

Archie looked at the photograph and said, "Print it off and ask Fergus' neighbours if they've seen either of them hanging around, especially on the day of the murder."

"Will do."

"I'll be back later. I'm going to interview the pair of them."

***

A couple of hundred miles away, Seb and Rolf had settled in to the hotel. The receptionist had insisted on a name and address for both of them when Rolf signed in, so Seb had given them the first name he had thought of – Edward Thatch - and Rolf's address. The two rooms were identical with their purple bed cover, TV and tea making facilities.   As the two poured over a map of the Somerset Levels which was spread out on the bed, Seb declared that it didn't need the two of them to go around together and in any case, he wanted to keep a low profile.

"I'll keep the car," he told Rolf. "You can hire a bicycle. It will be easier to get around. It's very flat – well, it would be I suppose." That was lost on Rolf. "The roads here are very narrow, it's far easier on a bike."

"But it's my car," Rolf said.

"I'll look after it. I'd be no good on a bicycle. You can ride, can't you?"

"Well, yes, I can ride a bike."

"There you are then."

Rolf began to protest, but he knew Seb of old. If he wanted something, he always got it.

"Take this photo of Esther with you and show it around the shops, that sort of thing.   Ask around. Jonathan's been back to me – he's contacted the convalescent homes, but he's drawn a blank, so you can leave those. Here, I've made a list."

"What if I see her. What do you want me to do?"

"Don't let her know you've seen her. Ring me straight away. Follow her and don't lose her."

"That will be difficult if she's in a car and I'm on a bike," Rolf said.

"I'll be somewhere nearby. Just ring me if you find her."

***

Esther was getting ready to go to the folk club. The others were already in the people carrier and Ray was drumming his fingers on the wheel impatiently while Esther tried to decide whether to wear the bright red lipstick or just put on a bit of lip gloss. She settled for the lip gloss. She couldn't even remember what make-up suited her. All she had were a few pieces the girls had discarded as no longer being fashionable, or perhaps they had grown bored with them: lipstick and lip gloss, a little bit of black mascara and some pink eye shadow.   She had no idea whether she used to wear a lot of make-up or none, or what colours suited her; whether she usually straightened her naturally curly hair, wore flat shoes or heels. It was very strange to have no memories, no past.

When she got outside, she saw Leanne had taken the front seat again (it was only ever her or Fiona; the others never got a chance to sit at the front).   Yasmeen was at the back with Rachel.   They tended to stick together, both outsiders by virtue of belonging to a different religion. Yasmeen was a Muslim and Rachel a Jew.

She climbed in beside Fiona and they set off, Yasmeen and Rachel occasionally whispering something to each other that Esther could not hear. Leanne was laughing at something Ray said and Ray had his hand casually on Leanne's knee. From where she was, Esther could see the disgust on Leanne's face, but she didn't tell him to stop. Perhaps that was the way she got round him and got to do whatever she wanted. Esther shuddered inwardly. She'd rather take Ray's punishments than submit to that.

Ray drove carefully along the narrow roads, almost too carefully. The town, when they arrived, was heaving with people out to enjoy themselves on the warm Friday night. People milled around the shops or sat outside the cafes eating, while buskers played on the pavement outside the churchyard. The pub was busy and the barman directed the group through to the function room, a large room with solid wooden panels covering the walls on which were hung various shields or coats of arms. It was dim, the only light coming from the wall lights with their heavy red material shades, which reminded Esther of the fire torches in the medieval castle. She hesitated in the doorway, wondering whether there had some sort of time slip and she was back in the castle.

"Come on," said Fiona behind her. "What's the matter?"

"It looks like a medieval castle," Esther said.

"So what?" asked Fiona giving Esther a shove. "It's just one of those theme pubs."

Most of the chairs and tables were occupied, but Tom had reserved them a seat at the front. Leanne's music could be heard pumping out of her headphones as they threaded their way through the tables, and a number of people glared at her. The audience was a mixed bunch – different ages, some looking dishevelled and untidy, others well groomed, but they all had one thing in common. They were all wearing jeans and T-shirts. Esther wished Tom had told her. She had no idea there was a type of 'uniform' for folk

55

clubs. People were staring. None of them looked as if they belonged in a folk club. Yasmeen had put on a long skirt and top that hid everything while Leanne's skimpy top left nothing to the imagination. Rachel had on her new shoes with pink polka dots and very high heels that she could hardly walk in. Esther and Fiona had put on jeans, but their tops were a little dressy. Ray had put on a suit and looked the most out of place of all of them.

They did not have long to wait until the organiser introduced *Buskin.* The band consisted of Tom, two other men and a lady. They were wearing the same 'uniform' too: jeans with different coloured checked shirts. Tom picked up his guitar and began strumming the introduction to *Whisky in the Jar*, a song the audience clearly knew very well as they joined in, clapping and stamping their feet. Esther waited until Ray started tapping his feet and she knew they were safe to join in too, all except Leanne who was moving to a different beat. Tom nodded at the little group in the front, and Esther risked a smile. Ray's chair was slightly in front of hers and she didn't think he would notice, but in any case, he was too busy leering at the singer in her tight jeans. Esther forgot everything and immersed herself in the music. It took her into another world, one where there were no lost memories, where the past did not matter. There was only the present and the joy of the music.

When it was time for the interval, Ray went to the bar to buy drinks and the girls went off to the Ladies, leaving Esther alone. She knew it would be a brief respite and willed Tom to come out from backstage and talk to her. She wanted to speak to him alone, and Ray would be back in a minute.

She scratched her finger where the eczema had reappeared, as it did whenever she was anxious. She was relieved to see Tom appearing from behind the stage. Glancing at the bar, she saw that Ray was talking to someone next to him, still waiting to be served. The girls would not be long. If she was going to say anything, she had to do it now.

As Tom drew up at the table, she blurted out in a hoarse whisper, "Can you meet me tomorrow, the same time as before?"

Tom looked a little puzzled but rallied and said, "Yes, of course."

Ray was coming back. Esther's eyes glazed over. She looked imploringly up at Tom, willing him to understand that he was not to say anything, not to give the game away. Tom looked from her to Ray, a puzzled look in his eye, as if he was trying to work something out.

Now Ray was glaring at Esther and saying, "I could do with a hand with the drinks." Esther got up quickly to help and when she returned, Tom had gone. The girls came back from the Ladies and Ray sauntered over to the stage to look at the CDs and pick up a leaflet about the band's future gigs.

When the second half came to an end, Ray was in a hurry to get home. Fiona sat in the front of the car this time humming *Whiskey in the Jar*. Yasmeen was whispering to Rachel about how much she had enjoyed the night out and Leanne was lost in her own world of music, leaving Esther alone with her own thoughts. Ray said, "That was OK, but I don't want you thinking you're going out every week."

"Funny, I thought you were really keen on the music," Leanne said, picking up the leaflet about the band.

The next day, as Esther made her way to town for another visit to the voice, she reflected that it was the only relief from the boredom of her existence. She had no memories of what she had done before she had come to the house, but now her days consisted of household chores, gardening or, if it was wet, reading. One of Ray's rules was that she could not go beyond the drive; she did not know why, as the other girls came and went as they liked.

Starting with Love and Friendship, a collection of fictional letters, she planned to work her way through all of Jane Austen's books: Pride and Prejudice, Emma, Persuasion, Sense and Sensibility, Northanger Abbey and Mansfield Park were still to come. She had no idea whether she had read any of them before, but in any case, it didn't matter, because she would not remember the plot.

She had been confused and worried when she first found herself in the medieval world, but looked forward to going now. She still did not understand whether it was a waking dream or whether she had actually travelled hundreds of years back in time; she had no memory of whether time travel was possible or not. She liked the fact that there were no restrictions: she could walk where she wanted and talk freely to Estrila. In the castle, her lost memory did not matter. If she could help Estrila simply by being there, letting the girl tell her story, being the companion she had longed for, if she could immerse herself in this other life, it made her time at the house more bearable.

At the sound of the voice, she slipped easily into the passageway, eager to see where she would come out today. As she stepped through the wooden door, the air was fresh, with no unpleasant smells, which meant that nobody was working at the tanning pits. She was standing on an incline above the castle, a position from which she was able to see that the castle had an inner courtyard garden. She thought how pleasant it would be to walk there one day, or in the small, private garden to the side, surrounded by a willow fence. She recognised some of the plants growing there – sage, fennel, chives. Beyond that was a more open garden with roses and marigolds.

She turned her attention to the church, which lay straight ahead. Beneath the large rose window, Estrila stood in the ornate porch in a sumptuous blue dress thickly embroidered with silver, blue ribbons in her hair and a garland of orange blossom around her head. The man who stood next to her had the slightly stooped posture of an old man. He was dressed in a thick velvet tunic and cloak, lavishly embroidered and trimmed with fox fur.

In front of the church, a large crowd had gathered, people of all classes, from peasants dressed in thin woollen tunics and scuffed boots, to noblemen in silks and furs and fine shoes. Women in their old, thin dresses held children on their shoulders and young men climbed the trees to get a better view. Esther left her position on the hillside and went towards the crowd, realising that this was Estrila's wedding day. She wanted to beg the priest not to marry these two, but he would not have heard her, even if she had dared to speak.

Goran's voice rang out strong, with authority and carried to the back of the crowd. "I receive you as mine, so that you become my wife and I your husband." Estrila made a similar declaration, but her voice was little more than a whisper and people at the back called out, "Speak up!"

The villagers dispersed as the wedding guests entered the church for the wedding mass. The church was full, with no spare seats, but in any case, Esther would not have risked sitting down among the crowd. She propped herself against the cold stone of the wall at the back and listened, but could understand nothing the priest said. Eventually she went outside and sat in the sun, waiting for the service to finish.

After the mass, the guests made their way to the castle for the wedding reception in the Great Hall. It was looking splendid, bedecked in pale yellow and white roses, great baskets of them. Above the huge fireplace was the family's coat of arms: two winged horses either side of a shield and two wild boars above. Tables had been placed down the length of the hall, with one across the top on a raised platform. The bride and groom and their families took the top table, while the other guests seated themselves on the side tables. They had each brought their own knife, spoon and cup and placed them on the table in front of them, but apart from that, it was not that different from a modern wedding. Servants brought out food from the kitchen into a side passage, and pages carried it from there into the hall, where each dish was shared between six guests. First came plates of scones, followed by strawberry soup and pottages. The meat course consisted of several stuffed swans, a boars' head, woodcocks and pheasants, all surrounded by fresh fruit. There were eels, tench, a whole tuna, various pies and pastries, and platters of cheese.

Musicians played from the gallery while the guests ate. Esther recognised some of their instruments - recorders, a violin, a triangular harp and something that looked like a bass guitar - but she had never seen the curved wooden instrument that sounded like bagpipes before.

Estrila picked at the food. Only once did her serious face break into laughter as the minstrel embarked on a very long tale.

One day a fair maid did espy
A snow white squirrel, pink of eye
Young man, come lie beneath the tree
A curious sight I will show to thee

When it finished to rousing cheers, Esther whispered to Estrila that it was time for her to go, and she would be back soon. Estrila nodded slightly in acknowledgement. To the wedding guests, it simply looked as if she was nodding in agreement at something her husband had said.

CHAPTER 7

Esther emerged into the daylight of the twenty-first century, the crumhorn still ringing in her ears. She was on the side of the hill, beside a garden. Cars passed close to her on the narrow road, but even the petrol fumes smelt better than the foul smells of the unwashed crowd outside the church.

She still had a little time before meeting Tom, so she decided to have a look around the garden. Going through a metal gate, she followed a curved gravel path and, turning a corner, she passed through the rose garden, the beds full of old fashioned yellow and white blooms. At the back of the bed, the stone garden wall was covered in a shower of wild roses. She paused, drawing in the heady perfume which filled her nostrils; for a moment, she thought she was back with Estrila.

She left the rose garden and followed the sloping path gently upwards, giving her a view in the distance of a steep hill rising from the flat valley. The landscape had changed little in the last seven hundred years, and it was unmistakably the same view she had seen from the castle windows. The fields were much larger now, but the cattle still grazed on the flat land, sheep decorated the hillside, and the farmer ploughed the fields, this time with a tractor.

She followed the sound of trickling water and, going through a stone archway, came across a quiet, shaded area where she could sit among the ferns and contemplate the stream which ran through this part of the garden. Watching her was a stone statue of a lady sitting on a crescent seat, her long hair spilling down in curls and her long dress swirling in the wind. Esther peered at the statue's face. It looked just like Estrila.

Deciding to explore the place more the next time she was in town, she left the garden and went down to the High Street, looking forward to meeting Tom again. He was waiting for her outside the café he had taken her to the first time they had met. "I was worried you weren't coming," he said as she reached him.

"I'm sorry, I lost track of the time," Esther said.

"Do you mind if I go and buy a book first?" Tom asked. "The book shop emailed me to say the one I'd ordered was in and I'd like to get there before the it shuts." Unbidden, a memory came into Esther's head of the time she had gone shopping with someone, a man, she didn't remember who he was, perhaps her husband, if she had one. She had tried on a pale blue dress, tight at the waist, with a skirt which flared out, showing off her shapely legs. When he had seen it, he had said, "You're too fat for that, go and take it off." It wasn't so much the memory of the words which stung, but the way it made her feel: small, ugly, unloved and unlovable. If this was an example of the memories that lay in waiting to pounce out at her when she was passing, she would rather not remember.

"Here it is," Tom said, arriving at a shop that sold New Age supplies. Crystals and wind chimes hung in the window, moving slightly in a gentle breeze from the open door, their tinkling sounds reaching out into the street. Hanging from the door were several long, flowing gowns of the sort that the ladies had been wearing at the festival for St Cullen.

"It's a book on heraldry," Tom said. "They have quite a collection in here."

While Tom went to get his book, Esther looked at the display of crystals of all different types and colours. A green Moldavite was, she read, from outer space and "helps to awaken and accelerate spiritual awareness and cosmic consciousness." As she put it back, she noticed a stone with brown and orange stripes, highly polished but unmistakably her talisman stone. She picked it up and held it tight, thinking back to the wedding ceremony and the celebrations in the Great Hall.

"Tiger's Eye," Tom's said behind her. "It allows the wearer to see everything, even through closed doors. Could be useful." How very true that was! Her talisman stone had opened the door to the past and allowed her to enter a world that was hundreds of years old.

"Time for a coffee?" Tom asked. Esther paid for her stone and as they left the shop, he tucked her arm through his. She felt like a fraud. She had asked Tom if he would meet her because she felt she owed him an explanation, but now the time had come, she had nothing she wanted to tell him. Her secrets, whatever they were, were best kept where they were, locked away where she could not think about them.

They went to the café with the blue painted fascia again. When they were seated with their drinks, Tom asked, "Did your friends enjoy the music?"

Esther nodded. "Yes, very much."

"So who is this Ray, then?" Tom asked. "Are you married to him?"

Esther put down her cup with a clatter. "Oh no, did you think that?"

"You were clearly nervous when he came over and I was talking to you. You wanted me to go," he pointed out.

Esther blushed. "I'm sorry." She hung her head and waited for her punishment.

Tom reached over and touched her hand. "You don't have to be sorry," he said. "I just need to know."

"I'm not married to Ray," Esther said. "That's one thing I do know. I'm not involved with him, except that …"

"Except that?" Tom prompted.

"I'm not married to anyone, at least …"

Tom withdrew his hand. "I just need to know, Esther, whether I'm wasting my time."

Esther felt herself beginning to withdraw, to the place she went to avoid being hurt. She had been foolish to think that she could be with a man. She wasn't ready for that. She stood up quickly, spilling her coffee on the table.

"I'll go and get a cloth," Tom said. When he got back, she was gone.

***

As the tyres crunched over the gravel of the drive, Esther was relieved to see that Ray was not waiting for her to get back this time. As she hung her jacket on the blue plastic hook in the hall, he beckoned her into kitchen. "Come in here," he said, his voice unnaturally calm and controlled. Somewhere in the depths of her mind she knew that voice, remembered that it meant danger. She sat down on the small metal steps, the ones Ray used to get things out of the top cupboards, on alert as Ray picked up a knife and continued chopping vegetables.

"What is it?" Esther asked.

"I checked. Your appointment finished early. Where have you been all this time?" Esther followed the movement of his knife as he waved it in her direction. She stood up, ready to run.

"You know what this means. You've broken the rules. You'll have to go back."

"Back where?"

"Back where you came from."

She remembered nothing about that place – where it was, why she was there – but she knew there had been pain, terrible pain.

"No, don't send me back," Esther said, wringing her hands. "Not back there."

"I have to tell them."

"It was just this once. I won't do it again."

"How do I know that? It was that Tom, wasn't it? I knew he was trouble when I saw him at the folk club."

"I know, you're right," Esther said and Ray looked at her sharply.

"Is this some sort of trick?" he asked.

"No, I did meet him, you're right, but I realised I'd made a mistake. I'm not ready for that. Please, I won't do it again." How on earth could she have imagined she would get away with it?

"I might, but on one condition."

"Anything."

"I will drive you there and wait for you and bring you back."

Esther sighed with relief. She didn't even mind her punishment. With Ray there, she would not have to speak to Tom even if she did see him.

***

As he drove home, Tom was in a bad mood. He liked Esther (he didn't know why, she was so infuriating!). He

66

wanted to get to know her, but he didn't understand what the problem was. If Esther *was* involved with someone else, she should tell him and stop playing these mind games. He was so preoccupied, he nearly ran over a pheasant, only noticing the distinctive blue and red plumage as the bird plunged into the hedgerow.

He had wanted to invite Esther to the Ham Hill Medieval Fair to be held next weekend, but before he had the chance, she had disappeared again. The Witcombe Valley was a hundred acre valley, inhabited until the sixteenth century. There had been a small hamlet of around ten houses, each farming a small plot of land. The village had disappeared long ago, but the park rangers had reinstated the medieval pond and stream, which at one time was diverted through underground pipes, but now ran once again through the valley. Arriving home, he made a decision. For his own peace of mind, it would be best not to bump into Esther any more. He would keep away.

Home was a cottage in the village of Stoke sub Hamden which he had bought two years previously. He had looked at the view of far reaching countryside from the back garden and had made an instant decision to buy the place. Soon after he moved in, a black cat had come to visit, eyeing him hopefully, making it plain that he wanted to live with him. He smiled wryly. It was a bit like him and Esther. He was the cat, watching, waiting for an opportunity, hoping for a kind word and to be let in.

He rubbed the cat under the chin before opening the gate. Predictably the cat got down and followed him up the path, as it had every day since he had bought the house. He was just taking a bag of frozen peas out of the freezer when there was a knock at the door. When he saw the police constable on the doorstep, his mind instantly went to Esther.

"Have I done something wrong?" he asked.

She shook her head. "No, sir, I just need to speak to you."

"What is it? I'm just cooking my dinner."

"I'm sorry to disturb you, but it really is important. Perhaps I could come in for a few minutes."

Tom shut the door behind her and retreated to the kitchen to turn off the cooker. The kettle had just boiled. "Do you want coffee or tea or anything?"

"Nothing for me," she said. When he came out of the kitchen with a steaming cup of coffee, she was still standing by the front door.

He led her into the lounge, where the cat was stretched out on one of the chairs, looking pleased with itself and licking its paw. He noticed how untidy the place would look to a stranger: papers all over the table, CDs scattered over the chair, the rug in front of the fire in need of a clean. He wasn't very handy at housework. He picked up the CDs and motioned her to sit. She perched herself next to the cat, stroking it absentmindedly as she talked to him.

She introduced herself as PC Wilson. "We're making some enquiries about a lady called Esther. I believe you know her."

Tom blinked. He had only met her briefly. How could they know about that?

"What's this all about?" he asked.

"I'm sorry I can't give you any details, but any information you have would be helpful."

"I don't have any details. We've just had a coffee a couple of times. I bumped into her in town – quite literally."

"What did she tell you about herself?"

Tom's thoughts were racing ahead, but whatever the problem, he couldn't help because he didn't know anything. "Nothing," he said at last. "I asked her if she was married and she was a bit vague. That's all."

"So is she married then?"

"I don't know, as I say, she was a bit vague."

"It's really important. Please try to think back to that conversation. Did you get the impression that she *was* married?"

Tom replayed the scene in his mind. "She said she was not married to a man called Ray. I don't know what their connection is, but she definitely said she wasn't married to him."

The constable nodded. "Anything else?"

"Her exact words were – let me get this right. *I'm not married to anyone, at least –* "

"At least what?"

"That was all she said. At least. She didn't say anything else after that."

"I see." She stood up. "You've been very helpful, thank you. I'll come back to you if we have any more questions, but here is the number to call if you remember anything else."

***

A hundred and thirty miles away, Archie had gone to interview the parents of the girl who was suffering from brain damage.

Mr Tindall worked in the RBS bank in the High Street. On the day of the murder, the bank manager confirmed that he had been working all day as usual. He had gone out at lunch time and returned an hour later. Archie reflected that this would have given him ample time to get to Fergus' house and back.

Archie spoke to Mr Tindall who said he usually went to one of the many eating places on the High Street. His favourite was the Twins' Coffee Shop, but he didn't know whether he'd been there that day.

He went to see Mrs Tindall. She had just returned from a visit to her daughter and was in no mood to talk. "It's about Fergus Cormac," Archie told her.

"That liar!" Mrs Tindall said. "He's the reason the driver's walking around instead of rotting in prison. Someone should make him pay for what he did."

Both of them had a reason to hate Fergus. Maybe they just went round there to talk to him, try to get him to change his story and it got out of hand. He would wait to see what the door-to-door enquiries brought.

CHAPTER 8

Esther felt guilty about the way she'd run out on Tom. She was not being fair to him, she knew, but life was so confusing. She didn't know who to trust, she couldn't even remember *how* to know whether someone was trustworthy. She realised how much people rely on their past. It was there that people learned what they needed to know, from social etiquette, to how to recognise a conman. She would do everything that Ray said, in the hope that in time she would understand, or her memory would come back. She certainly did not understand his rules or his punishments at the moment and had no way of knowing whether he would stick to what he had told her: that he would not send her back as long as he took her to town and brought her home again. She wasn't interested in meeting Tom any more.

She was in the middle of ironing when Leanne said, "Come for a walk with me, there's something I want to show you."

"No, I'm sorry, I can't."

"It's just beyond the drive."

"I'm not allowed out there."

"Don't be so stupid. Nothing's going to happen to you." Esther continued ironing and Leanne said, "How about helping me with my hair then."

"I must finish this. Maybe in half an hour's time."

Leanne knocked the pile of ironing off of the chair as she went by. "Sorry," she said, laughing as she went out the door.

Ray came in. "Leanne tells me you asked her to go for a walk with you later," he said. "I told you you're not allowed out there. Do that again and I'm definitely sending you back."

Later, Leanne walked into Esther's room without knocking. "You never paid me for that pink leather handbag of mine you wanted," she said.

"You gave it to me. You said it was a present."

"You stupid liar. I did no such thing." She grabbed the bag from the bed and searched inside. Finding two pound coins, she pocketed them and threw the bag back.

"I want more next time Ray gives you money," she said.

Esther lay on her bed, tears falling. She was alone in a world she didn't understand.

Perhaps because she knew Ray was outside waiting for her, or perhaps because she was upset at Leanne's tricks, her next trip to the castle did not go well. She went through the passage and found herself in the Great Hall. It was empty and still and she wasn't sure she was even in the same castle. There were logs in the fireplace but no fire. The floor was unswept, the tables littered with remains of food. In the corridor leading to the kitchen, all the doors were closed. She opened each door cautiously but everywhere was deserted. In one room, a heavy book lay open on a table as if someone had just been reading; in another, someone had been writing at a desk and had left half way through a sentence. The writing, which was in a foreign language, trailed off, the final three letters drooping as if the scribe had suddenly lost concentration.

She wandered around the deserted castle until she came to a room that she recognised as the one where Robert and William had been talking and plotting. There was nobody there, but a book carousel was slowly turning, as if someone had brushed past it before leaving.

She made her way downstairs to the kitchens, where a large animal lay pierced on the roasting spit above a fire that had once been lit, but was now a pile of ash. Half cooked bread lay in the bread oven and a swan hung from a hook in the ceiling. A big pot of honey stood open on a large wooden table, dead flies stuck to the inside. In the laundry room, a pile of clothes was heaped in the sink. Esther stalked the silent corridors until she came to a door to the outside, swinging loose on its hinges. She looked out. Even the village had gone. Where houses had been, there was just a dirt track leading through scrub land.

The gardens she had seen from the hillside were on this side of the castle, untended, with weeds choking the plants. She walked through the herb garden into an orchard. Struggling to walk through grass which grew several feet high in place, she opened the door of a small, conical shaped building with gaps all around the walls. It was a dovecote. The sides were thick with excrement but there was no sign of any birds.

She made her way back to the castle with a sense of loss. Where was Estrila? What had happened to her? Would she ever see her again? She walked back through the passageway and wakened to find herself laying on the couch in the back room of the terraced house in Pilbury.

When she left, Ray was leaning against the car, arms crossed. "What were you doing in there?" he said. "I didn't know you were going to take so long."

It had taken less time than usual, but she did not argue.

As they set off, he said, "You'd better cancel those sessions, I can't be driving to and fro like this, and you're not going on your own."

Esther felt her stomach knot. That was unfair. "But Ray," she began in her best, sickly sweet voice.

"No buts. That's my decision."

Esther held back the tears. She wouldn't let him see her cry and besides, after the way Leanne had treated her, she had remembered that it was not safe to let anyone see that you were vulnerable.

When they got back to the house, there was an ambulance in the drive and two men were supporting a pale and bleeding Leanne, helping her into the vehicle. She had cut her wrists.

Inside, the girls were in a state of shock. Yasmeen was reading the Koran and Rachel the Torah. Fiona sat staring into space, her mascara running down her face.

"Why didn't you look after her while I was gone?" Ray yelled. "Can't you get anything right? You knew she wasn't well."

Esther went into the kitchen and began to put the groceries away. She understood nothing. Fiona was shouting, "You can't blame me. It's not my fault."

Dinner was late that day. Ray ate in his office. The girls ate in silence until Ray came in with bowls of apple pie and ice cream and slammed them on the table.

"I want the kitchen cupboards cleaned, inside and out," he said. "There will be no TV this evening."

When he had gone, Fiona said, "He's punishing us for what she did. It's not fair."

Rachel said, "We'd better just do as he says."

Esther said nothing. It was just one more confusing thing that had happened in this house. She did not wish Leanne ill, but she was glad that she was no longer around to torment her.

She cleared away the plates and washed up, then called the others in to help her with the cupboards. She began by lining up the sauce bottles on the worktop – brown sauce, tomato sauce, salad cream, barbecue sauce (when had they ever had a barbecue?), mustard…

It was gone midnight by the time Esther got to bed, exhausted but unable to sleep. She picked up Sense and Sensibility from her bedside table, but she couldn't focus. The room revolved and suddenly she was standing on the top of a very steep hill.

People down below were snaking their way up, looking like a line of ants following a sticky trail. They wore long hooded cloaks made of rough woollen cloth tied around the waist with a rope, and cowls pulled around their faces. When they came close to Esther, they reached up with bony fingers and pulled their hoods back. None of them had a face. She shrank back in horror and fell off the hillside.

She woke with a start. The dream had been so vivid. She lay still, staring at the ceiling, feeling sick. Someone knocked on the door.

"Esther, Ray is asking where you are." Esther swung her legs off the bed and onto the floor. The door opened and Yasmeen's concerned peered in.

"Yes, I know," she said. "He likes us all to eat together." She pulled her clothes off the chair and said, "I'll be straight there."

Rachel had almost finished her breakfast as she had to catch a bus into town, where she had a part-time job in an estate agent's. Yasmeen sat looking out of the window, nibbling on a piece of toast. Fiona drummed her fingers on the table until Ray glared at her. Esther slumped down in her chair and tried to eat but her head felt as if it was attached to her body by nothing but a few loose stitches.

When Rachel had gone and Ray was in his office, Yasmeen helped Esther clear the table and wash up. They worked silently, aware that Ray was only a few feet away. As they left the kitchen, Yasmeen said, "I leave soon. I will miss you very much."

"Leaving?" Esther said. She had been about to go upstairs, but she sat down on the first step instead and looked up at Yasmeen. "How can you leave?"

Yasmeen sat on one of the hall chairs. "Your government tells me I can stay in your beautiful country. They give me job and home and even paint it for me. You have such wonderful government."

"I didn't know it was possible," Esther said.

"Oh yes, they have – what do you call it? Granted me asylum." She stumbled over the difficult phrase.

"I didn't know it was possible to leave *here*," Esther said, silently adding, I am a prisoner. I can't even go beyond the drive, let alone leave.

"Of course, perhaps you will leave soon also. Perhaps you ask Mr Ray. He will know."

"How long have I been here?"

"You do not know?"

"I cannot remember."

"Just a few weeks."

A door banged. Ray had opened his office door so violently, it had smashed against the wall. He stood in the hallway, glaring at Esther. She stood up quickly and went upstairs, followed by the sound of Ray's voice calling up to her. "You know what will happen if you stop the others from getting on with their work."

As she reached the top of the stairs, she heard Yasmeen's quiet voice. "Oh no, Mr Ray, it was not Esther's fault."

Ray was already heading back to his office.

Later, Yasmeen knocked quietly on Esther's bedroom door and told her things she had never told anyone: how she had watched her entire family being slaughtered, and the perilous journey to England. Esther prayed that she would not discover such horrors when her own memory returned.

CHAPTER 9

As he watered the plants in his office, Archie noticed that the rubbish in the garden at the back of the antiques place was being cleared. He hoped it wasn't going to be turned into a place for customers to park, like some of the other gardens at the backs of the shops. Soon there would be no corridor for the wildlife to roam.

PC Jessica knocked and entered, looking pleased with herself. "Sir, I thought you'd like to know straight away that a traffic warden has just rung in as a result of the piece on the TV. She says she remembers a car being parked in a residents' parking bay on the day of the murder, but it drove away before she could issue a ticket."

Archie looked at her keenly. This could be promising. They needed a lead. Two of the team had shown the Tindalls' picture to Fergus' neighbours but the best they had come up with was, "They look familiar, but I'm not sure."

Hopefully this latest information would prove more helpful. "Did she get the registration number?" he asked.

"Not all of it. She was just about to write it down when the driver left. But she remembers part of it. There was an F and Y at the start. She knew the time it was in the road, because she issued a ticket a few minutes before in the next street. That time puts the car at the scene around the time of the murder."

"So she didn't hear any disturbance, didn't see anyone going into Fergus' house?"

"She says not."

"Did she notice what sort of car it was?"

"She said it was a Citroen C4. She was quite certain about it."

"She'd make a more reliable witness than the member of the public," Archie said. "And juries always believe traffic wardens, even though they hate them. Follow up on the car, then, and let me know what you discover."

"We're already on to it, sir."

Archie hoped it turned out to be a good lead. Up to now, they had made no more progress on the murder than they were with knowing who Esther was. He hoped Kenneth would have some new thoughts.

The police psychologist looked up as Archie entered. "I've just been looking at the latest report on Esther," he said, "The one where the castle's empty."

"Have you had any thoughts about that?"

"There are several possibilities. It might represent some sort of loss in the past – a parent, a husband, or perhaps some other loss that was felt on a deep level. The memories that have begun to surface in Esther's mind could be so upsetting that her mind has switched off, for her own protection. It might mean that she simply doesn't want to talk to us."

"I see. Apparently Ray decided to drive Esther to the sessions and wait for her, although no-one authorised it. He was worried about security risks, and a man called Tom."

"That could explain things. Esther could resent what she sees as Ray's interference and it's her way of not cooperating with us. Did you check out this Tom?"

"Yes, we sent a constable round there. He seems like a normal guy, no criminal records."

"It's important that Esther is allowed to go to the sessions without any interference from Ray."

"I'll make sure it happens."

Archie made his way back to his own office, where Jessica was waiting for him. "I've been checking a few things," she said as he came in. "When Fergus' mother went into a nursing home, she signed a power of attorney over to Fergus. When the father died, Fergus had control over all financial matters. He was named as executor of his father's will too. When his brother Kiernan learnt that Fergus was dead, he came down and is staying in his father's house. He found a copy of the will and it wasn't what he expected. A third went to him, a third to Fergus and a third to a Mrs Dora Abbott of Kentish Town. Kiernan had never heard of her."

"When was the will signed?"

"About three weeks ago, a few days before the elderly Mr Cormac died."

***

Ray had been in a foul mood since Leanne's suicide attempt, but Esther needed to talk to him about the visits. She waited in the kitchen, coffee at the ready. The moment the clock hand clicked onto eleven, Ray opened the office door.

Esther poured the coffee and looked up at him, tilting her head to one side. "Can I speak to you?" she asked. She watched his face carefully, looking for a flicker of anger or flush to the cheeks that would indicate danger. "Did you really mean that I should not go to Pilbury anymore?"

"Yes."

Esther pulled at her hair, twisting it around her fingers. "They said I had to go."

80

Ray shrugged. "That's not my problem."

She risked going on, even though his lips had tightened.

"Ray, will I get out of here one day?"

"Who knows?" He turned and went back to the office.

Esther shrank into herself. She wished she understood what was happening and why they recorded everything that happened with Estrila. Was she being used in some kind of experiment? Perhaps it wasn't the details of what happened hundreds of years ago that mattered, but something else. Could Ray be putting a new drug in her food that gave her hallucinations? She'd heard of such things.

***

Ray picked the phone up almost before it had rung.

"Ray, what's going on there? I'm told you insisted on taking Esther to her last appointment. Why did you do that?"

"Well, I just thought… "

"We got nothing out of her last time."

"She was getting back at all times, I didn't know where she'd been. She might have been seeing that Tom or somebody else. I've been told to keep her safe at all costs."

"You know the police are watching us, so don't mess this up. You've made one serious mistake already. You're lucky Fiona found Leanne and called the ambulance in time."

"That wasn't my fault," Ray began, but the man on the other end cut across him. "You might have jeopardised the whole operation. She's not telling us anything now. Just let the girl go to her appointments as before – and don't make any more decisions without running them past me. If she doesn't speak again, it's you who'll get the blame – and the sack."

Ray slammed down the phone. They didn't have any idea of what it was like here. It was he who had to deal with the everyday problems, with no proper instructions and no training. He had half a mind to walk out.

Back in her bedroom, Esther took the Tiger's Eye crystal from the bottom of her underwear drawer where she had hidden it. She suspected Ray searched her room while she was in Pilbury, but with his dislike, phobia even, of all things feminine, he would never go delving in there. She held it up to the light and traced her finger along the stripes of brown and gold, wondering whether she could visit the castle without the help of the voice. Holding the crystal in her palm, she lay down on her bed with her eyes closed, listening to the sounds of noises of the twenty-first century – cars speeding along the bypass, the refrigerator with its intermittent hum, the sound of the vacuum cleaner coming from Fiona's bedroom. She did not slip into the castle, but she did have an idea.

She got up and took the plastic bag that had held her possessions from the bottom of the wardrobe, filling it with a change of underwear, her precious notebook, the Tiger's Eye and a spare toothbrush. She replaced it in the wardrobe, covering the contents with a pack of tampons. Ray kept a calendar on the kitchen wall with details of where everyone would be. It showed that Rachel and Fiona would be at work tomorrow, the day Yasmeen was leaving. There was a note in the margin: 'Yasmeen, 10 a.m. Taunton station'. Ray never allowed her to stay in the house on her own, and would be expecting her to accompany him, but she had other ideas. She had gone over and over the plan and could not see any flaw.

The next day, she lay in bed, knowing that someone would soon come by to tell her it was time to get up. When she heard the loud knocking on her door, sounding like gunfire, she knew it was Ray. "I'm not well, it's my period," she called out. She knew he would not stay for a further explanation. He grunted and said, "You can have fifteen more minutes then I want you dressed and downstairs."

She got dressed and waited the allotted time. Looking in the mirror, she saw that she looked too healthy: her cheeks were red, her eyes bright. She used mascara to smudge dark bags under her eyes, put on her sunglasses and left her hair unkempt. When she entered the dining room, the others were tucking into plates of fried bread, mushrooms and tomatoes.

"You look awful," Fiona said.

"Let me get you a coffee," said Yasmeen, reaching for the coffee pot.

"I think I've got a temperature, I feel terrible. It gets to me like this sometimes." She sat down at her place and nibbled at a bit of toast and sipped at the coffee.

"I'm not dragging you around like that," Ray said. "You can stay here until I get back." He had been given instructions to never leave her alone in the house, but nothing would happen to her. He had drummed it into her that she was not allowed beyond the drive, and it didn't take much to make Esther do as she was told.

"Do you need anything?" Yasmeen asked.

"I could do with some more tampons," she said.

"That's enough," Ray said angrily. "You don't talk about that stuff in front of me."

Rachel leant over and said, "I've got some you can have."

It was the one weak spot Ray had, his one vulnerability. He couldn't stand "women's stuff". That one vulnerability had been her key to getting out of here.

After breakfast, Esther went back to her bedroom and watched from behind her curtain. The single decker white bus appeared and disappeared along the line of the hedgerow but there was no sign of Fiona or Rachel. If they missed it, there was another hour to wait and that would ruin her plan.

She continued to watch. A little later, Yasmeen, Rachel, Fiona and Ray left the house together. Yasmeen's voice drifted up: "But I want to say goodbye to Esther."

"Hurry up," was all Ray said. "I've got to drop the others off first."

She got in the people carrier, sitting in the front for the first and last time, watched by Esther from her bedroom window. Esther was sorry to see her go.

CHAPTER 10

The house was silent except for the gentle noises from outside: the rustling of wind in the trees, a blackbird's distress call. Now that the time had come, the time when she was going to escape, uncertainty began to creep in. Although she could not remember any details of her life, the feeling persisted that if she broke the rules, something terrible would follow.

As she sat down heavily on the bed, an inner voice began to taunt her. 'Where will you go to anyway?' it asked. 'You know nobody, you have no friends'. Suddenly, from the depths of her forgotten memories came a face, a heart shaped face with straight blond hair.

More painful memories floated to the surface, crowding each other, jostling for position. 'You've always been a liar,' the woman was saying. 'When we were little, you were always getting me into trouble. It was you who scratched all over the brick wall in the porch, but Mum and Dad blamed me when you said you hadn't done it. I don't believe a word you say now.'

Another face crowded into the scene. It had the same heart shape but was older, harsher, the hair grey. 'You've been spreading tales, you wicked girl. You've got to stop that.'

Esther struggled to catch the elusive memory as it passed into her conscious mind for a moment before disappearing. She wanted to know what she had been telling them, but it remained out of reach, showing her only a younger self, tears glistening in her eyes, crying, 'I'm telling the truth.' Esther lay on her bed and curled up like a baby in the womb.

The voice wouldn't stop. 'You won't get round me like that,' the older woman said. 'I know your tricks.' Esther felt the pain of that day and suddenly, here was the memory, forcing its way through the thick layers of amnesia, demanding to be heard. She had been trying to talk to someone about … Esther shook her head. It was gone again, but the feeling that she could not go to her family remained with her. No, these were not people she could look to for help.

There was one person, the only person she knew, Tom, but she had run away from him twice. She could not expect him to help her. As she threw her bag back in the bottom of the wardrobe, another voice spoke to her, a different voice, a voice of a stronger Esther telling her that she might never get another chance to leave. She could worry about the details later. The important thing now was to get away.

With renewed purpose, she hurried downstairs and into the car, put the key in the ignition and turned. The engine groaned and died. She tried again. Nothing. She stared at the dashboard as if it could tell her what the problem was. As her glance fell on the petrol gauge, she saw that it was on zero. That couldn't be right, she'd filled it up last week and she hadn't been out since. Ray never used this car. He preferred sitting up high in the people carrier, lording it over everybody on the road.

She tapped the gauge and tried again. Nothing. There was only one conclusion to come to. Someone had either been on a long journey, or drained the car of petrol.

She went back indoors slowly. The sneering voice was back. *How foolish to think you could get away with it*, it chided her. *You've always been powerless. You know you must always do what other people want. You're not capable of thinking for yourself, you need someone to tell you what to do.*

Her mind began to taunt her with memories of her own helplessness: she was a toddler in a big hall somewhere, sitting quietly with her mother. She heard music, music that made her want to dance and move around. She slipped down from her chair and for a moment, she was lost in the moment. Suddenly, her mother's hand pulled her hard. "Come and sit down," she hissed. "Don't draw attention to yourself." She had never danced since.

What about your father, the voice inside her head went on, it was the same with your father. Here she was again, a teenager, watching a comedy on Channel 4, laughing out loud. And here was her father, storming angrily into the room and switching off the television. "We don't watch Channel 4 in this house," were his chilling words.

Remember how he used to lock the door at ten p.m. every night, the voice reminded her, *how the other girls would laugh at you when you told them you couldn't go to a nightclub or party with them, or even the school dance. After a while, they stopped asking you.*

Esther covered her ears and tried to blot out the voice, reminding herself that she was living somewhere else now. The sunlight bounced off the white walls and a sparrow looking in the window with its head to one side. The voice had gone, but it had left its words behind, like footsteps in damp sand. She had known since she was tiny that her place in the world was to do what others told her to do, that she counted for nothing. She had learnt to hide beneath a thick, protective layer, to pretend to be someone else, act a part, be the 'someone' others wanted her to be.

It was all coming back now. Small incidents, which seemed just part of life at the time, but there had been so many, they had been like a dripping tap, wearing away at her confidence. Both her parents' insistence that she did exactly what they wanted had eroded her very self, until she became like a puppet, never thinking for herself. Others had controlled her life for as long as she could remember, drumming in the message that she was unimportant and must do what they wanted.

The sound of the tyres on gravel cut into Esther's reverie and the memories slunk back into the slime of her subconscious. Ray was back. All she could do was resign herself to never getting out of here. She had to accept that seeing Estrila had been the one time she had been free, and now even that had been taken away from her.

The front door shut noisily and Ray called up the stairs. "Esther, come down here!".

She decided to ignore him. If he said anything later, she would say that she had been asleep. She'd get up this afternoon and do some gardening. It always lifted her mood to see the plants she had sown growing up strong. There was a quantity of ripe fruit and vegetables that she needed to pick and freeze for the winter too. Nobody else would do it.

She jumped as Ray banged on the door. "Esther, get up. They've changed the time of your appointment. You're to go straight away," he said.

Esther was startled by the news. There was nothing she would like to do more, but there was no way she could drive there.

She opened the door. "There's no petrol in my car," she said. "I'll have to take a can to the garage first."

"What are you talking about?" Ray said. "You filled it up last week."

"Are you coming too?"

"No. Now hurry up."

Not quite believing what was happening, Esther got into her car and put the key in the ignition. The petrol gauge moved. She had a full tank.

***

Dora Abbott's address turned out to be a luxury penthouse. Archie and Jessica took the lift to the top floor and knocked on the door. It was answered by a short, tired looking woman in her mid thirties, dressed in a cheap track suit and carrying a broom. Archie assumed she was the housekeeper but said, "Dora Abbott?"

"You're the second person who's come looking for her. You've got the wrong address. I've never heard of her." Archie could see that behind her, the flat was completely without furniture. At the back, a balcony stretched along the side of the property with extensive views over London.

Archie checked he had the right address, then said, "Do you live here?"

"No, I'm just looking after it until the owners move in."

"And your name?"

"Mandy Davis."

Archie took the picture of Fergus from his file and said, "Do you recognise this man?"

"Yes, that's him, the one who was looking for this Dora Abbott. He said she was his half sister. He looked upset, said he hadn't known about her until a few days before."

"You're sure it's him?"

"I don't forget a face. What's this all about?"

"Just making enquiries."

As they walked back to where Archie had parked his car, he said, "Go round to the address she gave later, see if she was telling the truth."

***

Seb didn't like to admit it, but he had assumed that the Somerset Levels was a small area and he would easily be able to find Angela, but in fact it was over thirty miles across. He had driven around for a bit rather aimlessly, passing through many small villages with unusual names, such as Othery and Westonzoyland but he needed a better plan. At lunch time, he met up with Rolf and told him to ring Jonathan Whicher.

Jonathan was not surprised to hear from Rolf again. He had passed on Cynthia's message and been told his involvement was finished, but he had learned a long time ago that sooner or later, people who thought they could do his job would always come back to him. It wasn't as easy as people imagined. You needed contacts, you needed to know how to talk to people so they gave you the information you needed without realising it.

"Do you want me to come down there and help look for her?" he asked.

"Yes. Can you come straight away?"

"All right, I'll be there later," he said. "I'll let you know when I've arrived."

He left his office and stood behind Silvie, ruffling her hair, which was beginning to show the grey roots. Time for another visit to the hairdresser soon. "I'll be away for a few days, old girl," he said.

"Somerset?" Jonathan nodded. He had learned years ago never to react to the things clients did. That had been Sylvie's influence. When he was younger, he would get in a rage at some rudeness or injustice, but Silvie had calmed him down. Gradually he had learnt from her not to react, but to quietly work towards the result he wanted.

Human nature is a funny thing, she used to say. The people who came to him were all worried, upset, searching. For some, that came out in being rude, downright obnoxious sometimes, and with others, it meant phoning him up every five minutes, being ingratiating, but the message was always the same. They wanted him to perform miracles.

"I've never believed Rolf's story. Could you make some enquiries this end?" he asked. "Start by going to that address he gave, see what you can find out."

As he went out the door, she said, "Be careful, won't you," as she had done every day they had worked together.

CHAPTER 11

Esther stood on a gently sloping hill. She didn't recognise where she was. There was no sign of the castle and the only water was a slow moving river making its way down the valley. The harvest had been gathered in and the bare fields looked like strips of corrugated cardboard spread across the landscape.

A water wheel turned steadily and the blacksmith's metallic hammering rang out in a steady beat. A village nestled in the shelter of the valley, the wooden framed wattle and daub houses looking as if they might fall down if there was a strong gust of wind. A church stood nearby, a simple stone building with a small tower from which a single bell was suspended. Rain clouds gathered in the distance and there was a chill in the air. Esther pulled her thick woollen cloak tightly round her.

A path led upwards from a large manor house and disappeared into a slightly elevated wood. A number of men in faded blue woollen tunics could be seen snaking along the path, leading silent dogs. Back at the courtyard in front of the manor house, tables had been set out, laden with bread and flagons of wine. All the village seemed to have gathered here, the peasants grabbing handfuls of food and eating hungrily.

Nearby were the stables, a stone building that could house twenty or more animals. They were all out in the yard, being saddled up before being led to the courtyard where the riders were waiting. Next to the stables was a smaller building that housed the dogs. A group of big animals, black, tan and white hounds, waited in the grass enclosure in front of the kennels, their long tales waving like trees in the wind. From another building, two men brought out hawks and falcons, which sat still on their handler's arms or moved their heads from side to side.

Esther was surprised to see that a number of women were mounting the horses. She had assumed only men rode in those days. Some had replaced their headdresses with caps and others were bare-headed, their long hair braided and fixed tightly to their heads.

A man dressed in a black cloak edged with black and white fur and a horn slung round his shoulders, emerged from the manor house, stooping slightly but carrying himself with an air of authority. Lord Goran. Peasants bowed low as he passed and young boys scampered out of his way. The dogs were let out of their enclosure and ran eagerly to the courtyard, milling around under the horses, who lifted their legs and stamped on the ground. Goran raised the horn to his lips and the group followed him out of the courtyard, gathering speed over the rough countryside.

When the group had disappeared into the wood, there was still one horse left in the courtyard, a black stallion. It took two men to restrain it as it reared and pulled at the rope. Back at the village, a smartly dressed man left one of the bigger houses and walked towards the manor house. He spoke a few words to the groom, shook his head and seemed to be arguing with him. Shaking his head again, he moved slowly to the wooden mounting block. As soon as he was on the animal's back, it skittered sideways; the man slipped but managed to stay on the horse. He pulled hard on the reins, gained some control of the horse, sat firmly in the saddle and pounded out of the gate, already at a canter. The horse and rider disappeared from Esther's view for a few seconds, before emerging in an open field. The man was lying over the horse's neck, holding on tight to its mane.

As the grooms and dog handlers dispersed, a lady was left in the centre of the courtyard, watching the rider on the black stallion until she could see him no more. She turned to face Esther and began walking purposefully towards her, holding herself in the strange pose the ladies of this time favoured, with their belly protruding. She came up to Esther and without slowing her pace, she said "Walk with me, or the others will question why I have stopped". Esther was surprised by how much older Estrila looked, and wondered how much time had passed.

"Oh, I am so afraid." Estrila's voice was so quiet, Esther had to strain to hear. "Lord Goran has sent Sir Ranuulf on an errand. He ordered the black stallion to be made ready. Even Lord Goran does not ride the black stallion."

"You fear for his safety?"

"The horse is too strong for him."

"The man I saw riding out?"

"I believe that Lord Goran means him ill. I wished to stop him, but I have no power to influence my lord."

She turned to follow a path that could not be seen from the village, holding her hands over her belly.

"You are pregnant?" Esther said, but it was more of a statement. She instinctively knew it.

"I am with child," Estrila said.

"It is your first?"

"I hope this one will live," Estrila said. "I have been burdened with six miscarriages and two stillbirths." Her voice had not wavered as she spoke. She had expected nothing less.

Her breathing was heavy and her pace had slowed. "Let us sit for a few minutes," she said, pointing to a large, flat stone. "I must rest."

"I hope your baby lives," Esther said.

"Lord Goran is angry. He wants a son," Estrila said. Esther thought about this lonely girl facing the miscarriages and stillbirths on her own, without the comfort of her husband. The ghost of a memory passed like a shadow across her mind, but she let it go. She would catch it another time.

"I'm sorry," she said.

As if in answer to a question, Estrila said, "My lord is often away fighting for the king." She was silent for a moment before speaking more quickly. "He has ordered that a young boy's hand be cut off for snaring rabbits. He is only seven years old." She buried her head in her hands. "I cannot bear it."

"I am so sorry," Esther said then went on, "But what about you? Does he hurt you?"

"He does not beat me now I am with child."

"Can you not leave him?" It was a foolish question, Esther knew. Estrila's every movement had been dictated by her father and then her husband since she was born, but in any case, even in the twenty-first century, women were still unable to escape from men who abused them.

They sat in silence, looking at the scene below. Far in the distance, they saw a hart break cover and race across the open fields. When it could no longer run, it turned to face its enemy. Lord Goran dismounted from his horse, took his spear and walked slowly towards the animal.

"Why have you come?" Estrila asked.

Esther turned away so she could not see the killing of the deer. "I do not know. The voice tells me to enter a passage and each time I am led to you."

"Where have you come from?"

"From the future."

"This I know. But how far in the future? What is it like in your time?"

"In some ways, it is not so different from yours," Esther said.

"Do you have a child?" Estrila asked.

Esther's head began to pound. A memory was trying to push its way to the surface, but it was accompanied by fear. She felt instinctively that it was better not to remember. She put her head down between her knees until she felt better. When she looked up, Estrila was gone and she was sitting on the ground, overlooking a valley. The village and the manor house had both gone too.

She remembered standing on the hillside watching the hunt, and Estrila's worry for the man riding the black stallion, but nothing more. She blinked and looked around her, realising she was in the garden in Pilbury she had visited before. The sound of traffic hummed reassuringly in the distance and an aeroplane flew overhead, its vapour trail leaving a streak across the sky. She did not know how she had managed to get here. I must not visit Estrila again, she thought, it is too dangerous. One day I will not be able to find my way back.

More than anything, she wished Tom were here with his smiling face and cheery greeting. She'd thrown away his card, but not before she'd memorised his phone number, but she knew she would not ring him, not after the way she had behaved towards him.

She was not late going home, but her heart beat faster as she approached the house, afraid of Ray. As she drew into the drive, she saw him washing the people carrier and prepared herself for another lecture. As she got out of her car, Ray said, "Fix the hose will you, it's come loose." She tightened it where it fixed onto the outside tap, took a deep breath and said, "Ray, can I stop going to this appointment?"

Ray came towards her and she drew back. "Why? You were all keen to go the other day," he said.

"It's dangerous," Esther said.

"Nonsense," Ray replied. "You're completely safe. You know what will happen if you don't go. They will come and get you. Do you want to go back there?"

Esther didn't, but it was all so confusing. Yesterday, Ray had told her she couldn't go, now he said she had to.

CHAPTER 12

Silvie locked the office and set off for the address Rolf had given Jonathan. When she arrived, she wondered whether she had come to the right place. The houses to either side of Rolf's were well looked after, with neat gardens and pretty curtains at the windows, but the garden of Rolf's house was full of rubbish. The bin was overflowing, several black bags had split open and the contents dragged over the garden, probably by a fox. The windows were dirty and at the front, two dirty curtains were hanging off the curtain rail. The front door was filthy and the path broken and uneven.

Silvie trod carefully up to the door and searched for a bell. Finding none, she banged on the door and waited. Eventually it opened and a tall, thin man dressed in track suit bottoms and a vest and with several days' stubble on his chin stood before her.

"Yes?" he said, rubbing his eyes.

"Sorry to disturb you. Are you Rolf?"

The man shook his head and began to close the door. Silvie put one foot inside and said, "Do you know when he'll be back?"

The man said nothing and Silvie went on, "What about Angela. Is she here?"

"I not know anyone called Angela," the man said.

Silvie withdrew her foot. "Sorry, I must have the wrong address."

Back at the office, she checked the files. She had written the address down correctly. It was probably false.

People did that all the time. Archie rang to say he had arrived in Somerset and was not surprised to learn that Rolf's story of living with a girlfriend was untrue. There was something very strange about Rolf's tale. He showed very little concerned that his girlfriend had gone missing.

***

Archie sat in court, wishing he could be back at the office rather than spending the afternoon waiting to be called as a witness in a fraud case. A financial advisor had been fleecing little old ladies. He had travelled up and down the country persuading widows that he could give them a better rate of interest if they would pay their savings into his personal bank account instead of writing a cheque out to the various companies he recommended. He chose women whose husbands had always dealt with money and did not know what they were doing, the ones who were grateful to him, and had no idea of the consequences of entrusting their money to him.

What he was doing was completely illegal, of course. Once they handed over the cash, he gave them a good income for a few months and then told them that the company had gone bust. Most of the time, the ladies accepted it. They did not realise he had stolen their money until one day they opened the door to a policeman.

The financial advisor had operated his scam one time too many. He'd tried it out on a lady who had decided to fight back when he told her the money was gone. She'd gone to the police, who had investigated and found, to their astonishment, that the man had operated his scam hundreds of times up and down the country. He regularly went to the races, gambling hundreds of pounds at a time, and drinking champagne. "The Harold Shipman of the financial world," the papers called him, when the story came out. Harold Shipman was a doctor who had been convicted of killing fifteen elderly patients with an overdose of morphine, but an inquiry after the trial had shown that he was responsible for at least two hundred and eighteen deaths.

When he got back to the office, Jessica told him she had called at the address given by Mandy Davis at the penthouse but nobody had heard of her or Dora Abbott. Archie wasn't surprised.

"Check out the penthouse, see if she's still there. If not, there will be security cameras all around the building. See if you can get a picture of her," Archie said.

He glanced at an email from Kenneth. "It seems from Esther's latest visit," he had written, "that she could have a child. It is possible that she has had at least one stillbirth or miscarriage too."

He asked Jessica to check out the hospitals and police stations and see if anyone had reported a child wandering about without a mother. "Check the schools in the area too, see if there's an unexplained absence," he said. If a child *had* gone missing and nobody reported it, the chances of finding that child alive would be remote, he knew, but he still felt a slight lifting of his mood and a note of optimism creeping into his thoughts. He looked out of the window and saw that even the scrubby piece of land his office looked out onto was looking more optimistic. The rubbish had been taken away, the grass had been cut and there were a few flowers in pots near the back door.

Archie turned to the murder case. Acting on a hunch, he searched for information on the files of an organisation called Action For Justice. Its published aims were to bring injustices to the attention of the public by peaceful protests, social media, petitions and the like. They had led the protest outside a hospital where doctors wanted to turn the life support machine off of a terminally ill baby. Archie suspected the organisation of more violent protests, although nothing had been proved. As he thought, the Tindalls' tragedy was mentioned, with a quote from Mr Tindall that, "We just want justice for our little girl." That proved nothing, but of more interest was the link to Action For Justice on the Tindalls' Facebook page, urging readers to "support this organisation and help bring down those who protect criminals." It was time to bring Mr Tindall in for questioning.

***

Esther could not remember what it was like before she came to the house, although one thing was certain. Whenever she thought about it, her body began to tremble. Wherever she had been before, whatever she had been doing, it was somewhere she did not want to go to again. Ray's threats to send her back there made her nervous, and thoughts of escape once more filled her head. She wanted to get in the car and drive away, a long way from here, where nobody could tell her what to do. The thought was becoming more pressing, a definite need to go somewhere she would not be forced to do someone else's will.

Gradually she realised that this was not her imagination at work; that the feeling was based on a memory. It had actually happened. She was standing at the ironing board, ironing the blouse she had been wearing when she arrived at the hospital, the only thing she had from that 'other' life. It must have set off a memory.

A film began to play itself out in her head. She stood the iron down carefully on the ironing board and sat on the nearest chair. Her memory was beginning to return, and she wasn't sure she wanted it to. She wanted to turn away, switch off the film, but it kept rolling.

A scared woman sat at the wheel of a car, driving too fast. Next, a flashback to a Chinese restaurant: red walls decorated with golden dragons, Chinese lamps hanging from the ceiling, silk covered screens, nodding cats in the window, a slim waitress in a tight-fitting dress with a mandarin collar, her shiny black hair and pretty almond eyes. The woman there with her husband, feeling fat and ugly beside this beauty.

The film continues rolling: the man ordering wonton soup for both of them, followed by Peking Duck *('I'll choose, you get to choose every day of the week,' spoken rather menacingly.)* The waitress turns to the man, smiling, showing her neat white teeth in her rosebud mouth. "Now that's what I call a *real* woman!" the man says.

The next scene. A different camera angle. The waitress returns with the soup, and the man winks at her. "Want to meet me round the back when you've finished?" he asks. The woman smiles and the wife hides her tears. Close-up of her face: she is hurt, embarrassed, angry and wants to slip beneath the table. The man speaks to his wife. "You miserable cow! I wish I'd never brought you here."

The film moves on. Now the man and woman are at home. The man grabs her roughly, forcing her to stand in front of the hall mirror. "Who'd want to be married to *that*!" he exclaims. "Do you blame me for fancying other women? Do you really blame me?"

102

The man goes off to bed while the woman stays downstairs, staring at the wallpaper. The camera pans to the clock: two a.m. The woman gets up, leaves the house, gets in her car and drives. She does not notice it is raining, but she knows she is tired and upset and shouldn't be behind the wheel, but she just wants to get away. She is driving too fast. There she is, skidding round a corner and crashing into a garden wall.

A man comes out the house, a coat over his pyjamas, but she stays in the car, cowering. He opens the door, fearing she is hurt. She waits for the beating which she knows will comes, but the man just says, "Are you all right?" His wife is standing at the front door now, inviting her to come inside to warm up. They are so kind, taking her into the house, giving her a hot drink, it makes her cry. They ask her where she lives and the man insists on taking her home. "We'll sort this out in the morning," he says kindly, pointing to her damaged car and the damaged wall.

Now they are back at her house. She walks unsteadily up the path, the man supporting her under her arm, thinking it is the effect of the accident, but the viewers know she is afraid to face her husband. He has been woken from his sleep and looks confused, invites the man into the house and hears the story of the accident. He smiles and ruffles his wife's hair, but the viewer knows it is only an act. "As long as you're not hurt," he says, as if he is the most caring husband in the world.

The man leaves and the audience holds its breath. As soon as the door is shut, the husband flies into a rage, fists flying. The woman falls to the floor, draws up her legs and covers her face with her arms to protect herself. The man is clever. She will be covered in bruises from neck to toe the next day, but nobody will know. He has not broken anything or touched the face. The film fades. Esther blinks and tells the pile of ironing, No, I will not try to escape again.

She had not seen the man's face. Could it have been Ray? He had not shown any signs of violence so far, but it could just be a question of time. If not Ray, did it mean she was married to someone else, or was this a memory from the past? There was no way of knowing, unless Ray could tell her more.

She did not know how long she had been sitting on the settee, staring into space when her reverie was broken by the sound of Fiona calling her.

"Esther, are you all right?"

Esther shook herself. "Yes, I'll be fine."

She took a red T-shirt from the ironing, but Fiona said, "Leave that for a minute. Rachel's got something she wants to tell us." Esther hesitated. Ray would be angry if the jobs weren't done.

"It's all right, we'll just be a few minutes," Rachel said. "Come and sit down. I want to tell both of you." Esther perched on the edge of a chair, listening out for Ray, ready to jump up if she heard him coming. "Oliver's found us somewhere to live," she said, as if she expected Esther to know who Oliver was.

Esther looked blank. She had no idea what Rachel was talking about.

"Have your parents accepted him now?" Fiona asked.

"No. My father wrote me a letter telling me that interfaith marriage has achieved what Hitler could not: the destruction of the Jews, and that if I continued with my plan to marry Oliver, I would never see my family again."

"That's gross! What does Oliver say?"

"He thinks once the babies start coming, they'll change their minds. My mother might. She won't want to miss out on the grandchildren. But they'll never forgive me if I don't bring the child up in the Jewish traditions."

"What does Oliver say to that?"

Esther covered her ears with her hands. Babies. Children. Grandchildren.

CHAPTER 13

"I don't want to go to the castle today," Esther told the voice.

"Are you afraid? What are you afraid of?"

"I don't want to go. I might not get back."

"That is not possible. I will always bring you back."

"How do I know that?"

"You are feeling stressed. I will show you how to relax."

"You won't make me go anywhere I don't want to go?"

"That is not possible. Now close your eyes."

Esther did as she was told and the voice told her to imagine she was walking through a meadow. It described the scene: tall grasses, waving in the gentle breeze. "Your favourite flowers are there," it said, and Esther imagined them growing all around: ox-eye daisies with their black central eye, lady's bedstraw with its frothy yellow flowers and heavenly scent of new-mown hay. Devils-bit scabious stretched up through the grass, inviting butterflies and bees to come to its nodding purple head. She sniffed the air and breathed in the pungent smell of the pink musk mallow.

The meadow was filled with butterflies, the blue wings of the Common Blue and the maroon of the Camberwell Beauty contrasting with the yellow flowers of St John's Wort on which they rested. The sound of birds was all around: the familiar blackbird, the cuckoo and the thrush, the chorus mixing with the sound of running water from a gentle stream. It was getting hot now, the sun directly overhead in a cloudless sky. The meadow was edged with wild roses and beyond was a wood where wild cherries grew. Seeking shade, Esther crossed the meadow, the tall grass tickling her legs, and entered the canopy of trees. There ahead, sitting on a fallen log, was Estrila and beside her, a young man.

Esther panicked. It was a trick. Where was the passageway? How would she ever get back from here without it? "Do not be concerned," the voice said. "I will bring you back when it is time. You have the talisman." Esther felt something hard in her hand. She opened her palm and saw the Tiger's Eye glinting in the sunlight, radiating orange and brown in all directions.

Estrila's long sleeve was rolled back to expose a mass of purple bruises. The young man looked up, then continued rubbing ointment into her arm.

"Oh, Lady Esther, you have come! It has been so long."

"When did you last see me?"

"It was on my wedding day three years ago," Estrila said. "This is Ranuulf, physician and astrologer."

The man stood and bowed. "Good morrow, my lady,"

"You can see me?" Esther asked.

"Indeed, my lady, I see you clearly."

Esther turned to Estrila. "You are hurt," she said.

Estrila bowed her head. "By my own carelessness," she said. Esther looked at Ranuulf for confirmation.

"It is as my lady says," he said.

"Have I seen you before?" Esther asked. "You look familiar." There was something about him, the line of the chin perhaps. "Were you at the castle owned by Estrila's father?"

"No, Lady Esther, I have lived in this village all my life."

It suddenly came to her. He was the rider on the dangerous black stallion. She had seen him on the day of the hunt. Lord Goran had sent him out on a dangerous horse, knowing he would not be able to control it. Estrila was in danger. Some time in the future, Lord Goran would discover the pair together.

Ranuulf held Estrila's arm, applying the ointment gently, while Estrila watched. Goran was an old man, a cruel, heartless man while Ranuulf was young, handsome, caring. With Goran away so much, love had a chance to grow, but Goran made a dangerous enemy.

"You must be careful," she said. "Both of you."

Estrila blushed. "We meet only in the woods here, where even the pigs do not roam. There is nobody here, just the wild boars and the foxes."

"I will take care of Lady Estrila," Ranuulf said. "I do not fear Goran. We have been waiting for you to come to ask for your help so that Estrila may escape from him. There is a treasure that was stolen several hundred years ago. You could help us find it, if you are willing. Once I have this treasure, I will take Estrila to France where I have a cousin in the court of Philip Augustus. We will be safe there."

"What is this treasure?"

"It is a special cup, a golden cup much prized. When Jesus visited this country with his uncle, he visited Estrila's ancestors. They had in their possession a golden cup given to them by the Druids, which they gave to Jesus to drink from. Many people desire objects that Jesus has touched and in the year 1012, it was stolen."

"You say that Jesus came here?" Esther said, trying to control the bemused smile that crossed her lips. "I have not heard of this."

"Yes, he came with his great uncle and guardian, Joseph of Aramathea. Joseph had a thriving business, exporting tin from Cornwall to the Roman Empire. While Joseph was engaged in his business transactions, Jesus studied with the Druids."

"I do not know this story."

"It is said that there is an ancient manuscript which tells of it, in a place known only to the Druid masters."

"I thought that the Druids were uneducated."

"Oh no, my lady. The Druids are philosophers, teachers and judges, masters of mathematics and astronomy."

"You are a Druid?"

"Alas, no. I have much to learn before I can call myself a Druid, but one day I shall attain that privilege, if God be willing."

"Tell me more about the treasure. Will you sell it if you find it?"

"No, my lady. Philip Augustus has promised to grant Estrila a divorce when I bring him the treasure. To me, he will give lands and his permission for us to marry, so that we may live our lives in peace and comfort."

"There is a story about Jesus in our time," Esther said. "People are searching for the Holy Grail, the cup which Jesus drank from at the Last Supper. They say it is somewhere in the West of England. Whoever possesses it has power over everything."

"The treasure of which I speak is a large golden cup given by the Druid king to Estrila's ancestors. At times of great feasting, the cup would be filled with wine and passed among the honoured guests. Jesus was present at the great Feast of Lughnasadh, the first day of the harvest, and drank from the cup."

"There is also a story that Joseph of Arimathea struck his staff in the ground and it grew into a thorn tree," Esther said, remembering a pamphlet she had seen at the garden in Pilbury. "It is a special tree that blossoms twice a year."

"I know of that tree," Estrila said excitedly. "It is close by my father's castle. I often sat under its shady branches when I lived there."

"The story of Jesus coming to England is sung in churches throughout the land," said Esther. She began to sing.

And did those feet in ancient time,
Walk upon England's mountains green:
And was the holy Lamb of God,
On England's pleasant pastures seen!

"Will you help us find the treasure, lady Esther?" Estrila asked. "You may walk unseen in places we cannot go."

"Where should I look?" Esther said.

Estrila said, "Nobody but the Lord of the Manor and his most trusted knights knew where the treasure was kept and they guarded the secret for many years. It was said that the cup was locked inside a heavy metal box which no dagger or spear could penetrate, no locksmith could break open and no one man had the strength to lift.

"It is not known how the thief was able to penetrate this sanctuary, but one day the guardian of the cup was disturbed by the thief and gave chase. In the steep hillside by my father's castle there is an underground entrance, a large cave. From here, many tunnels run under the castle. The thief entered the first cave and ran into one of the tunnels. The guard listened carefully to his footsteps to determine which way he had gone. As he stood listening, he felt a great earth tremor beneath his feet and the sound of falling rock.

"He turned to go. As he came out of the labyrinth of tunnels, the rock ceiling collapsed behind him. He was certain that the thief could not escape and was buried alive. Many have excavated the tunnels, but neither the man nor the cup have ever been found."

"Then how can I find it?" Esther asked.

"The cup will be discovered on 19th July 1893," Ranuulf said. "If you search, you will find a record of this discovery. My lady, if you will come back to tell us where it is found, we will dig there and soon have it in our possession."

"Please," said Estrila, "it is our only hope."

"Of course, I will do what I can."

"Lady Esther, while you are here, there is something I would like to ask you that is close to my heart," Ranuulf said. "I have thought for many moons that there must be twelve planets, a ruler for each sign of the zodiac. Many people mock my idea. Do you have knowledge of this?"

Esther bent down and drew on the ground: Sun in the centre, surrounded by Mercury, Earth, Mars, Venus, Jupiter and Saturn.

"That is not correct, my lady," Ranuulf said. "You have drawn the planets revolving around the Sun. I have heard this said, but it is mere foolishness."

"Oh of course, you don't know that yet," Esther said.

"It will be found to be so?" Ranuulf said.

111

"Yes, in several centuries from now."

"That is a most important discovery."

She continued, drawing in the three outer planets, Uranus, Neptune and Pluto.

"You have knowledge of three more planets?"

"Yes. Pluto was the last, in 1930. That's all of them – at least all we know about."

"You have placed these three planets beyond what the eye can perceive."

"Yes indeed. We have many instruments that can look far into space."

"It is a great honour to be born in your time and see such wonders," Ranuulf said.

The light was fading. Esther could only just make out the shapes of Estrila and Ranuulf. Beyond the meadow, the sun was low in the sky. "I am grateful for your wisdom," Ranuulf said. "I shall convey it to the Druids who will guard it carefully and keep the knowledge secret until the time has come to reveal it."

"We will leave you here," Estrila said, "and pray we will soon meet again." As Esther watched the two disappear into the darkness, a cold wind blew across her heart.

She turned to go back the way she had come as the sun disappeared below the horizon. She was plunged into darkness, with no moon to show her the way. She stepped forward cautiously, calling out to the voice.

"Where are you?" she cried. "How can I get back?" Her voice rose in the darkness like a nightjar at sunset. There was no response. Esther feared she would trip, and sank to the ground. The grass grew above her head and bent over, pressing down on her.

Suddenly the light of the twenty-first century burst through. She shielded her eyes against the sun and looked around. She was sitting in the garden, on a grassy hillock. Around her, the wild flowers grew, and the sound of trickling water rose above the hum of traffic. A blue butterfly settled on a buttercup nearby. Below her, the thorn tree shimmered in the heat and a squirrel sat on its haunches watching her.

CHAPTER 14

Living at the house with Ray and the girls, her past a mystery, Esther felt alone, painfully alone. If she had any friends, she did not know who they were. Now that Leanne, Rachel and Yasmeen were gone, Fiona tried to talk to her about boys she had known and boy bands she admired, but Esther had nothing to say.

Estrila was her only friend, the one person who could take away her loneliness. She felt connected to her and Ranuulf; they were part of her. She was certain that it was not a dream or her imagination at work. Two different times had converged, their destinies linked. Time was not linear, travelling from here to there, from past to present to future. Different times, different centuries existed side by side, and by some technique that man had not yet mastered and she did not understand, she had travelled between the two worlds.

But what of her recent past? If she was ever to find peace, she needed to face up to her memories, but apart from the scene in the Chinese restaurant and the car crash, they had remained on the edge of her conscious mind. Ray said he knew nothing about her past, but she did not know whether to believe him or not.

***

Archie was feeling relaxed after a pleasant weekend. On Sunday, he and Mary had gone to Brighton and wandered around the narrow, twisting alleyways in the area called The Lanes. When they had come to the chocolate shop, Mary had been in heaven. She'd spent a whole hour in there admiring all the hand-made treats, the cake garden with its garden shed, the Witches Kitchen and the Empire Room with its tiger's head throne. They had left with bags full of presents for the children and grandchildren (and one or two for themselves).

The view from the office had improved over the weekend. Someone had planted a eucalyptus tree in the middle of the grass. It looked rather out of place, but perhaps, Archie smiled to himself, it was to blot out the view of the policeman who liked to look out of his window.

Archie made his way along the corridor to the incident room for a team meeting. Kenneth was already there, a file open on his lap. As Archie sat down, he said, "Let's deal with Esther first. She mentions bruises. That is a significant part of the story. It is clear from the narrative that this was not a one-off, but Lord Goran regularly beat his wife. You will recall that, in an earlier report, Estrila said Lord Goran did not beat her now she was pregnant."

Archie said, "Esther had bruises when she went to Accident and Emergency, but according to the doctor, they were all freshly made. There was no evidence of any old injuries or beatings. The doctor confirms that her injuries were consistent with falling and hitting her head on something sharp."

"We've made enquiries, but there was nobody of the right age who had been taken to hospital for unexplained injuries in the last few months," Jessica said.

Kenneth continued, "Abusers are usually clever at hiding what they do. Bruises, cigarette burns and puncture wounds from something like a screwdriver or small tool can be hidden and don't need the victim to go to hospital. The evidence disappears within a few days. The victim is

115

usually too embarrassed to go to the doctor or seek help from a family member or professional. They have low self-esteem, and when they are told that they are bad people, that the abuse is their fault, they believe it."

"Until Esther remembers who she is, it's going to be difficult to follow up on that line of enquiry."

Archie asked, "How likely is it that a husband or boyfriend would attack Esther and then leave her to wander about?"

"Abusers do not usually intend to kill their victims. Some do, but more often than not, they fly into a rage – they call it a red mist – and they're not aware of what they are doing. He could have come out of the mist and found her gone."

"She could have fallen anywhere, even in the street, making her way to hospital."

Archie said, "This is all supposition, of course, but I don't rule out the possibility that Esther was being abused."

"On another point, in this latest report, we have another indication that Esther has a child," Kenneth said. "I assume you've found nothing yet?"

"No, not yet, no missing children or unexplained absences from school, but we are continuing to make enquiries along these lines."

"Esther also says that it is the finding of the treasure that will save Estrila. She is quite clear about that point. I am not sure at this stage what the treasure symbolises, but Esther will feel compelled to search for the treasure, the druid's cup. It is important that she be allowed to go wherever she wants in the search, or she will slip even further from reality and we may never know the truth." He looked around at the group before saying, "Has any part of her memory returned yet? Unrelated episodes from the past, for instance?"

"Not as far as we know." Archie said. "She has said nothing to Fiona or Ray about her past, no clues to who she is."

"I consider this latest development, the story of the Druid's cup, to be highly significant," Kenneth went on. There are two possibilities. The first is that she is talking about an actual, valuable object. This need not be a cup. It could be a piece of jewellery, something like that. The second possibility is that the treasure is a symbol of something of great importance to her, like a child. You've heard the phrase, 'she's a treasure'."

"My mother says that about her cleaner," someone said.

"Could there have been a robbery and she fell while she was trying to stop the thief?" one of the team asked.

"Surely it would be unusual for a robber to break into a house during the day when somebody is there?"

"They prefer to break in when there's nobody there, of course, but he might have got it wrong."

"It's a long shot," Archie said. "But get onto the local jewellers, see if they've been offered anything suspicious, especially something of great value."

"Is there anything else before we move on?" Archie asked. When the team shook their heads, he said, "Let's consider the case of Fergus then. I've interviewed Mr Tindall who insists that on the day of the murder he did not change his routine. He was at work all day apart from the hour he spent in a local café. He named three that he regularly went to, but said he might have been in any of the cafés. We need to see if anyone remembers him being there that day and take a look at the CCTV tapes, if they have them."

***

During that period between wakefulness and sleep, a time when the subconscious romps around the playground of the mind, stretches itself and imagines itself somewhere else, Esther entered into a conversation with Ray in which he explained everything. When she was fully awake, she knew it would never happen. If she was going to find out anything, it would be by her own efforts.

She had a difficult thing to ask Ray and wasn't sure he would agree. She waited until Fiona had left to catch the bus, and put the coffee machine on. Ray came into the kitchen on his way to his office. She had to act quickly. "I was wondering if I could go to the library," she said.

"Aren't there enough books here?"

"I want to look something up." Ray hesitated and Esther thought he was going to refuse, but instead, he said, "I'll think about it."

He went into his office and she could hear him talking on the telephone. A few minutes later, he came out and said, "You can go this afternoon, but don't take too long about it."

So it seemed that Ray did not make his own decisions. There was somebody else in charge. Who were these people who controlled things, and why were they so interested in Estrila? Were they after the treasure? Was someone planning to steal it once she had discovered where it was? Perhaps this was what her imprisonment was all about: she had some information they wanted. Did that mean that as soon as she had found the treasure, they wouldn't need her anymore? She shuddered. At that point, she would know too much and they would have to silence her….

Suddenly the day wasn't so bright. Her joy of being free to go out soured with the thought that someone might be watching her every move, someone who might want her dead, as soon as they had what they wanted.

As she drove away from the house, she put on the car radio, turning it up to drown out the thoughts that were crowding into her mind. At the end of the drive, instead of turning right as usual, along the road that took her to her appointment, she turned left, heading for nearby Portlake. She parked in the car park by the river and, as it was a pleasant day, decided to stroll in the sun before going to the library.

She felt fairly safe here: there were a few people walking dogs who she could call on in an emergency, and she could see anyone who was on the path all the way to a bridge in the distance. It was peaceful. She searched the bank, hoping to see a kingfisher, but saw only a water vole slipping out of the bank and into the river. The kingfishers, with their handsome plumage, were as elusive as her memories.

An elderly lady stood by her garden gate, holding out a letter she wanted posted. "It floods here every winter," the lady said. "When I was a girl, it used to freeze over and we could skate for miles."

Esther realised this lady was a fellow sufferer, locked in a silent world. Unlike her, the lady had a lifetime of memories, but she had nobody to share them with, they were trapped inside her. Esther was happy to listen, to soak up someone else's memories, to feel again that sense of

119

being connected to the past, even though it was second hand.

As she came to the bridge, the bank flattened out into a small stony area where mothers sunbathed and children dipped their nets in the water. She sat on a low, flat stone, enjoying the happy laughter and the children's excitement when they caught a tiny creature and plopped it into the waiting jam jar.

CHAPTER 15

It was not going to be easy to find the girl, Jonathan thought. He had checked the convalescent homes (and there seemed to be more per head of population than in other parts of the country). If she wasn't there, she could be anywhere within two hundred and fifty square miles of grassland dotted with numerous small villages that made up the area called The Levels. As long as the weather held, he didn't mind the search. There were worse ways to earn a living than walking around one of the most beautiful areas in the country.

He started by trawling round the bed and breakfast places and pubs which offered accommodation. Most people who turned up somewhere like that with a picture of a young girl he was looking for would be sent packing, but he knew how to get round people. That was why he was so successful. You couldn't just shove a picture in their faces and ask if they'd seen her, you had to reel them in slowly, get their confidence. He had drawn a blank everywhere he'd gone, but it was just a question of time. Sooner or later, someone would know something.

Despite all his efforts, it was while he was taking a break, treating himself to a relaxing walk along the river, that he spotted her. She was sitting on a flat stone, her face to the sun. He continued walking casually, trying to look like any other holidaymaker, but when she turned and saw him, there was something about him that seemed to unnerve her. She jumped up and began walking quickly back the way she had come.

He was sure he had the right person. Every detail of the photo Rolf had supplied was ingrained on his mind. Keeping her in sight, he took out his phone and rang Rolf. He spoke quietly. "I've found her. I'm following her now. What do you want me to do?"

"Just don't let her out of your sight," Rolf said.

***

Every time Esther looked, the man was behind her, always the same distance away. He could be following her or simply walking along the tow path, but she wasn't taking any chances. She was glad when she arrived back at the town and saw a crowd of people of the grass ahead, a group of cyclists who had dismounted to eat their sandwiches. It made her feel safer.

The path ended at the cycle hire shop and gave onto the main street through the town. She stopped for a moment and leaned against the bridge, turning slowly to look at the man, as if she was admiring the view. He had stopped and was talking to a lady walking a dog, but as soon as she walked on, so did he.

She hurried along the High Street looking for some way of losing him. When she came to a charity shop, she dodged inside and pretended to look through the records, keeping her eye on who went by outside. When the man came into view, she dodged down behind a rack of clothes, relieved to see him go by without looking in her direction.

"Are you all right?" the assistant asked.

"Oh yes, but I think there's someone following me."

"Would you like me to call someone, a friend or the police?"

Esther shook her head. "No, he's gone by. Hopefully he'll go on his way and not bother me anymore."

The assistant said, "Stay here are long as you like. You can wait in the back room, then if he comes back, he won't see you."

The back room was separated from the shop by a curtain. It was the place where the staff sorted out the donations, ironed the clothes and separated stuff they could not use into piles of recycling or rubbish. Esther stepped inside and the assistant pulled the curtain across firmly. The room smelled musty and damp. A large table in the middle of the room was piled up with books, bric-a-brac, CDs and clothes waiting to be sorted. Around the walls stood shelves weighed down with plastic boxes stuffed with toys, shoes, scarves, more books and jewellery. Esther stood listening at the curtain and heard voices. Peering out, she saw the man who had followed her talking to the assistant, asking her if she had any fishing reels.

When he left, the assistant stayed at the window, pretending to set up a new display so she could keep watch. A few minutes later she came into the back room and told Esther that she had seen the man drive off. Esther opened the door cautiously and peered along the road to where a couple of ladies stood chatting. Leaving the charity shop, she sprinted the few yards to the library and hurried in through the glass door.

Jonathan had seen Esther going into the charity shop. His instructions were to find her and report back to Rolf, which he had done, but he did not believe Rolf's story and would have liked to talk to her and find out what she was doing here. She was clearly nervous of being found.

He pretended to lose her, walking up and down as if he was searching for her. He went into the charity shop to get the assistant's attention, then got in his car and drove off. With any luck, she would think he had left the town and would be lured out. He parked round the corner, covered his black T-shirt with the orange waterproof jacket he kept in the boot and put on his straw fedora. He looked like just another walker on his way to the moors. He wandered back up the High Street and saw her come out of the charity shop and go into the library. She was looking for a man in dark clothes, and paid no attention to him.

The library was small and Esther could see at a glance that the man was not in here. In one corner, a lady was reading a story to a group of children and in another, two elderly men sat at a table reading the newspapers, but the library was otherwise deserted.

She explained to the librarian that she was looking for information on druid kings and druid treasure and was directed to a shelf of books with titles such as *The History of Druids, The Legend of Arthur* and *Walking the Ancient Way*. She took a pile of books over to a table and sat facing the door so she could see who came in. In *Joseph of Aramathea*, she found an illustration of the thorn tree which flowered twice a year. On the same page was a woodcut of Joseph striking his staff in the ground and a number of religious paintings. She read that Joseph of Arimathea had landed in the West country and built the Church of St. Mary in Somerset, the first Christian church. It was as Ranuulf had said, but there was no mention of Jesus coming with his uncle.

The Bible Fraud told how the Church of Rome began destroying important historical documents in 1415. In 1550, the Pope repealed permission for priests to read the Talmud which he said contained "hostile stories about Jesus Christ". That was interesting. It was after Estrila's time, so it could well be that her story of Jesus coming over to Britain was true and had later been erased from the history books.

She was on her way over to the desk to ask if she could take some of the books home to read, when she realised that she would have to join the library and give them an address. It would be a foolish thing to do under the circumstances but in any case, she still did not know where she was living.

She put the books back. "I was really looking for information about some treasure that was dug up in 1893 somewhere in this area," she told the librarian.

"You could go to the museum in Pilbury," the librarian said. "It has a lot of exhibits with local interest. They might have some information on it."

As Esther left the library, she whispered, "Don't worry, Estrila, I am on the trail of your treasure. I won't let you down."

She did not notice the man in an orange jacket following her to the car park and making a note of her car registration number.

Jonathan returned to his car and moved it so that he could see every vehicle that went into the car park. When a battered Skoda entered, belching fumes from the exhaust, he recognised Rolf, who was driving, but not the other man. Rolf drove to the far corner and stopped. Jonathan got out and began walking towards the Skoda – he particularly wanted to get a good look at the passenger - but Rolf came hurrying towards him and stood between him and the other car.

"We go this way," Rolf said, taking hold of his arm and shepherding him out of the car park. When Jonathan looked back, there was no sign of the enigmatic passenger.

125

"You have my girlfriend?" Rolf said. "You have found Angela?"

"Sorry, she gave me the slip. I saw her driving out in that direction." Jonathan pointed in the opposite direction from the one Esther had taken. "By the way, who was that other man in the car with you?"

Rolf hesitated, slightly before saying, "I came alone."

"I saw another man in the car with you."

Rolf spoke quickly. "No, you are mistaken. We go back now, I show you."

Jonathan was not surprised when they returned to the car and it was empty. "You see, nobody," Rolf said.

"You'd best try and follow her," he said. "You'll soon catch up with her – there aren't too many side roads she could go down."

"You tell me if you see her again," Rolf said.

He watched Rolf drive off. Whoever the other man was, he was no doubt waiting at a rendezvous point somewhere up the road.

***

The knowledge that she had been followed scared Esther. She had no idea what anyone wanted from her. It was not necessarily anything to do with the treasure. It could be entirely innocent, a family member trying to find her, maybe even someone from the Salvation Army, who helped trace missing people. Whatever it was, she needed to find the treasure quickly, before the man caught up with her again. She was certain that the treasure was the clue to everything, that finding it would unlock her memories.

The next visit to Estrila was harrowing. When she passed into the castle, she was in a first floor corridor, looking down through a gap in the wall into the Great Hall below. Estrila's father sat on a large, throne-like wooden chair on the raised platform addressing a peasant who cowered on the floor below. "You are accused of stealing a rabbit," William said. "How do you plead?"

The prisoner hung his head. He knew that whatever he said, he was likely to be found guilty and punished. Without one of his hands, he would be unable to work and would be at the mercy of the rest of the village.

Esther noticed a little girl watching further along the corridor, about eight or nine years old. Without turning her head, the girl said, "Hello. Who are you?"

"Not guilty," said the peasant down below.

The girl seemed to lose interest in the scene in the Great Hall. She turned to Esther, her violet eyes bright and a smile on her face.

"Estrila?" Esther asked.

The girl nodded. An older girl entered the corridor. "Come, you must try on the dress for my wedding."

The girl turned and skipped off with her sister. With a shiver, Esther noticed an elderly man lurking in the shadows staring at the girls, licking his lips, a leer on his face. She followed Estrila, wondering how she could protect her from the future she knew was coming.

At this age, Estrila was a normal, happy girl, but the future was already written for her in the eyes of the old man who had been watching her with such obvious desire. She wished she could pick Estrila up and take her with her back to the twenty-first century where she could look after her. Perhaps the secret of helping Estrila lay not in finding the treasure, but in protecting her from the men who thought of nothing but their own desires, safe in the

127

knowledge that if anyone found out, it would Estrila who would be punished. But how could she achieve that?

Estrila skipped up the corridor, unaware of the danger she was in, singing a familiar nursery rhyme:

London Bridge is falling down, falling down, falling down
London Bridge is falling down, my fair lady.

Esther followed the sister into a small room. A lady sat sewing and nearby, two dresses were draped carefully on a chair, a pale lilac silk dress richly embroidered with gold thread and a maroon velvet dress with a fur trim. She stayed and watched for a while as the girls tried on their dresses. Estrila particularly looked beautiful in the lilac dress which complemented her bright eyes.

The girls had left the door open and Esther saw the man in the shadows watching as the girls removed their daytime dresses. She pushed the door shut, making the seamstress jump. "My word, that was a strong gust of wind," she said.

CHAPTER 16

Archie was frustrated. Jessica had been to the cafés. Nobody remembered Mr Tindall, but of course that did not prove he hadn't been there. Only one of the cafés had a working CCTV camera and there was no sign of Mr Tindall at any time on the day of the murder. They had found neither Mandy Davis nor Dora Abbott.

The team had checked the schools for a missing child, but there were no unexplained absences. They had no idea how old the child might be and were now checking up on anyone who had missed a post-natal appointment right through to the age of five. They also asked the health visitors for help. So far, they had drawn a blank. Different scenarios flew around Archie's mind, all of them filling him with dread. Had the child witnessed the murder? Was the child with the murderer? Whatever the circumstances, they needed to find out what had happened, and fast. When Archie saw Jessica's smiling face peering round the door, he hoped it was good news.

"I've been calling up the playgroup leaders to see whether a child had been absent for any length of time. The Happy Bunnies leader said she hasn't seen one of the children for several weeks. They weren't concerned. It sometimes happens. The family goes on holiday and doesn't tell them, or the mother decides not to come again. It's quite an informal arrangement. They don't usually check up if a child is absent, but they do keep records. They gave me a name and address. Of course, it might be nothing to do with Esther."

Archie was already picking up his jacket from the back of the chair.

The address was in the artistic, liberal part of London called Hampstead, close to the heath, an area Archie could not hope to live in on his salary. Someone had told him there were more millionaires here than anywhere in the UK. He could believe it, with the size of some of the houses. The same person had told him that the painter John Constable had bought a house for his family in the area.

The house was a moderate, end-of-terrace property, one of six similar houses, but Archie knew that it probably cost well over a million pounds, at least four times more than the same thing back in Yorkshire. It was smart and well looked after with its recently painted wrought iron gate and matching black front door with a semi-circular window above. A red Lexus car was parked outside. Archie made a note of the registration number and the mileage.

There was no answer to his knock. He peered through the living room window at magnolia walls, leather three-piece suite, oversized TV and a box of toys. He noted the layer of dust on the shiny surface of the coffee table and went round the side of the house to look over the fence into the back garden. The grass was about a foot high, with a smattering of dandelions, buttercups and daisies and the flower beds were untidy and needed weeding. He guessed that nobody had been in the house for several weeks.

He returned to the front and fixed a thread across the door, an old trick he had learnt when he was just starting out as a constable. If anyone went through the door, the thread would break.

Archie had noticed a curtain twitching next door when he arrived. A nosy neighbour – just what he needed. He knocked at the house and was pleased when an elderly lady opened the door. Retired people were the first know what was going on in the neighbourhood. Younger people were too tied up in their own lives and families, or out at work all day.

He explained who he was, showed her his card and waited while she checked his identity. She came back, satisfied, and introduced herself as Mrs Williams. He showed her a picture of Esther taken at the hospital.

"I need my reading glasses," Mrs Williams said. "Don't stand on the doorstep." As she went up the hall, she called out, "Cup of tea?"

"Love one, thanks," Archie said. The longer he was here, the more she would remember. That was how it worked, especially with lonely widows.

Although the house was identical to the one next door on the outside, the inside couldn't have been more different. Flowery wallpaper, two worn but comfortable chairs either side of a gas fire, small china ornaments covering every surface (mainly dogs of various breeds), photos of people on the walls (presumably family) and a large Prayer Plant in the corner.

Mrs Williams returned with a tray which she put down on a fifties-style table with a tiled top (probably original). She picked up the picture of Esther and said, "Oh yes, that's her. It's not a very good picture, but there's no mistaking it, it's her all right. Is she all right?"

"You know her?"

"Yes, she lives next door, with her husband and daughter. She's very quiet, but he's a very nice man, always has time for a cup of tea and a chat. Charm the birds out of the tree, that one could. Is she in trouble?"

"Not at all. We're just making enquiries. When did you last see Esther?"

"Well, it was some weeks ago. I'm not sure exactly when."

"And she's not been back?"

"No, nobody's been here at all. I thought they must have gone on holiday, although they usually tell me so I can look after the place."

"Do you know anything about her family? Her friends?"

The woman shook her head. "No, I never saw anybody come to the house. They were very private."

"Does she have a child?"

"Yes, Abigail. I sometimes babysat when they went out. She was so good, I never had any trouble."

"How old was the child?"

"Nearly three. She was very excited about her birthday party coming up. She's all right, isn't she?"

"There's nothing for you to worry about." Archie drained his cup. "I'm very grateful to you," he said. "If you think of anything else …."

"I've got a spare key if you want it."

The day was getting better all the time. "That makes things easier," Archie said. "I'll take the key and be back when I have a search warrant. You've been most helpful."

He drove back to the station feeling pleased. They could now start to piece together the different strands of Esther's life. He had always known that Jessica would make a good detective, from the moment he'd been transferred here. She was bright and showed initiative. She had checked the playgroups before he had asked her to and it had really moved the case on.

When he got back, he called her into the office. She sat opposite him, occasionally glancing up at the abstract picture on the wall by a Polish artist – splodges of red, yellow and purple. It had been here when he was given the office and he'd moved it behind the desk so he didn't have to look at it.

She was frowning. "Sir, what do you think the latest report of Esther's visit means? Is she telling us that her daughter has been abused – or maybe that *she* was?"

"Esther uses Estrila to tell us what happened to her, so as the abused child is a young Estrila, I think we have to assume she was abused as a child." Archie hated thinking about it. Please God they weren't dealing with another Ian Brady and Myra Hindley, the notorious Moors Murderers who abused and killed at least five children. Not for the first time, he wondered if Fergus' murder was connected to Esther's disappearance. If Fergus had discovered something, that would certainly be a reason for killing him. Or maybe Fergus was the abuser and the murderer had discovered something about *him.* Whatever the truth, Esther was the only one who could tell them.

"Another thing," Jessica said. "I've been going through the reports and there's something wrong. In this one" – she drew a sheet of paper from the pile in her hand – "Estrila talks about her mother being dead and how she couldn't warn her about putting Lady's Mantle on her bed post."

"I wouldn't take too much notice of that," Archie said. "It's not likely to lead anywhere useful."

"I know, sir, but I've been studying the medieval period, I thought it might help and the point is, in the Middle Ages, ladies of noble birth did not have much to do with their children at all, they were brought up by nursemaids."

"I see, so you think the detail is wrong?"

"Yes, it is definitely wrong, but the question is, why did Estrila say that about her mother?"

"You have a theory, I am sure."

"I went to speak to Kenneth, and he said it's possible that the mother is not actually dead, but the two are estranged for some reason. Maybe Esther feels her mother didn't look after her very well as child."

"That would fit in with the abuse theory." Archie pulled out a picture from the file. "This is a much more solid clue," he said, regretting it as a flush passed over Jessica's face. "I had a word with the DVLA. The red Lexus is registered to a Malcolm Dayton. They've emailed a copy of the driving licence. Archie pushed the copy across the desk to Jessica. "What do you make of him?"

Jessica studied the photo. He had the sort of brooding good looks that would get him a lot of attention from women: dark hair flopping over his forehead, chiselled features, a charmer. He was a lot older than Esther, a good twenty years, she guessed.

"We haven't been able to get in touch with him yet," Archie said. "It's possible he's away and doesn't realise his wife's missing, but as soon as we find him, we should be able to wrap up this case."

CHAPTER 17

Esther wandered around Pilbury looking for the museum, mistaking the stone building with a large porch for a church. When she realised her mistake, she wondered if she had been sent to the right place. Surrounded by an apple orchard in which sheep and pigs foraged, the museum was dedicated to rural life: displays of farm machinery and old cheese making equipment and descriptions of willow coppicing, mud horse fishing and peat digging. There was a second building, a "magnificent 14th century Abbey Barn, one of only four surviving barns which belonged to the Abbey".

Finding nothing that related to any treasure, she wandered back to the entrance and asked the lady at reception if she knew anything about an archaeological dig in the nineteenth century that had revealed some valuable treasure. The lady shook her head. "I don't know about that, I'm afraid," she said. "You could try the abbey museum. It has a magnificent sixteenth century bishop's cope." She saw Esther's bewildered expression and said, "That's a long cape, is that what you're looking for?"

Esther shook her head and the woman went on, "There's the Lake Village Museum, but that's all about life in an Iron Age settlement. I don't think they'd know. If anything valuable was dug up, I think would go up to London. The curator would know more, but she's on leave. Give me your telephone number and she'll ring you when she gets back."

"I don't have a phone," Esther said. "I'll come back and speak to her." It seemed like a dead end. She was not even allowed her own phone and Ray would never let her use the one in his office.

"What about the newspaper offices?" the lady said. "It might have been reported at the time in the local paper. They keep the back copies in an archive."

That sounded more hopeful. The only problem was, it meant asking Ray if she could go on another trip.

She left the museum and made her way to the high street, noticing that everyone she passed had mobile phones. Some appeared to be talking to themselves as she went by, others were leaning against the shop windows sending texts. One person was using it to find directions. She suddenly remembered she had never had a phone, not just here, but before, when …. the memory eluded her, but she knew with certainty that she had never had her own phone.

When she was nearly back at her car, she passed a phone shop. She stopped and looked in the window at the bewildering array of phones. She didn't even know how they worked. She stood in the doorway, trying to summon up the courage to talk to the shop assistant, who looked as if he had just left school. "Come in," he said, "you're welcome to browse."

"I - er – don't know anything about phones," Esther said.

The assistant began talking too about SIM cards, roaming overseas and Bluetooth. Esther had no idea what he was talking about. "I'd just like to make a phone call sometimes," she said.

The assistant showed her a fairly simply model and asked for her bank details so he could set up a direct debit. Esther shook her head. For the first time since she had woken in the hospital with amnesia, she wondered what had happened to the money she must surely have had before the accident. Ray gave her a small allowance each week for petrol and cosmetics and other things and that was the only way she could buy what she needed. She couldn't even remember whether she had a bank account. As she turned to leave, the young man said that she could pay for the calls as she went and could top it up at the local Co-op for cash.

"You only have to put a few pounds on it when the credit's running low," he said.

Esther turned back to face him. She would have her phone after all.

***

Jonathan saw the girl going into the phone shop. He'd been acting on a hunch. Sooner or later, everyone visited Pilbury and it wasn't far from where he had last seen her. It was an interesting town with its medieval merchant's house, its octagonal Market Cross, the fifteenth century inn and a spring that had been bubbling up from underground for at least two thousand years. It was a place where the Christian society sat side by side with the New Age community and myths of King Arthur and the Holy Grail. On the one side was the abbey and on the other, a whole wealth of shops selling New Age supplies. Spanning the two was the local Anglican vicar.

Jonathan had spotted her coming out of the museum and followed her, waiting near the phone shop, timing it so that when she came out, he 'accidentally' bumped into her.

137

Some feeling, something in his gut, told him there was something suspicious about this case and he wanted to get to the bottom of it. He had been used once before by a client who'd spun him a line. He'd found the man he was looking for, told his client and the next day, he had been shocked to hear on the news that the man was dead, murdered. He had never forgiven himself for not taking more care. He was certainly not going to have another innocent person on his conscience.

"I'm so sorry," he said, quickly scanning her face. It was definitely her, Rolf's girlfriend.

"It's all right, I'm not going to hurt you," he said as the woman backed away. "I want to help you. Someone's trying to find you."

She gave him a darting glance and said, "What do you know about that?"

"Let's go and have a coffee, talk things over."

Esther hesitated, looking around at the pavements crowded with tourists before nodding briefly. They set off down the road, heading for the café where she had sat with Tom. Somehow it made her feel safe, knowing they had sat there together.

She ordered a coffee and sat down near the door, where she could escape in a hurry if need be. "Who are you?" she asked when Jonathan sat down. He looked a kindly, fatherly sort, but she knew she knew that appearances could deceive.

"Jonathan Whicher. I'm a private investigator. A man hired me to find you."

Esther put her coffee down, picked up her handbag and stood up.

"Don't run away, please," Jonathan said. "I want to help you. At least listen to what I have to say."

Esther remained standing and said, "You could have lured me here to give him time to come and get me."

"I could have," Jonathan said, "but I didn't. Anyway, you're safe here. There are plenty of people about." Esther sat down on the edge of the chair as Jonathan went on, "A man who said he was your boyfriend hired me to find you. He is Polish. Do you know him?"

"I don't know."

"There's no hurry, take your time."

"I don't remember anything. I've lost my memory."

A couple of scenarios flashed through Jonathan's mind: the girl had stolen something from Rolf or she had some information he wanted. Whatever it was, if she couldn't remember, it was a frightening place to be.

"So you don't know why he's trying to find you?" A shake of the head.

"You followed me before, by the river," Esther said.

"Yes, I did, but I sent Rolf off in the other direction when you left."

"Why would you do that?"

"I'm not satisfied that he was telling me the truth when he said he was your boyfriend."

"How can I trust you?"

"I'm going to give you my card. If you need anything, if you're in trouble, just ring me."

He held out one of his business cards, but she did not take it and he put in down on the table between them.

"I need to get home," Esther said, finishing her coffee.

"I'll walk you back to your car."

139

"No," Esther said, so vehemently that the couple on the next table looked up, ready to come to her aid. "And don't follow me."

When she had gone, Jonathan phoned Rolf. "Whicher here. I've just caught a glimpse of your girlfriend in Norton Fitzwarren," he said. That would put him off the trail. Let him go chasing her in the opposite direction. It would give him more time to find out what was really going on.

"Do you follow her?" Rolf said.

"Unfortunately she disappeared round a corner and by the time I got there, she was gone."

"So she slip out of your grasp again," Rolf said.

"Tell me again what happened," Johnathan said, "why you are looking for her."

"I tell you, we had an argument. She left and I do not see her again. I ring but there is no answer. I am afraid something happen to her."

Jonathan had a photographic memory. It was one of the things that made him good at his job. He remembered every word of the conversation in his office. Rolf had said nothing about an argument back then.

Rolf rang Seb to give him the news, waiting while Seb looked Norton Fitzwarren up on the map. "It's miles away," Seb said, a note of annoyance in his voice. Stay where you are and I'll pick you up."

They were on their way to Norton Fitzwarren, the bicycle tied to the roof rack. Seb was driving too fast, braking suddenly whenever he came to a sharp bend. Rolf was trying to follow their route on the map, clinging on to the seat as he was thrown around, unable to see properly out of the windscreen wipers. He had never known it rain so much. It had been a heat wave when he'd left London and he had only brought a light jacket with him, expecting to be away a week at the most. He had just been getting ready to go to Yeovil and buy an anorak when they'd got the news that Angela was in this strange sounding place. He was getting sick of the search for Seb's wife and wanted to go back to London and his building work.

Reaching the village, they began their enquiries on foot, starting at the local pub. Seb handed round a photo, but nobody had seen a woman of that description. They went on to make enquiries at the medical centre, the school of driving, the garden centre, and questioned a couple putting flowers on a grave in the churchyard. Nobody knew anything.

They returned to the pub where Seb downed a pint of beer in record time. "I don't believe she's here at all," he said. "I need to talk to Whicher, find out what he's up to."

CHAPTER 18

Esther hid her new phone in the carrier bag at the bottom of her wardrobe when she got home, then took out her notebook and wrote an account of what had happened the last couple of days: meeting a young Estrila in the castle, the visit to the museum, the man who had bumped into her on the way out of the phone shop, the same man who had followed her along the river bank. *Do I have a Polish boyfriend?* She wrote in large letters and underlined it.

Jonathan had told her that he had been hired to find her. With most of her memories still lost to her, she had no way of knowing why anyone would be looking for her. She wondered briefly if Ray would know anything about the man, but Ray could be part of the conspiracy, whatever it was.

Strangely, in the last couple of days, Ray had changed a little. He was slightly more relaxed, and she wondered if it could be a trick. He had been keen for her to go to the library and the museum – anywhere she wanted, in fact. Was he hoping she would lead him to something, the treasure or something valuable? Really, there was no reason why she shouldn't just get in the car and go wherever she wanted without telling anyone, except that she had been primed from an early age to do as she was told. That's how it had always been, doing what others told her to, but perhaps it was possible to change. She didn't always have to be that way.

She sat heavily back on the bed. Her memory provided no details, but there was something she understood now. In a strange way, her memory loss provided her with a way to alter things. Unhampered by the knowledge of whatever others had done to her to make her so compliant, she was free to do what she wanted - almost. The early conditioning was still there, but she wanted to use her memory loss as a springboard for a new Esther. She could do whatever she wanted to, be whoever she wanted to be, if only she were brave enough!

She went downstairs in buoyant mood. "You're looking happy," Fiona said. "Wait until you hear what Ray's got in store, you won't be smiling then."

She had to wait until dinner time as Fiona refused to say any more. When they were all tucking in to steak and kidney pudding, Ray said, "There's a medieval festival tomorrow at Weldon Castle, so be ready to leave early."

Esther's heart jumped. A medieval festival. Perhaps she could learn something about Estrila's life there.

"I'll come, but it's not my sort of thing," Fiona said, as if she had a choice.

You'll enjoy it," Ray said. "It's a big event, with a jousting show, archery competitions, birds of prey, minstrels, jesters, clowns …" He thought it was a hair-brained scheme himself, but he was just following orders. *"It might help Esther remember. Take Fiona with you and make sure you all stick together."*

"All right, we get the picture," said Fiona.

The next day, the sun rose in a clear sky. Ray chose the people carrier rather than the smaller, more compact Fiesta, "so we can spread out." Although it was not yet 10 a.m. when they set off, it was already hot inside the car and getting hotter as the sun rose higher in the sky. They made steady progress at first, but as they approached the venue, the traffic increased and still had three or four miles to go when they came to a halt. From then on, it was slow going. They crawled along at a few miles an hour, trying to ignore the noisy children in the car ahead of them who waved and stuck their tongues out. As they turned a corner, the top of the castle came into view on the horizon, half hidden by trees.

Fiona was looking up the event on her phone. The castle was surrounded by water, more of a lake than a moat. There were two buildings: the older one that was partly in ruins was almost completely surrounded by water. A narrow bridge lead to a newer, larger part of the castle. There was a large lawn in front of the building which, Fiona read, would once have been used for jousting competitions and by knights on horseback teaching children the art of warfare.

Esther closed her eyes and thought about Estrila, wondering what she was doing now: whether Goran had returned and whether she was still meeting up with Ranuulf. She was startled out of her thoughts by Fiona nudging her and saying, "Look at this". It was a picture of a handsome man dressed as an archer in white padded jacket, black and red trousers and a metal helmet.

After another half an hour, they saw signs directing them to a large field where they could park. There were already at least ten rows of cars and more were coming in all the time. "How are we going to find the car again?" Esther said anxiously, but Ray did not answer.

There was a long queue to get in. Restless children ran round, knocking into the crowd. Esther worried about who else might be here and looked around anxiously, her earlier confidence beginning to seep away. In this crowd, she could easily get lost or parted from the others. What if the man who was following her was here? What if this Polish man Jonathan had spoken about was waiting to kidnap her?

As if she had spoken aloud, Ray said, "Stick close. I don't want you getting lost." It made Esther nervous, especially when he turned to Fiona and said, "You're to keep an eye on Esther, make sure she doesn't wander off." Did he know something she didn't?

"We all stick together," Ray repeated as they shuffled towards the people taking the entrance money.

Ray handed out leaflets. Esther turned the map around but could not make any sense of it. Her head hurt and she wished she'd brought a sun hat with her. Not that she had one. There were so many things she didn't have. Yesterday she had washed her hair and looked for a hairdryer, the one with the diffuser, before she remembered everything from her old life was gone. Remembering the hairdryer was a good sign, though.

Ahead of them was, according to the leaflet, a "full sized tiltyard" where there would be jousting competitions in the afternoon. To the right was an area where various demonstrations would be held during the day: dog agility, a Long Netting display by Victorian poachers, ferret racing, carriage driving. There was a separate tent for gaming and fish cookery demonstrations and face painting (surely not an authentic medieval experience!), fire eating and juggling, weapon making and clay pigeon shooting. Ray wanted to see the archery demonstration to be held after lunch and Fiona asked if they could see the falconry demonstration later.

"We've got plenty of time to see it all," Ray said. "What are you interested in, Esther?"

145

"I'd like to see the knights again and perhaps the musicians," she said.

"You've been to one of these before?" Fiona asked and Esther realised her mistake. She'd given something away in saying 'again'.

"I think I must have done," she said vaguely and was relieved when nobody asked any more questions.

They made way their way slowly towards lines of colourful, striped tents. Esther searched the crowds for danger, frequently losing sight of the others as people cut in front of her. They reached a man demonstrating how to fit all the different pieces of armour onto a padded undergarment or the Arming Jack, naming each piece as he carefully fixed it with straps: Gorget, Spaulder, Cuirass, Greave, Poleyn.

Esther made sure the others were close to her before stopping to watch. She was fascinated to see how everything fitted together. A horse covered with red and yellow cloth was tethered nearby, waiting to carry the man away once he had all his armour on. It occurred to Esther that a man might easily disguise himself as a knight if he did not want to be seen. As they moved off, Esther took Fiona's arm.

There was everything for sale that the medieval lady or gentleman might need: swords, shields, armour, bows and arrows, leather and pewter tankards, jewellery, frankincense, soap, wooden bowls and platters, knives, candles, toys, sheep skins, dresses and wooden boxes. Esther was drawn to a cloth doll dressed in a pink medieval style dress, with long hair. Something began to tug at her, a feeling that there was somebody she would like to give this to. She held it close to her heart, struggling with herself.

Part of her wanted to remember, but another part was afraid to.

"Would you like that one?" the stallholder asked, bringing Esther out of her reverie.

"Oh yes, please," Esther said, handing over the money.

Ray and Fiona wandered to the next stall. Esther turned as a man pushed his way forward, blocking her view. He was dressed in a leather doublet, decorated with metal rivets over a mail shirt, leather breeches and a balaclava made of chain mail. He might have been anybody, but Esther panicked. A memory had leapt into her mind, an image of her and a man, going to a fancy dress party with another couple. She was dressed as a sexy swashbuckler, in knee high black boots, a dress which came well above the knees, and a hat with a feather. He went as a medieval knight, dressed a bit like the man who stood before her. The thing she had remembered was the man telling the couple they were with that he was mad to get married. "Don't ever have kids, whatever you do. It's sheer hell."

"Don't ever have kids." How many did she have?

Suddenly Ray was there, pulling her away. "Keep up, will you," he said angrily, keeping hold of her arm.

When they were tired of wandering about, they sat on straw bales, eating ice cream and watching a medieval puppet show telling the story of John Lambton. John was a rebelliously character who skipped church one day to go fishing but instead of fish, he catches an eel-like creature with a head like a salamander. An old man appears who tells him he has caught the devil. On his way home, John throws it down a well. Years later, while he is off fighting in the Crusades, the creature escapes and roams

147

countryside, killing sheep. John's father appeases the creature by supplying it daily with the milk from nine cows for seven years, until John returns and kills the creature.

Esther sat in a daze, feeling memories stirring the depths of her mind, like the creature at the bottom of the well. Her memories were rising to the surface, threatening to overwhelm her and create devastation.

When the show was finished, Fiona said, "Let's go and have our future read. There's tarot readers over there." She pointed to a reader with large, round ear-rings and a colourful silk scarf wound round her head.

Esther shook her head. She did not want her fortune read. The tarot reader might know the secrets that were trying to worm their way up into her conscious mind and she did not want to learn them here, in this crowded place, with others listening.

"We'll wait here," Ray said, sitting down again.

Fiona went off and could be seen shuffling the tarot cards. As the reader began to spread the cards across the able, a woman sat next to Esther. She was striking in a green silk dress with wide sleeves, her long curly hair falling down her back. Esther felt the woman's eyes on her, turned – and was surprised by a face that she had seen before. She frowned, puzzled. She could not be here, not here like this. It wasn't possible, but there could be no mistake – the violet eyes, the slim, pale face, the plucked eyebrows and the high forehead. The hair was a slightly different colour and shorter, but it was unmistakably Estrila.

"My name's Eloise," the woman said. "It's beautiful day, isn't it?" Ray shifted in his seat and stared at the stranger.

"You remind me of someone I once knew," Esther said.

"I feel we have known each other before too," said Eloise. She took hold of Esther's hand.

Ray's fists clenched. "What are you up to?" he said.

"I was going to read her palm."

"No you don't," said Ray, pulling Esther to her feet. Esther tried to push him away, but he was too strong. "I wanted to talk to her," she protested.

"No you don't," Ray said. "You don't know who she is. She could be anyone." He was worried it was a trick; that sooner or later the woman would get Esther to go off somewhere he couldn't follow.

Esther did not see the woman again and began to wonder if she had imagined her, but on the way back, Fiona asked, "Who was that woman in the green dress you were talking to? She was rather striking."

"Eloise," Esther said in a strange, detached voice. She had so wanted to talk to Eloise and didn't believe she was there to hurt her.

Ray said, "It was a trick," but Esther knew better. How would anyone know what Estrila looked like? It had to be her.

As soon as she got home, Esther made a hot drink for everyone then took hers upstairs to her bedroom. As she got undressed, she felt something in the pocket of her jeans, a piece of paper. She drew it out. It was Eloise's name and her telephone number.

She took out the doll out of its carrier bag and studied it, trying to remember who she had bought it for. The memory would not come. She placed the doll carefully in the bottom of the carrier bag in the wardrobe, tucking Eloise's card down the side, along with phone she had

149

bought. At the first opportunity, she would hide it in the boot of the car, underneath the spare wheel, so she would be ready to go at a moment's notice.

CHAPTER 19

Archie returned to Esther's house in Hampstead with Jessica, the spare key and the search warrant. The place looked just as deserted as before. The thread he'd placed across the door was intact and the car hadn't moved. Nobody had been back here since his last visit.

Archie slipped a photo of Malcolm standing beside a surf board out of its frame. It was strange, but there were no photos of his wife and child anywhere in the house. There were a few circulars on the doormat, but nothing important. There seemed nothing out of the ordinary until he went into the bedroom.

He returned to the station feeling sick. When he'd walked into the bedroom and opened the wardrobe, he had been met with an array of torture toys and bondage gear. He issued an order that on no account was Dayton to be informed of his wife's whereabouts when he returned from wherever he'd been. He wanted to speak to the man first, or better still to Esther.

Lots of people used these things and it didn't have to mean anything bad, but, with Esther covered in bruises when she walked into the hospital, he wanted answers fast. He asked Jessica to fetch the CCTV tapes from the hospital for the time of Esther's stay. They needed to go over them with a fine-toothed comb.

The hospital security office was easy to find, being situated in a corner of the reception area. It was a cubby hole really, with room for a desk and not much more.

Jessica read the name on the office door, Daniel Foster, and knocked.

"Mr Foster? I wonder if you could help me?"

Daniel swivelled his chair round to face the policewoman, glad of the interruption. He was a large, heavily built man, his shirt stretched tightly over his chest and flesh hanging over his chair, but his voice was surprisingly thin and high pitched. He listened to what Jessica had to say before taking down a file and flipping through it. "There's no report that security was called that day, but I can get the tapes for you."

When she had the tapes, Jessica went to the ward where Esther had stayed and interviewed the nurses who had been on duty during her time in hospital for the second time. Each one said the same thing as before – they had no recollection of anybody acting suspiciously during the days that Esther was there. They were all so busy, they didn't have time to scrutinise every visitor closely, but they would have noticed something out of the ordinary. When she had finished with the nurses, Jessica spoke to the porters and cleaning staff for that ward, but nobody knew anything.

She was about to leave when the Ward Sister came in with her rota and said. "Did you talk to Miss Torres? She's an agency nurse. She wasn't due on that week, but at the last minute, we had to call on her, just for one day, the day that Esther left. I don't know if she can help you. I'll give you her details."

Jessica rang the agency who told her that Miss Torres was currently working in the Paediatrics Department.

Maria Torres was a small woman with a big smile. She'd come over from The Philippines two years previously and loved the work and the country. She didn't understand why the British kept complaining about the NHS. She thought it was marvellous. She had seen so many people in her own country who could not get proper treatment. Her own brother had an operation on his foot that was not very successful, and now he walked with a limp. In her country, only the very rich or the foreigners (mostly Americans) could afford to have replacement knees or hips or medicines when they needed them. The rest had to rely on people with a natural talent, such as her brother who was a gifted healer, or the Chinese doctor.

Working here, she was able to visit her sister and send money every month to her mother back home to help the family. She was proud of the face that she had been able to pay for her nephew to go to college. He was hoping to come over here to work too one day. She wanted to find a nice English man who would ask her to marry him, then she would be sure of staying in the country, but she hadn't found him yet.

She smiled at the tall policewoman and shook her proffered hand. In the staff room, she listened to the questions about a particular day when they had brought in a lady who had lost her memory and thought back.

"I know it was a while ago, but even the smallest detail, something that seems insignificant, can help," Jessica said.

There was only one thing Miss Torres didn't like about the British. They had no hesitation in showing when they were angry. In her country, you were taught to be pleasant and charming, whatever you were feeling inside, but the British were apt to shout and yell.

Maria said, "Yes, there was a man, he want to know where his girlfriend go. He thump the desk and is angry when I did not say him. I pick up the phone to call security, but he go away."

"You didn't call security?"

"No, he just get in the lift and go."

"Did he tell you his name?"

"I ask his name," Maria said, "but he does not say."

***

"Don't ever have kids." Esther tossed and turned. Sleep would not come. The same words revolved around and around her mind, but she could not remember who the speaker was or why he had said it. She imagined herself getting ready for the fancy dress party, putting a child to bed and giving the babysitter instructions, but the memory remained aloof.

As she drifted into sleep, she saw herself on a beach. In one hand she held a toddler, in the other, a pushchair overflowing with a number of bags. A man, perhaps her husband, walked several feet in front of her while she struggled to move the pushchair over the dry sand. Reaching the steps up to the promenade, she saw the man disappearing along the esplanade. She struggled up the steps and hurried to catch up with him.   When she drew alongside him, he said, "You walk too slowly. I'm not going to shuffle along with you", and hurried away." Who was he? She hadn't seen his face, but he had Ray's build and dark hair.

In her dream, she bent down and turned the child to face her, but it was blank, like the figures on the hillside in her other dream. She began to scream, she was fighting for breath now, struggling to wake up. Bursting out of the dream, wondering where she was, the dream images still felt real. Where was the child now? Who was the man who

154

refused to walk with them? Her mind raced on to other thoughts. Had she dreamt up the man in the castle lusting over a young Estrila? Did that mean that the figure in the pushchair was her daughter and she was being molested, perhaps by her very own father? Please God no, she said out loud, burying her face in her pillow. If she had a child, she must find her. Why did her mind refuse to deliver up the very information she so desperately wanted and which might protect the child from harm?

Her last thought before sinking into a dreamless sleep was that, for some reason she didn't understand, finding the treasure was the clue.   Once she had the treasure, everything would come right.

CHAPTER 20

The passageway opened onto the Great Hall. Esther stepped through and shivered. It was cold, despite the large fire in the fireplace. The windows were covered with thick cloth, but through a gap, Esther saw there was snow on the ground. A young Estrila sat near the fire sewing a dress, while servants cleared away the remains of a meal.

"Hello," said Estrila.

Esther looked at the servants clearing the tables and sweeping the floor. "It's all right," Estrila said, "They will think I'm talking to myself. I am always talking to myself." She concentrated on a difficult stitch before saying, "My sister will soon be married. She is two years younger than me. I should have been married first."

"How old are you, Estrila?"

"Thirteen."

Thirteen. That number meant something. Thirteen. Suddenly she had it. "I met a man when I was Thirteen," she said. She could feel a dam breaking in her mind and memories sweeping into her conscious mind. Images were coming thick and fast, demanding they see the light of day. "I went to a cinema with a friend – "

"What is a cinema?"

Esther tried to explain, but Estrila did not understand. "We have many people travelling around the country telling us stories, but we cannot see them once they have gone," Estrila said. "Are you a witch, do you do magic?"

"Oh no," Esther said. "There are many, many things that are possible. A man walked on the moon in 1969."

Estrila looked up from her sewing. "Father would beat me if I said such a wicked thing," she said.

Esther fell silent while the memories revolved around and around her mind, looking for an exit.

"What happened at the – cinema?" Estrila went on, stumbling over the strange word.

"While we were waiting to go in, we got talking to a boy and his father. When we got inside, the father bought his boy some sweets, and some for us, too. We sat together and when we came out, the father said he'd see us home. After that, I used to see the father when I came out of school, even though his son didn't go to the same one.

"There are many words that I do not know," Estrila said, "but I think I understand the story."

"I liked the father a lot. He explained that his wife died the previous year and he missed female company. I used to go to his house and cook meals or listen to him playing – he played the piano – "

"I do not know this *piano*," Estrila said.

"Never mind, it doesn't matter," Esther said. "He bought me things my parents couldn't afford, special trainers – shoes and clothes."

"Ah, yes, this is the way to attract a lady's attention," said Estrila.

"We got very close."

"You married this man?"

"I was only thirteen, so no, not at the time."

"You may not marry at the age of thirteen?"

"No, not until sixteen, and only then if your mother and father agree, otherwise eighteen."

"You may marry without your father's consent?"

157

"Yes, if you are eighteen or older. My parents did not like me seeing this man because he was so much older than me. They told me not see him anymore, but I ignored them."

"You ignored them?" Estrila repeated. "Your father must have beaten you very hard when he found out."

"No, he didn't find out, but in any case, he wouldn't have beaten me."

"When I was sixteen the man asked me to marry him, but my parents refused to give their consent. I was very angry. They said I was too young to make this decision, that I would change my mind."

"So you must wait until you are eighteen," Estrila said.

"We ran away to Scotland," Esther said. "There, we were allowed to get married."

"There is much trouble between the English and the Scots," Estrila said. "I have heard my father speak of it often."

Esther felt tired. There was so much more to tell, but the memories had begun to slip beneath her conscious mind again. It was like a shoal of fish. Occasionally one or more would come to the surface and leap into the light before splashing back down in the water and disappearing.

The flames in the fireplace were dying down. The servants had finished clearing up and had disappeared. The Great Hall was silent and darkness was descending. She could barely see Estrila now. The scene was slipping into the shadows and would soon be gone. Esther turned to go back. A single candle broke the darkness, a pinpoint of light. She followed its light and came into the passageway where she stepped through into her own time.

158

She leaned against a wall while her mind adjusted to being in the twenty-first century, thinking about the things she had remembered.

***

Jessica left the hospital and made her way back to the station, wondering how Archie was getting on. He had gone to see Dayton's mother, to see if he could find out where he might have gone.

The door was answered by a smart, stylish woman, a brunette who introduced herself as Melanie, Dayton's sister. She took Archie into a lounge that smelt of dog, and made him a cup of tea. He sat on a rather old settee facing the mother, Hilda, who had a pinched, tight face and hair dyed a dirty straw yellow colour.

Archie showed them the photo he had taken from the house. "Is that your son, Mrs Dayton?"

The woman nodded.

Melanie said, "What's this all about?"

Archie said, "He's not in any trouble, but we just want to ask him a few questions. When did you last see him?"

Melanie looked at her mother whose slight shake of the head did not go unnoticed by Archie. "It was a while ago. We don't see him very often. What's happened?"

Mrs Dayton peered at him closely. "You sure you're a policeman?"

Archie showed her his warrant card for the second time. "When did you last hear from him?"

"It's been a while, he's been busy," Melanie said, tight-lipped.

"What about Esther, do you keep in touch with her?"

"Who's Esther?"

Archie looked from one to the other. They genuinely did not seem to know.

"The woman Malcolm lives with."

Mother and daughter looked at each other and shook their heads. "How long has he been living with a woman?" Melanie asked at last.

"I'm not sure," Archie said. He never volunteered information.

"He used to come round and do things for me," Hilda said. "Little jobs I couldn't do myself, putting up a shelf, painting, that sort of thing. But just lately, he hasn't been so often. I've heard of women like that, jealous of the man's family."

"He didn't mention the girl then?"

Hilda looked close to tears, but she sat up straight, gathered herself together and said, "No."

"She must have forced him to keep quiet. She didn't want us involved," Melanie said, adding, "Nasty piece of work."

"You know her then?" Archie asked.

"No," Melanie said quickly. "I just meant -." She turned to her mother. "He wouldn't have behaved like that, he was a very caring son."

She paused then went on, "Has she hurt him? Is this what it's all about? Where is he?"

"Please calm yourself," Archie said. "We have no reason to think he has come to any harm."

"Why are you here then?"

"Just routine enquiries."

Archie left soon afterwards, wondering what exactly had gone on in the Dayton household. Had it got it all

160

wrong. Was Esther's memory loss an act to disguise - what? That Esther had killed her husband?

The computer technicians had been all over Dayton's computer. They'd discovered the details of Dayton's business. The only bank account was a personal bank one and nothing had been withdrawn for several weeks. Archie wondered whether Esther really was capable of murder. He wouldn't be surprised. Sometimes the most unlikely people, when roused, committed the most dreadful crimes. Often it was the person you expected the least: the quiet elderly man next door, the polite middle-class woman. It would explain Dayton's absence.

In this age of technology and social media, Esther and Malcolm were fairly invisible. Esther did not appear on Facebook, nor did she have an email account. None of the phone providers had an account in Esther's name. There wasn't much on Dayton either. His emails were mostly about work, although there were a few to his sister, with no mention of Esther or the child.

CHAPTER 21

The treasure was the key to everything, Esther thought. If she could find the treasure, she would remember what had happened to her children. The first step was to go to the newspaper office in Yeovil to look at the archives. She did not want Ray to know. He had said she could go anywhere, but she still did not trust him. The drawer containing the key to the Fiesta was kept locked, but the last time she had gone to Pilbury, she had had a duplicate made.

Since the medieval festival, Ray had become quite solicitous, but she did not expect it to last. He was up to something, she was sure. Testing him out that morning, she had left the washing up after breakfast and sat in the lounge reading. He had come out of his office at coffee time and seen the dirty dishes piled up in the sink and instead of shouting like he would have done before, he had said in quite a jovial voice, "Don't feel like washing up today?" Esther had no idea why he had changed. Was it possible that Ray was part of some plot, was he lulling her into trusting her, so that he could more easily deliver her into the hands of some gang?

She slipped out of the house, closing the front door quietly. As she started the car and moved off, Ray opened the front door and stood on the porch, watching her. She looked at him in the rear-view window and he waved. He actually waved!

Arriving in Yeovil fifteen minutes later, she headed for the car park in the centre of town. It was raining quite hard and she had only her thin jacket on. She pulled up the hood and headed for the green and white striped awnings of the nearby market to buy an umbrella.   With no memory of a previous visit to any market, the brightly coloured stalls selling materials, sweets, plants, watches and toys were a delight to the senses. She bought a jam doughnut at the bakery stall and savoured each mouthful, licking the sugar from her lips. The umbrella stall was colourful. There were all sorts of designs: polka dots, butterflies, blue, black and bright pink, stripes. She chose a black one with rain drop shapes that changed colour as they got wet – all the way through the rainbow, from red to violet.

She walked towards the newspaper building, stopping to look at a stall selling hair accessories where her eye alighted on a pink unicorn hairbrush. As she held it in her hand, a memory struggled to get out.

"Do you want that, love?" the stallholder asked. She paid for the brush, looked around to see whether anyone was following her, and set off the for the newspaper office.

Reaching the right building, she negotiated the revolving doors and spilled out into the reception area with its low chairs, copies of the latest newspaper, and advertisements for the paper's coach holidays. Two minutes later, she was on the way out. She chided herself for not ringing first. The archives were not kept at this office, but at Bristol. Bristol! Even with her new-found confidence, it might have been the moon! Just as hard for her to get there.

As she stood on the steps putting up her new umbrella, she nearly stabbed a man as he made his way up the steps. She froze, recognising the man who had bumped into her as she came out of the phone shop in Pilbury.

"You're following me again," she said.

"No, really, I wasn't," Jonathan said. "I'm going back to London. I was just looking for a present for my wife." Too late, he realised it was a feeble excuse. He wouldn't find a present in the newspaper office.

Thinking on his feet, he said, "We had our honeymoon down here and I wanted to get her the paper for the day we married." Actually, it was a good idea. Silvie would like that.

Esther frowned. "Have you told them where I am? Is that why you're going back?"

"No. I haven't told them, but you need to be careful. Always make sure somebody knows where you're going. It's best if you don't go anywhere on your own." Jonathan wondered if he'd said too much. He didn't want to terrify the girl, but the feeling that she wasn't safe just kept on growing.

She looked at him closely. "You know something, don't you?"

Jonathan settled for the truth. "I don't believe the story that Rolf told me, about trying to find his girlfriend. Just be careful, won't you."

Before she could ask him whether he was certain she really was the person he was looking for, he turned and strode off towards the centre of town, pulling his collar up against the rain. She didn't see him take a small mirror out of his pocket so he could see where she went.

Esther drove fast. On the edge of the town, a car came out of a side street and turned in her direction. Esther gripped the wheel, and put her foot on the accelerator. When she got to Ilchester, she heard an ear-splitting roar and a fighter jet came into view, nose pointing towards the ground, engine screaming, heading straight for her. It looked as if it was going to crash on the car roof. At the last moment, the pilot pulled out of the dive and skimmed over Esther's head, just inches away. She stopped the car, her hands trembling too much to drive. Surely they weren't trying to kill her from the air?

She was glad to be home, even though Ray was standing at the end of the drive, peering along the road. "What's happened?" he asked. "You look terrible."

"A fighter jet," she said, trying not to burst into tears.

"Probably practising for the air show," Ray said. He peered at her. "Scared you, did it?"

She said nothing and went up to her bedroom. She took out the pink hairbrush from her handbag and put it in the carrier bag with her phone and the medieval doll.

A loud knock on the door startled her. "Esther, can I talk to you?" Ray said, in a voice he used to reserve for Leanne. "It's all right, you're not in trouble."

Seeing the door handle already turning, she leapt to the door, opened it and went outside. Ray's mouth was twisted in what could have been an attempt at a smile, but might have been a grimace or a leer.

"I just wanted to say - I don't want to restrict where you go," Ray began. He had had a call that afternoon telling him to say that. They had also told him to watch Esther and to let them know if there were any signs of violence. Meek little Esther, who had been spooked by a low flying aircraft, could, it seemed, be dangerous if she wanted to be.

"You mean I can go anywhere I like?" Esther asked.

"But you've got to be careful," he said.

"Why, Ray, why do I have to be careful?"

165

"You've lost your memory."

"Is someone after me?"

He shifted on his feet. "No, not as far as I know. But the doctors don't know a lot about amnesia. I wouldn't want you to go somewhere and not know how to get back."

"I think you know more than you're telling me." Ray began biting his nails and Esther felt a rush of power. For some reason, he was suddenly *nervous* of her.

She went back into her bedroom and shut the door in Ray's face. Nothing made sense.

She drew out her notebook and made a list of her visits to the castle.

1. Just before the wedding
2. Three weeks later
3. The wedding
4. ??? (that was the strange visit where the castle was completely empty)
5. The Hunt. Esther left that one for the moment; she had no idea where that fitted on the timeline
6. Three years after the wedding
7. Estrila, eight years old
8. Estrila, thirteen

The day of the hunt must have been later than all the rest. She surmised that Goran had discovered the couple and sent him to his death, so she rearranged the visits in order: eight years old, thirteen years old, sixteen years old (two visits) – wedding – three years later – the hunt - ? empty castle. She stared at it for a moment, but nothing came to her.

CHAPTER 22

Jonathan decided to go home. Rolf had got quite unpleasant when he told him Esther had given him the slip. It was time to bale out. He ate a good breakfast, settled up his bill with the b & b and packed the few possessions he had brought with him. He was making his way to the car when his phone rang. Seeing it was Rolf, he almost left it. Later, he would regret his decision to take the call.

"Mr Whicher? Can I meet you somewhere? I have someone who wants to meet you," Rolf said.

"Is it important? I was just heading back to London."

"I have been working all this time for someone else and he want to meet you, he want to give you the right story so you can help him."

Jonathan was not sure he believed this latest story, or that the 'other person' was about to tell him the truth. He weighed up his options and decided he would go. He owed it to Esther to find out if they meant her harm. He agreed a time and place and rang off.

He was first to arrive at the Halfway House pub, almost mistaking it for a private house with its stone walls, porch and small, square windows. Inside, the slate floor was cool underfoot as he made his way to the bar. He glanced at the menu, rejecting the faggots and mash and settling for a salt beef and horseradish sandwich and a Hopback beer. He sat in the garden to eat. From here, he could see every car that entered the car park and a few minutes later, the battered Skoda drew in. Rolf got out of the car and came over, standing by the table as Jonathan took a swig of his beer.

"Why don't you sit down and have a drink?" Jonathan said. "They have excellent beers here. They've been Camra's pub of the year numerous times."

"You're to come with me," Rolf said.

"Where's this other person who wants to see me?" Jonathan asked.

"He is in the car. He want to talk to you somewhere private."

Jonathan insisted on finishing his lunch before going anywhere. He didn't want to stop for food on the way back to London. When he was ready, he followed Rolf to the Skoda, which was parked in the corner, engine running.

Rolf opened the front door and Jonathan climbed in. The man at the wheel turned. "Seb," he said.

"Nice to meet you at last, Seb. I understand it's *your* girlfriend we're trying to find, not Rolf's."

Seb locked the doors and put his foot on the accelerator, flinging Jonathan backwards. "Hey, steady on," he said as Seb raced out of the car park, just missing a car coming in.

Jonathan had a bad feeling as they flew through several deserted villages. Speeding along a stretch of road, Seb suddenly turned the steering wheel and they almost skidded. The road was a rough track now, leading to a deserted car park surrounded by trees. Jonathan caught a glimpse of a sign for a nature reserve and Seb said, "Bird lover are you?"

"I'm a city boy myself," Jonathan replied, wondering where on earth this conversation was leading.

"Let's take a little walk," said Seb, "See what we can see."

Rolf led the way with Jonathan in the middle and Seb at the rear. The further they went into the wood, the more Jonathan felt that no good was going to come of this. They came to the hide, deserted at this time of day. Rolf held aside the flap and Seb pushed Jonathan inside, motioning to Rolf to stand in the doorway. Bird watching, Jonathan knew, was the last thing Seb had on his mind.

"Where is Angela?" Seb said.

"Why are you looking for her? I want to know the truth."

"Rolf told you the truth, except that she is my girlfriend, not his. Now, where is she?"

Jonathan looked around for anything to use for a weapon, if need be, but there was nothing, just plain empty walls covered in a couple of posters for birds and a couple of pairs of cheap plastic binoculars chained to a bench.

"You didn't find her at Norton Fitzwarren?"

Jonathan wasn't expected the swift blow to the stomach which knocked him to the floor. "You know I didn't. Now you're going to tell me where she is."

Jonathan groaned and tried to get up. "Stay there," Seb growled. "Now, where is she?"

Jonathan rolled onto his side and drew his legs up to protect his body. He would die rather than tell them where Angela was.

Seb kicked out. "I said, where is she?"

Gasping for breath, Jonathan heard Rolf say, "Look at his phone. He will have picture on his phone. Maybe it tell us where she is."

169

Jonathan flinched as Seb bent down but he only took hold of his coat and rifled through his pockets. He found the phone, and handed it to Rolf while he stood guard over Jonathan.

A few minutes later, Rolf said, "Look, I am right. Here is picture of her getting into her car."

Seb took the phone and studied it. In the background was a sign which was too small to read. He zoomed in on it. "I've seen this before. I know where this is."

Seb said, "So, old man, you thought you'd cheat me, did you. I suppose you were taking money from her to send me all over the countryside on a wild goose chase. What have you got to say for yourself now?" With one final kick on Jonathan's prostrate body, the two left. Jonathan closed his eyes. I'm sorry, Angela he mouthed before passing out.

"We must call an ambulance, tell them where Jonathan is," Rolf said as they made their way back to the car.

"Don't be stupid," said Seb. "Do you want the police on to us?"

Rolf wasn't happy. When he'd agreed to help Seb, he hadn't been told he would be expected to beat up an old man. Except that he hadn't agreed to help, he'd had no choice. He thought of his father who had been beaten up many times and imprisoned for his political views. Tadeusz and had told him since he was a babe in arms of the violent suppression of demonstrations and the deaths of nine comrades who worked at the Wujek coal mine. Rolf had grown up hating violence. He had come to this country in the belief that he and his family could lead a peaceful life without such struggles. He did not want to go around looking for someone who didn't want to be found, or beating people up.

"I want to go back to London, to carry on with my work," Rolf said. "You don't need me here anymore, do you?"

"You're staying here," Seb said.

CHAPTER 23

Esther stood in Estrila's bedroom. All but one of the windows was covered with thick tapestry hangings, keeping most of the light out. A sweet smell rose from the herbs that were scattered on the floor and a large crucifix stood on a table next to the bed. Estrila sat on a stool in labour, attended by the midwife, screaming in pain. Around her neck she wore a large amber stone set in gold filigree, and on her right hand was an amber ring in an elaborately carved setting.

"Estrila, breathe deeply, it will help," Esther said, wondering how she knew that. She breathed with Estrila, in, out, willing the pain to lessen. I know what to do, she thought, I wonder if I have given birth myself. The thought disappeared as Estrila let out another heart-wrenching wail.

When the contractions increased in intensity and Estrila's eyes became wild, Esther began singing. Estrila stared round until her eyes locked onto Esther's. Esther sent her all the love she could through her eyes and the midwife busied herself laying prayer scrolls over Estrila's stomach.

It was nearly time. Estrila had stopped wailing. Her face was pale, her breathing laboured and Esther was worried whether she would survive the ordeal. As a look of pain crossed Estrila's face, Esther said, "Push, Estrila, we're nearly there."

The midwife said, "I can see the head. Not long now." With one last effort, the baby's head emerged. The midwife guided the baby's head as it turned and on the next contraction, the child was born. The three women waited, but there was an ominous silence in the room, unbroken by a sound or movement from the child.

"I'm sorry, my lady," the midwife said.

"No," Estrila screamed, clutching the baby to her, seeing the blueness around the mouth that had killed her other babies.

Esther moved towards the birthing stool saying, "Let me look," but the midwife was in the way.

"Go, fetch the doctor," Estrila said. The midwife hesitated, not wanting to leave Estrila alone. "Go now," Estrila ordered. "Hurry."

When she was gone, Esther quickly placed the baby on the floor and ran her finger around the baby's mouth to clear it of mucus before placing her lips around the tiny opening. Blow five times, compress the chest thirty times, she told herself, repeating a pattern she had heard only a few days before on a hospital programme on the television. Blow five times, compress thirty times. Careful as the bones are very tiny. She willed the baby to live and at last, felt a gentle movement under her fingers. The next moment, the baby took its first breath and began crying. Esther picked the baby up and put it into Estrila's arms as the door opened. The midwife had returned. "The doctor is coming," she said.

Estrila held the child close to her and squeezed Esther's hand. "God be praised, it's a miracle!" declared the midwife.

Esther left the room and sank down on the corridor floor. At the moment the baby had let out its first cry, Esther had remembered another baby, another cry. Pain flooded throughout her body and a deep sense of loss. She

173

did not know how old her baby was or whether he was even alive. Her whole body ached to hold him in her arms and never let him go.

Ranuulf came hurrying up the corridor. Looking to see that there was nobody about, he bent down to the prostrate form on the floor.

"Are you all right, my lady? What has happened? Estrila, the baby – "

"They're both fine. Go in now, she's waiting for you."

An angry shout came from somewhere further up the corridor. "I must beat the wickedness out of you," she heard. It was Goran's voice, she was sure of that. Ranuulf was already hurrying into Estrila's bedroom. Esther stood up shakily and moved up the corridor. With her ear pressed to the thick wooden door, she could just hear a slapping sound and some muted yelps coming from within, as if whoever Goran was beating was trying not to cry. She opened the heavy door. The hinges creaked, but neither of the two people in the room looked up. A young girl, knelt on all fours, her dress pulled up to reveal her lower half, her hair loose. Goran, in a state of excitement, bent over her half naked form, beating her with a piece of flailing metal. Already ugly red weals were forming on the girl's skin.

"No," Esther yelled, picking up a heavy brass candlestick from a nearby table and bringing it down with all her force on the back of Goran's head. Goran crumbled, sank to the floor and lay quiet and unmoving.

The girl pulled her dress down and stood up, looking around wildly. Esther suddenly realised what she had done. All the girl had seen was a candlestick flying through the air and hitting Goran on the back of the head. When people came to investigate, nobody would believe her story and the girl would be found guilty of murdering the Lord of the Manor.

She ran to Estrila's bedroom and asked Ranuulf to come quickly, explaining what had happened. When they got back, the girl was sitting on the bed, staring into space, perhaps seeing her future ahead of her. She could either wait until they found her guilty or she could leave now and wait until they caught her. Either way, she would be tortured and then killed.

Ranuulf put his face to Goran's mouth to check his breathing, while Esther felt his pulse. "He's not dead," she said. Ranuulf spoke to the woman. "He is alive. Go about your duties, and don't mention this to anyone. I will say that I found Lord Goran alone; that he must have fallen and knocked the table. I will say the candlestick fell on him. I do not think he will deny the story."

The woman looked at him, round-eyed. "You would do that for me, sir?"

"It wasn't your fault," Ranuulf said. "Go, you will not get into trouble, I promise you that."

The woman curtsied and left.

***

Esther stood in front of her car, not sure how she got there. The last thing she remembered was being in the castle, talking to Ranuulf. She felt painfully alone. The times she spent with Estrila felt like her real life. Living in the house was a dream, a nightmare. She wanted only to get back to Estrila, to stay there and help look after the baby, watch her grow and make sure she was safe from the lustful men.

She sat behind the wheel awhile, her mind still back with Estrila. She hoped Ranuulf could really keep the woman being beaten by Goran safe.

She jumped when someone banged on the window. It was a traffic warden. "Are you all right?" he asked. He pointed to his watch. "Your time's nearly up."

"Sorry," Esther said, flustered. He stood watching, waiting, as she moved off.

She had no memory of the journey, but twenty minutes later, she was turning into the drive. One thought went round and round her head. She must find her baby.

Going through the front door, she called out Ray's name. Fiona looked up from the magazine she was reading in the lounge, sensing a drama about to unfold. "Ray!" Esther yelled again, storming into the kitchen and banging on the office door. Fiona followed her, curious. Nobody had ever disturbed Ray when he was in there. Not even Leanne had dared to do that.

The door shot open and Ray stood in the doorway, glaring. "What do you want?" he shouted. "I've got work to do."

"I want to know if I have a baby."

"You need to calm down. I know nothing about a baby. What made you think of that? I've had a message, you're being transferred."

Esther froze, realising how foolish she had been to think she could have any sort of freedom, could do what she wanted. She supposed this was some sort of punishment for going to Yeovil the other day. She should have known. Ray had appeared so understanding about it, but all the time he was plotting to send her away. She did not want to be transferred, not now she was so near to the truth.

"Where are they taking me? I don't want to be transferred. I'm not going."

Fiona watched with interest as Ray stopped yelling and ran his hand over his face, wiping off the sweat.

"It's out of my hands," he said.

"No," Esther cried. "I am not going to a new home. You can't make me. If you try, I shall run away, I shall go somewhere you will never find me."

Ray looked scared. "OK, calm down will you," he said. "I'll make a phone call, see if I can find anything out. Just wait there."

"I don't believe you," Esther said. "What have you done with my baby?" She burst into tears, hot, frustrated tears and sank down onto the floor.

Ray told Fiona to make sure she didn't leave and went back into his office where he could be heard talking on the telephone. "OK I'll fetch the doctor, if you think that's for the best."

Esther jumped up when she heard the word 'doctor'. "They're going to drug me and take me back there," she said, opening a drawer and grabbing a sharp knife.

"Back where?" Fiona asked, shrinking back as Esther sprang forward. She rushed past her and in three leaps was out of the front door.

Ray came out of the office. "Where is she going?" he asked.

"I don't know," Fiona replied. "She thought you were going to drug her and take her back somewhere. She didn't make much sense."

177

Ray swore and hurried out the door. A few moments later he could be heard yelling. Esther had slashed his tyres.

Esther knew that the slashed tyres would not hold up Ray for long. He would soon have the others on to her. She thought quickly, trying to form a plan as she drove as fast as she dared round the blind bends. She cursed as she realised her phone was in the bag in the boot and she would lose valuable time if she stopped to get it. She was rushing instinctively towards Pilbury. She thought quickly. Who could she ring to help her? She had Eloise's number in her bag, but she didn't know anything about her. She might be one of the people after her. That could have been why Ray suggested the medieval pageant in the first place. How was she supposed to know? There was only one person she felt instinctively that she could trust. Tom.

Putting aside the voice inside her head that told her he wouldn't want to know her after she had treated him so badly, telling herself he would forgive her for the way she had been so far, she resolved that as soon as she reached the town, she would ring him. What could she do with her car, though? If she left it parked on the road, they would see it and know she was nearby.

She thumped her fist on the steering wheel. There must be something she could do. Yes, she remembered. There was a park and ride some way outside the town. They would never think of that. They would expect her to drive into the centre; but if she parked in the park and ride, that would mean taking the bus. That would be all right. None of them would be expecting her to arrive by bus. She was thinking fast. Go to the garden, to the hill where she would see anyone who was coming. There were places to

178

hide there, too, like the dilapidated shed at the back, hidden by trees, that she had found by chance one day.

She pulled into the park and ride and drove over to the far corner, where her car would be partially hidden by the trees which overhung from the neighbouring land. Keeping the engine running in case of trouble, she waited for the bus to arrive. When she saw it trundling into the car park, she switched off the engine, took her carrier bag from the boot and waited by the car until all the people at the bus stop had alighted.

Sprinting over to the bus, she leaped inside as the doors were closing, startling the passengers who looked up briefly, then went back to what they were doing. Nobody seemed interested in her, but that didn't mean they weren't.

She delved down into the carrier bag for her telephone. She had ripped up Tom's card so Ray wouldn't find it, but had memorised the number. She prayed fervently that he would answer as she punched in the digits.

"Hello."

"Tom?"

"Esther, is that you?"

"Tom, I need help," she whispered, anxious that the other passengers might hear her. A middle-aged man in a grey cardigan was taking an interest in the conversation but he looked away when she glared at him.

"OK, where are you?"

"On a bus going to Pilbury. Can you meet me there?"

"I'm afraid this line isn't very good." Esther's voice was so quiet, he could hardly hear her.

"I can't speak loudly, someone might hear."

Tom heard an edge to her voice, as if she was trying desperately to keep hold of her sanity.

179

"When does the bus arrive?" Tom said.

"About fifteen minutes."

There was a pause. "I'll be a bit longer than that, I'm some distance away. Will you be all right until then?"

"I hope so."

The bus stopped at the bus station and Esther remained in her seat until the other passengers had got off. She scanned the crowded streets. Nobody she recognised, but with her loss of memory, that meant nothing.

She hurried towards the garden, feeling exposed. There were very few people on the street. It would be only too easy for someone to stop a car and grab her.

The road ran alongside the garden, which was bordered by a wall that was too high to climb. She followed the boundary for some distance but could find no way in. Throwing her bag over the wall, she took a frantic leap, managing to reach the top with her finger tips. Pushing her feet against the bricks, she shoved, hauling herself upwards until she was sitting astride the wall. The ground dropped away quite sharply here. To jump was to risk hurting herself. She turned round, lowered herself gently as far as she could go and let go.

As she landed, she rolled, grabbed a branch and came to a halt. She was not seriously hurt, just bruised and covered in dead leaves. She dusted herself down with a tissue, retrieved her bag from further down the slope and set off for the hill where she could observe the whole garden.

After a steep climb up the grassy mound, she crawled beneath the bench at the top. From here, she could still see anyone who came from the main gate, but they wouldn't see her.

She waited a long, anxious half hour before spotting a figure coming into the garden, pausing to do something on his phone. As hers rang, she jumped up, hitting her head on the bottom of the seat. It was definitely Tom standing on the path.

She began running towards him. When she was a few yards away, she called out, "I can't stop, they will be here any minute."

Tom matched his stride to hers and grabbed her hand. Panting, out of breath, she kept moving, tripping on the uneven path. Tom steadied her and they ran together towards the main gate.

As they came out into the street, they saw a man running towards them. They reached Tom's car and flung themselves in, pulling out into the traffic as the man reached them.

Putting his foot down, Tom said, "Who is he?"

"I don't know. A PI warned me. Someone's looking for me but I don't know why."

A myriad of questions came to Tom's mind, but he was too busy concentrating on his driving to voice them. He went as fast as he dared down the high street, screeching to a halt as a second man stepped directly in front of his car and banged on the windscreen. He pulled the steering wheel to the right and stepped on the accelerator as the man leapt out of the way.

Esther had covered her face with her hands and was rocking to and fro, moaning.

"Hold tight, I'll try to lose him," Tom said. In his rear view mirror he saw the man getting into a Skoda. He thought furiously, mulling over the routes ahead, hoping desperately that the men did not know the roads around here as well as he did. He had one advantage over the Skoda. His was a four-wheel drive.

He shot through an amber light. They turned red and the Skoda was stuck behind a green Nissan. As the lights changed, the Skoda pulled out, black smoke pouring from the exhaust, overtaking the Nissan on the narrow road and swerving to avoid a car coming the other way.

As they left the town, Tom picked up speed. Esther still had her head down. She was remembering how she had nearly had a crash on these very roads not so long ago. She stayed hidden until Tom turned the car onto a rough track lined with a thick hedge. The car lurched along the pitted and furrowed track, bouncing over holes roughly filled in with stones.

"Are they following us?" Tom asked.

Esther turned her head round as far as she could and said, "I don't think so."

They had travelled for a mile when the track divided. Tom took the left fork, which brought them onto an even narrower farm track. Without the four wheel drive, a car could get stuck in the mud.

They passed through the farmyard without losing speed, scattering chickens in all directions. After another mile, the track widened and a few yards further on, they bumped onto a road in the direction of Wells. They passed through a tiny hamlet and half a mile further on, Tom slowed the car.

"Here now," he said, turning into a driveway, opening the garage door with a remote key on his keyring.

One inside, he cut the engine and rested his head on the steering wheel for a moment before turning to Esther.

Her eyes were wild, her hands trembling, but her breathing had slowed. "Are you all right?" he said.

Esther felt his fingers closing over her own and felt strengthened, comforted. She waited in the kitchen while Tom checked the house and closed the curtains, distracting herself by trying to identify the flowers in the garden: hollyhocks, yellow loosestrife, lungwort, marigolds…. Tom poked his head around the door and said, "It's OK."

She followed him into the lounge where she sank down onto the sofa and closed her eyes. It had been a narrow escape. She heard him in the kitchen making drinks.

When he came in bearing a mug of coffee, she said, "The car registration. He will know where to find me." Her eyes were dull and lifeless.

"I thought of that," said Tom. "This house doesn't belong to me, it's a friend's house I use sometimes."

"Girlfriend," Esther said mechanically.

"Not girlfriend," Tom said, a smile playing on his lips.

CHAPTER 24

Archie was feeling relaxed after a pleasant lunch. He had bought sandwiches from a local café and taken them to a little wild nature reserve situated along a former railway embankment. Nobody else seemed to know of it and Archie wasn't about to advertise it around the station.

The summer meadow was in bloom with knapweed, field scabious and goatbeard. Bees buzzed and dragonflies flew over the pond. It was a peaceful place to take a break from the noisy traffic of the nearby road; but the feeling that all was well with the world lasted only until he got back to the station. Jessica was standing in his office, head bowed.

"I'm afraid we've lost Esther," she said.

"What do you mean, lost?" Archie asked. "What happened?"

"She heard Ray talking on the phone and drove off in the direction of Pilbury, slashing his tyres so he couldn't follow. He rang the local police station and they didn't realise the importance of it, but eventually he managed to get through to them that they needed to find her fast. They began searching and found her car in the Park and Ride. They showed her picture around and one of the bus drivers recognised her. She got off at Pilbury bus station but nobody knows where she went after that, although a number of people reported a man running up the road towards a couple who got in a car and drove off fast. The man tried to follow them, but witnesses think she got away."

Archie was thinking. Who did Esther know who might give her a lift? "This musician Tom is the most likely person she would have contacted," he said out loud. "As far as we know, he's the only person she knows. Get Somerset Police to put out an alert for his car and get Uniform to go round to his house and see if he's there."

"I've already contacted them."

"Tell them to keep an eye on the place and pick him up if he appears."

"By the way, we got a phone call from Berkshire division. Someone recognised the picture of Mandy Davis we sent round. They've been looking for her. She has a number of different names she uses. She cons elderly men out of their life savings by pretending she is their long lost daughter, then disappears. Sir, do you think Fergus realised what she was doing and she murdered him?"

***

The dining room and kitchen had been knocked into one large room. A cream coloured lace tablecloth covered the round, wooden table, which held two large, transparent Pyrex dishes. One held carrots, peas and sweetcorn and the other a fish pie. "Sorry they're only tinned," Tom said, dishing up a pile of vegetables onto Esther's plate. "I haven't had time to go to the shops." For the first time that day, Esther smiled. "Help yourself to fish pie," he said.

"But won't your friend mind you eating his food?" she asked.

"No, he always has something in the cupboards in case of unexpected guests."

"But this pie – it's home-made, isn't it?"

"Yes, he's a good cook."

"Will he be back soon?"

185

"No, he's away at the moment. You're quite safe. Nobody will know you're here."

Esther was hungry. It was 8.30 pm, hours since she had eaten anything. She said, "I didn't know whether to ring you after the way I behaved."

"I realised that you were in some sort of trouble that first day we met," Tom said. "I'm glad you called me."

"I must tell you everything," she said, and added, "Only I don't remember much."

"That's all right, you don't have to say anything until you're ready."

"The problem is, I've lost my memory. I can't remember anything, not before a few weeks ago, when I was taken to a house. I don't even know where it is, except it's somewhere outside Portlake. A man called Ray seemed to be in charge, but I don't know why I was there or whether I knew him before."

"They didn't explain anything?"

Esther shook her head. "Sometimes I almost remember things, but then it's gone. But there are a few things I *have* remembered."

There were many painful memories, waiting for a door in her mind to open. Now she was safe, she would let them come out in their own time.

"You asked me if I was married," she said. "I honestly don't know. I know now that I got married when I was sixteen. I ran away to Scotland with him because my parents didn't approve, but I don't remember if I am still married to him or not."

***

Esther lay on the bed, wondering where she was. Moonlight entered through a chink in the curtains, its soft

186

light revealing a blue bed cover with a red abstract design. As her eyes adjusted to the dark, the different coloured pieces turned into a picture of Superman. A plastic version of the hero was stuck to the wall and various cars and lorries were heaped up in a plastic box under the window. A little boy's bedroom.

She sat up abruptly, remembering how Tom had shown her to this room last night. As he had drawn back the dark blue curtains which matched Superman's costume he had said, "Sorry about the decorations. My friend has a young nephew who stays here sometimes."

She drank thirstily from the large tumbler of water Tom had thoughtfully placed on the bedside cabinet. 2.30 a.m. and she was wide awake. Her mind raced, thinking of a number of scenarios. Could this be her own house? Was Tom waiting to tell her some bad news about her family? Who was this friend he mentioned and could this really be his nephew's room? So many possibilities and no way of knowing which one was right.

She lay thinking about the events of recent times. She had always thought that she and Tom had bumped into each other by accident. He had said as much, but what if he had targeted her deliberately? Had spied on her or been searching for her? That might account for him being willing to see her, even when she had behaved in a way that would put any other man off. He had shaken off the man who had been chasing her, but what if the man had been trying to prevent him driving her away with Tom, in order to save her from some awful fate? Perhaps Tom was the person looking for her, the man the private investigator had warned her about.

She realised it was as dangerous here as it was back at Ray's. Until her memory came back, she could not rely on anything she was told. Tom seemed all right, but on balance, it was better to trust nobody. She must rely on herself. Every second she stayed here, she could be putting herself in more danger. She must get away.

She paused at the sight of her clothes on a chair, neatly folded. She always threw them over the back of the nearest chair. She went cold all over at the thought that Tom might have undressed her. She threw on the clothes and crept downstairs slowly, stopping when one of the treads creaked, holding her breath while she waited to see if Tom would emerge from his bedroom. His door remained firmly shut and she continued down to the hallway.

She stepped into the lounge, pulling open the curtain a little to let some light in. The gentle moonlight revealed her notebook lying casually on the coffee table. Why could she remember nothing about the evening and why was her notebook not safely tucked into her backpack? A chill ran down her spine at the thought that perhaps Tom had drugged her. She must get out now.

Tucking the notebook back in the bag, she moved quietly to the front door and turned the handle slowly. It remained firmly shut. It was locked and there was no key on the hall table or anywhere else she could see. She padded swiftly into the kitchen and tried the back door and the door to the garage. Both locked. With an increasing feeling of panic, she began searching the kitchen drawers. Cutlery, clean dishcloths, screwdrivers and other small tools – no keys.

She remembered her phone. Still holding a kitchen knife she had removed from the drawer, she retrieved her phone from the backpack where she had left it in the hall. It seemed an age before she was connected to the police and all the while she was listening intently for sounds from upstairs.

"Somerset Police. What is your name?"

"I'm being kept prisoner," Esther said in a loud whisper. "I can't get out."

There had been a team meeting only this morning about the girl who had gone missing yesterday afternoon, a girl who had lost her memory, a girl called Esther. Acting on a hunch, the telephone operator said, "Is that you, Esther? Where are you?"

Esther slammed the phone down. How did they know her name? If she could not even trust the police, her situation was hopeless.

"Esther? What are you doing? It's the middle of the night." It was Tom, screwing his eyes up against the hall light. Picking up the knife she had placed on the table, she held it out in front of her.

"What are you doing?"

"You read my diaries and now you're keeping me prisoner."

"You're not a prisoner."

"You've hidden the keys, I can't get out." The feeling of panic had gone and been replaced by an icy calm. She knew, now, what she was going to do. She would make him tell her where the key was and then she would kill him.

Tom moved towards her. She thrust the knife forwards. "You're not coming any nearer," she said.

"I was going to get the key. It's in the drawer of the coffee table. Have a look for yourself."

Keeping her gaze firmly fixed on Tom, she opened the drawer, feeling for the key. He kept his body turned towards her, his eyes on the knife.

"On the left-hand side," he said. She moved a few papers and saw a bunch of keys, three different keys on one key ring.

"Try them out," Tom said. "That big one is for the front door, the Yale is the garage and the silver one, the back door." Keeping hold of the knife, Esther picked up her bag and the keys and went into the kitchen. Taking hold of the silver key, she put it in the lock and turned. Nothing. "You liar!" she said, "You'll pay for this."

Tom's voice trembled as he said, "You have to turn the handle at the same time, pull it upwards."

"I don't believe you." She took the Yale key and tried it in the garage door. It opened immediately. "It's a different type of lock," Tom said.

"It's a trick!"

"Don't you remember anything about last night?" he asked. "You said you would tell me all that you knew. You took the notebook out of your bag and put it on the coffee table. Then you started talking to yourself – or somebody else. You were mumbling, I couldn't hear what you were saying, then you jumped up, took the Shepherdess off the coffee table and smashed it over my head."

Tom drew nearer. "Don't you remember?"

Esther buried her head in her hands and sobbed. "I don't remember anything."

"You are free to leave if you want to."

"I called the police. Tom, they knew who I was. How did they know?"

"I don't know. Did you give them the address?"

"I don't know where I am."

Tom touched her arm gently. "You can leave whenever you like. You keep the keys, I have a spare set."

Esther was exhausted. She had thought she understood what was happening, but now she realised that she knew no more than before. She let Tom help her back to bed where she lay awake, listening, waiting for the police to come.

She slept at last and woke to the sound of Tom preparing breakfast. When she went downstairs, he was laying the table, putting out cereal and fruit juice.

"How are you feeling this morning?" he asked as she entered the room.

Noticing the bruise on Tom's forehead, she suddenly remembered the scene in the castle when she had hit Lord Goran over the head with a candlestick.

"Oh, I must go back, I might have killed him."

"Killed who? Go back where?" Tom asked.

"Oh, I don't know how to go back. Only the voice can take me there but I can't go to Pilbury again, they will be looking for me."

"Esther, have some breakfast, then tell me from the start. I've cancelled all my appointments for the rest of the week. I realised when I first met you that you were in some kind of trouble, and I'm going to help you."

Tom made a big pile of toast and put out the butter and marmalade, but Esther only picked at the food, trying to make sense of what was happening and wondering whether it was safe to tell him the little she knew.

Tom waited patiently. As he swallowed the last of his coffee, Esher said, "I don't remember much, not anything before I was taken to the house." Tom nodded encouragingly and she went on, "I've started having flashbacks. I wrote everything down." She picked up her notebook and opened it at the first page. "I can't remember very much before they took me to the house, but whenever I think of my past, I feel frightened. I don't know why. Something bad must have happened."

She glanced at Tom's concerned eyes and moved a little nearer to him.

"At first, there were four girls at the house and me and Ray. I don't know who they were. Nobody ever told me, except that Yasmeen was a refugee from Syria – that's what she told me – and Rachel seemed to be in some sort of danger from her family, who didn't want her to marry the man she'd chosen. Then Leanne cut her wrists and they took her away. The girls kept asking me questions but I didn't know the answers and in the end, they stopped talking to me. Ray had his rules – no phone calls, don't go beyond the garden, but they didn't apply to the other girls, only to me. Nobody would tell me why I was there. I thought I must be in a kind of prison and the girls were my jailers."

Tom nodded and reached out to touch her arm. She leant towards him and put her head on his shoulders. "Take your time," he said gruffly.

"I had to go to an address in Pilbury."

"That's where you'd been the first time I saw you?"

Esther nodded.

"You were looking very confused," Tom said.

"It was very confusing. Someone would talk to me through headphones. I don't know who it was. I only ever heard a voice, I never saw anybody – except the woman who let me in. It wasn't her. Anyway, the voice told me to imagine I had just entered a passageway, and it was strange. I was actually *in* the passageway. I wasn't lying on the couch any more. Does that sound weird?"

"I understand," Tom said. "The imagination's a powerful thing."

"But that's just the point," said Esther, "it wasn't as if I was imagining it, but as if I was actually *there*."

"OK. Go on, then, what happened next?"

"There was a door off the passage and went I went through, into another world. There was a castle, knights on horseback, people in those dresses – like the people in the procession that time I first saw you."

"Medieval dress," Tom said.

"I'm frightened," she said. "I don't know what's happening."

Tom put his arm around her. "Don't worry, you've got me now. I promise I'll keep you safe."

CHAPTER 25

"I met Estrila. She was sixteen when I first met her, and about to be married. Each time I learned a bit more about her life. I made a list of the visits."

She showed Tom the notebook and he studied the page.

1. Just before the wedding
2. Three weeks later
3. The wedding
4. ??? (that was the strange visit where the castle was completely empty)
5. The hunt
6. Three years after the wedding
7. Estrila, eight years old
8. Estrila, fourteen
9. Estrila gives birth

"Nine visits," Tom said.

"They wanted to know everything that happened to me. It was as if they were trying to get some information out of me. Why would they do that?"

"Who do you mean?"

"The house at Pilbury, the voice, I don't know who they were."

"OK."

"On one of the visits, Estrila told me about a treasure that belonged to her family, the Druid's Cup. It was stolen and she wanted me to help her find it. Perhaps they were after it."

Tom's eyes had flickered with interest at the mention of the Druid's Cup and Esther hesitated. "You've heard of it?" she asked.

Tom shook his head and she went on. "Her friend Ranuulf worked out that it was going to be discovered on July 19th, 1893. If I could find a record of where it had been dug up, he would be able to go there and get it himself."

"Did you find the record?"

"I went to the museum but they didn't know anything. They suggested I went to Yeovil, to the newspaper offices so I could read the paper for that day. But when I got there, they said the archives were kept at Bristol."

"Did you go to Bristol?"

Esther shook her head. "I never got as far as asking Ray if I could go. He didn't like me going anywhere by myself, except the visits to Pilbury. Then he said I was being transferred but I didn't want to go anywhere else."

Tom gave her a squeeze. He felt helpless. Until she remembered who she was, he didn't know what he could do.

"Ray said he didn't know anything about my past. I don't believe him. He said he was going to phone someone and find out, but I heard him talking about fetching the doctor. I was afraid. They were going to take me back to the place I was before."

Tom fell silent. He liked to find solutions, but he didn't know what he could do for Esther, except keep her safe. He almost didn't hear whispering, "Don't make me go back, please."

Tom said, "I'm not going to make you do anything you don't want to do. I'm here to help you."

She looked up through wet eyelashes, longing to believe him, longing to feel there was some little place in this ocean of uncertainty where she was safe, some rock in this troubled sea where she could rest.

"Tom, I'm not mad, am I?"

"No, not at all. It's not surprising you're confused. You've lost your memory, so you have no anchor, it's like being at sea without a compass. You have no points of reference; you don't know where you have been or where you are going. There's just a mass of water, looking the same in all directions, with no indication of which way will lead you to land."

Esther nodded. "Yes, you're right, that's a very good way to describe it." She twisted her hair in her fingers. "They'll be looking for me."

"Don't worry, they can't trace you here." Tom pulled her gently towards him and kissed her on the forehead.

She watched Tom as he cleared up the cups from the lounge and washed up. She felt a little safer. If he had wanted to hand her over to some gang, he would surely have done so by now. She flushed whenever she saw the bruise on his head: maybe *he* should be wary of *her*. She was embarrassed, but he just smiled and said it had knocked some sense into him.

When he came back into the lounge, she said, "The problem is, even if I find the treasure, I don't know how I can get in touch with Estrila again to let her know."

"Let's not worry about that just yet," Tom said. "One thing at a time. A trip will do us both good."

Tom suggested going to the police, but she shook her head. "What could the police do? I don't even know my

196

own surname. They would ask all sorts of questions and I wouldn't be able to answer them."

"All right, we'll go to Bristol tomorrow, but when we come back, if you still can't remember anything, at least reconsider calling in the police." A wary look came into Esther's eye and he took her hand. "I'm not going to make you do anything you don't want to do," he said. "It's just a suggestion."

Tom looked out an adjustable garden seat from the shed, brushed away the cobwebs and suggested she relax in the garden. The only way in was through a gate and along a path that went around the side of the house, and that was secured with a padlock.

She was glad of a chance to sit quietly, to watch a squirrel darting up the silver birch tree and a speckled thrush searching for snails and slugs beneath the hazel and hawthorn. She was ready if her memories started to return.

A black cat appeared creeping low, making its way towards the bird. Esther clapped her hands to make the bird fly away. The cat wove in and out of the chair legs, rubbing his body round her ankles. Through the open window, she could hear Tom, talking on the telephone, arranging for a friend to look after his house and business for a few days while he helped Esther search for the druid's cup.

He finished the call and came out into the garden, removing several dead petunias from a hanging basket as he passed. Crouching down beside Esther's chair and absent-mindedly rubbing the cat's head, he said, "Ian's coming soon to collect the keys to the house. I'll fill him in on a few things I'd like him to do for me, then I'll be all yours. We'll drive over to Bristol first thing tomorrow – or this afternoon if you want."

Esther took his hand and held it tight. "Thank you," she said. "Tomorrow will be best. I want to have as long as I can to look through the papers."

She was still in the garden when she heard a car draw up. A few minutes later, Tom stood at the kitchen door and said, "Do you want to come and meet Ian?"

"I'll be in in a minute," Esther said. "I'll make you both a drink."

Her eyes began to close. She was still tired from her broken night. It was silent except for the murmur of Tom who was explaining his filing system to Ian, and the happy sounds from the two boys next door, kicking a football around. It was their last day of freedom: tomorrow they would be back to school.

When she heard a dull thump, she assumed a football had landed in the garden, but the next moment, she was fully awake, aware of a movement behind her. The cat leapt over the fence and a blackbird rattled its raucous alarm call. She stood up, knocking over the chair, but before she could turn round to see who was there, strong hands grabbed her and clamped something over her mouth. The last thing she remembered before everything went black was the smell of lemons.

***

When Esther did not appear, Tom went to check. There was no sign of her in the kitchen and the kettle was stone cold. Assuming she had fallen asleep in the garden, he stopped to empty the clothes from the washing machine into the laundry basket, took a box of pegs from under the sink and went out of the back door. There was no sign of

Esther and the chair was on its side as if she had stood up in a hurry. Tom dropped the basket and called her name. No answer. His blood ran cold. After what she'd told him, why on earth had he left her alone? He ran round the house, yelling her name, but she was nowhere to be seen.

He ran over to the fence and called out to the boys next door. "Have you seen Esther, the lady who's staying here?" he said.

The younger boy caught the ball that his brother had just thrown and said, "She fell to the ground and a man took her away to hospital."

Tom frowned. The older boy said, "Stop making things up." An argument erupted and threatened to escalate. Tom clenched his fists and said, "Stop arguing and tell me what happened." He felt dizzy and leant against the fence for support. "Who is this man you are talking about? Do you know him? What did he look like?"

The younger boy walked away and went back to throwing the ball, trying to get it into a basket that hung six feet up the wall of his house.

The older boy said, "We didn't really see him properly. He had his back to us. We thought it was you messing about."

Tom took a deep breath, forcing himself to speak slowly and said, "Tell me once more what happened – what really happened."

"We were playing ball. There was a noise, we looked up and saw a man holding your girlfriend. We thought it was you."

With rising panic, trying not to scare the boy, Tom said, "Go on, you're not in any trouble."

"She went all floppy so he picked her up and went round the front. That's all I know."

"Thank you," Tom said, as he turned back to the house, already on his phone, ringing 999.

Ian said, "Do you want me to drive you somewhere?"

Tom shook his head. "I've no idea where they might have taken her." His face crumpled. "From what those boys said, it sounds as if they drugged her. I shouldn't have left her." He sank into a chair then leapt up again and paced the room.

Ian went into the kitchen and filled the kettle. As he opened the cupboards, looking for cups, he heard Tom say, "I thought she was safe. I didn't think anyone could get in. The garden's completely fenced in and the side gate's padlocked. How did anyone know she was here anyway?"

Ian spooned coffee into two cups. "Perhaps the man came through the neighbouring fences," he said.

"Esther would have seen him coming."

Tom was surprised to hear a police siren approaching already. He was not to know that back at the call centre, they were primed to give priority to any message that included the word Esther.

Tom rushed outside, followed by Ian, as a young policeman got out of his car.

"They've kidnapped Esther," he said.

"Let's go inside and you can explain things to me," the policeman said.

Tom turned and hurried inside. He thought the man was wasting time, but wasn't going to waste even more by arguing with him.

"How long has she gone, sir," the constable asked.

Tom was so agitated, he could hardly speak. Ian said, "A few minutes, I think. Not more than half an hour. The boys next door saw a man take her."

"I'll speak to the boys in a minute."

"She's lost her memory," Tom said. Someone's been after her for a while. They were keeping her prisoner. I don't know how they found her."

"Don't worry, sir, we'll do everything we can," the policeman said. Like everyone else back at the police station, he knew all the details that the London Detective Sergeant had given them. He looked round the house and garden said, "Look, here's your problem." The lock of the side gate had been broken open.

He went next door to talk to the boys. "They should be trying to find her," Tom fumed, "instead of wasting time. Let's get in the car and go and look."

Ian said, "It's better to leave it to the police. We don't know where she's gone."

Tom paced about, sipping at his cup of coffee whenever he passed the table.

Next door, the older boy was elaborating on his story. "He grabbed her from behind. I thought he was just playing a game. Then she fell on the ground and he picked her up and carried her away."

The younger boy said, "I told you she was sick and he was taking her to hospital."

The policeman removed his helmet, looked at the boys and said, "Do you know he was taking her to hospital or is that just what you think?"

The boy glanced at his mother. "Just tell the truth," she said. "You haven't done anything wrong."

The boy looked down at his feet. "I just thought that," he said.

"You're a very observant little boy," the constable said. "Maybe you'll be a detective one day. Did you see a strange car in the street at all?"

The boys shook their heads. "We was playing football," the younger one said. The constable turned to the mother.

"No sorry, I was in the back, doing the ironing. You can't see over the fence from there," she said and added, "I don't know what goes on in that house. There's always different people coming and going. A lot of the time it's empty. I think you should look into that."

"Thank you, we will," said the policeman.

Back at the police station, the team was busy. Maps were laid out and a list made of any isolated building, farm or barn in the area. They would be making enquiries house to house too. The list was divided up into areas and each segment allocated to a member of the search party.

CHAPTER 26

Jonathan lay with his eyes shut. His body ached everywhere and he couldn't move his left arm properly. He listened to the sounds all around him: a television, a mobile phone, people talking, something that sounded like a trolley being wheeled around, but still did not know where he was. He was comforted, though, by the familiar smell of the perfume Silvie always wore. He thought he must be hallucinating.

He slowly opened his eyes – and looked straight into Silvie's concerned face.

"Oh, thank goodness you're awake," she said.

"Where am I?"

"You're in hospital, in Somerset. You were mugged. Don't try to talk now."

Jonathan's mouth felt like the bottom of a bird cage. Silvie helped him sit up far enough to take a drink of fresh water.

"Where was I when I was mugged?" he said.

"You were found in a bird hide. Did you go there to meet someone?"

"It was Rolf and another man. They wanted to know where Angela was. They beat me up but I didn't tell them."

Silvie took Jonathan's hand as it lay on the bedcover. "I didn't tell them," he said again. A look of pain crossed his face. "But they looked on my phone and saw a picture of her. Silvie, they've gone after her. You've got to tell the police."

Silvie was angry. They had left him in the bird hide to die. It was such a remote place, it could have been weeks until someone found him. Jonathan had been lucky. A few hours after the attack, a couple on holiday had decided to visit the local nature reserve.

"They were driving a Skoda," Jonathan croaked. Silvie took out a pen and paper and wrote down the registration number. "You've got to find her," he said, sinking back exhausted.

"I'll go and find someone straight away," Silvie said, squeezing his hand and pecking him on the cheek.

She went to reception to ask for the number for the local police station. When she got through, she told them, "They're dangerous. You've got to find them."

***

Archie turned to two reports on his desk, beginning with Esther's 9th visit. The first part was simple, the part about Estrila being in labour. They knew Esther had given birth to a daughter, Abigail. Archie frowned as he read through the second part. This was more complicated. Lord Goran was beating a semi naked woman. Esther stepped in and hit him over the head. Supposing Esther had gone round to Fergus' house and he had tried to rape her. She picked up an object and hit Fergus over the head in an act of self-defence. In the ensuing struggle, she had delivered a fatal blow. If that was the case, where was the object she had hit him with? They had carried out a search, looking for the weapon in rubbish bins and gardens but nothing had turned up.

Another possibility was that Fergus was abusing Esther's daughter and Esther had found out and gone to confront him.

The team had been through hours and hours of CCTV footage from the hospital, trying to find a clue to what had happened. On the day of the murder, a car had entered the car park, the passenger door had opened and a woman had stepped out rather shakily. She had her back to the camera all the time, but the registration number of the car was visible. The same car had entered the car park for the next six days but had not been seen since Esther left.

Unfortunately, the car was not registered in the UK and had no MOT or insurance in this country, which was going to make it harder to find.

Camera two showed the doors to the ward where Esther had been held, and also showed part of the reception desk. The visitors were mostly retired couples carrying bunches of flowers, or mothers with children. On the day Esther was admitted to hospital, nobody had visited her. However, over the next six days, until Esther was moved, one man had slipped in with a different group each day.

The strange thing was, he passed back through the doors just seconds after he had gone through. On the last day, the same man came out of the ward and stood at the reception desk talking to the nurses. Archie made a note to tell the hospital they should adjust their camera so that it showed the whole of the reception desk because, frustratingly, they could not see all that happened, or the whole of the man's face. This could have been the angry man Miss Torres had spoken to, but it was not possible to say for sure.

A picture of the man had been printed off from the CCTV camera. It was grainy, not very clear and the man's face was half hidden by the hood of his jacket. The computer guys had enhanced the picture, but it was still just part of the side of a face.

***

When Esther awoke, her head ached with the worst headache she had ever had. She was lying on a pile of cushions in a dark room, little lights bouncing in front of her eyes. The pain hammered as if it wanted to get out. She coughed and tried to sit up but it made the pain worse. She could just make out a figure sitting opposite on the floor, ethereal, fuzzy, swaying. She shook her head slowly, trying to clear the image.

"Hello, Angela."

Esther blinked hard and opened her eyes. She did not recognise the voice.

"I am not Angela."

"My name is Edward. Edward Thatch. You have led us a merry dance is the expression, I think."

Esther closed her eyes to stop the room swaying.

"How are you feeling now? I'm sorry that I drug you, but I think you do not come with me unless I drug you. It was my duty to save you. You were in a lot of danger."

Esther shook her head gently to try to clear it. "Danger from what?"

"You look for treasure, a Druid's cup," Edward said. "There is gang who wants to steal it, a very unpleasant gang who will harm you to get the information."

Esther couldn't think straight for the headache, but she knew one thing: the treasure she was after had been dug up a long time ago and should be safely in a museum by now. It would be very difficult to steal it.

"Tom was part of the gang," Edward went on. "He pretend to be your friend. I think he is succeeding."

Esther tried to think about Tom. He had always been kind to her, except that she had had her doubts but no, they had all evaporated. She didn't know what to think, who to trust.

"You could be right," she said at last.

"I am the good guy," Edward said.

"Are you the police?"

He nodded. "I work with them, help them sometimes. You are safe now, Angela, you have nothing to worry about."

"You've got me muddled up with someone else. I'm not Angela. I'm Esther."

"Esther, Angela, is all the same."

"How did you find me?"

"There is a farmer willing to tell anyone who listens, how you crashed through his farmyard, scaring his chickens." He tried unsuccessfully to mimic a Somerset accent. 'They could have killed us. I be driving the cows over to the milking shed when a car came shooting through the yard fast, scattering thee chickens. They'll be off lay for a week.' That track leads to just a few houses. I ask around. Ladies in your country are happy to tell a gentleman where he might find his girlfriend, the love of his life, his soulmate." He laughed.

"Do I know you?"

Something was in the back of her mind, struggling to get out. Suddenly, she remembered that she had been about to go to Bristol to look in the newspaper archives. "I have to go to Bristol. Can you take me?"

"Of course. We go tomorrow."

"I need to go today." She stood up but her legs would not support her. She sank down onto the cushions again.

"You need to rest today. You will be stronger tomorrow."

Esther closed her eyes. She was so tired.

When she woke, she thought there was something wrong with her watch. She had been kidnapped some time in the afternoon and her watch was now pointing to five o'clock. It was semi dark outside so it must be early in the morning. That would mean that she had slept for about fourteen hours. She was now lying on a blow-up mattress, covered with a single blanket but had no recollection of moving from the cushions. At least the headache was gone. She did not know whether to trust Edward but decided that if he took her to Bristol, she would know it was going to be all right.

As it grew lighter, it revealed a room empty except for a white carpet with several dents in the surface. She knew what this meant. The indentations were caused by a bed and dressing table that had stood on the carpet until recently.

She went through to the en-suite bathroom. Someone had lined up a number of products on the wide bathroom shelf: shampoo, soap, flannel, toothbrush, toothpaste, bubble bath, mostly samples taken from hotels, bearing their names. There was a soft white towel hanging on a hook on the door, embroidered with the initial S. She ran a bath and soaked for a while. It was still early and nothing stirred in the house. When she was dressed, she tried the door handle but it did not turn. She tried again, beginning to panic. She was locked in. She banged on the door and suddenly it opening to reveal Edward.

"The door was locked," Esther said, her throat tightening.

"Not locked," Edward smiled. "It's just a bit stiff. I've got your breakfast ready, then we set off for Bristol."

Downstairs in the kitchen, she surveyed the meal for one laid out on the kitchen table: an individual fruit juice carton, an individual packet of cereal, a small carton of milk, a yoghurt and a banana.

She ate hungrily. When she had finished, she cleared the table and began washing up. Opening the cupboards to see where things went, she found them empty.

Edward came into the kitchen and said, "We don't put things away." She watched as he poured the remaining milk down the sink and swept the remains of the breakfast into a carrier bag with the plate and cup. She thought it odd, but then, there was so much that was confusing since arriving at the house with Ray. Through the semi-transparent plastic of the bag, she could see the unused bottles from the bathroom, along with the toothbrush and toothpaste. It seemed they were not going to leave anything behind.

As she got in the car, she said, "What was that place? It was empty. Why did you take me there?"

"I need to take you somewhere safe and make sure we are not being followed. The police have many such places throughout the country." It had been Seb's idea to take her to this deserted place in case someone was on to them. He had been very clever. He had gone to an estate agent and said he was a cash buyer looking for a place he could move into quickly. The agent had shown him details of a house where the owners had already moved out. Seb had said he was interested in buying it and when they got there, he asked to look round by himself. The estate agent agreed. There was nothing to steal. He'd noticed the back door key hanging on a hook in the kitchen. He opened one of the downstairs windows a crack, then came back later, let himself into the house and left the back door unlocked so Rolf could get in later. Rolf had been concerned about breaking the law, but Seb had said, "Nobody's going to know, as long as you leave the place as you find it."

Esther got in the car and wound down the window. She felt light, free, her hair blowing in the wind. When she had found the treasure, she would go back for one more visit to let Estrila know. She was certain her memories would return and she was looking forward to getting her life back.

She didn't believe that she was in danger from Tom and wanted to let him know that she was all right, but her phone was not in her jacket pocket where it should have been.

"Have you seen my phone?" she asked. "Perhaps I left it at the house. Can we go back?"

"Don't worry about that, we will get you a new one," Rolf said.

Rolf was thinking that now he had his car back, he would drop the girl off then go back to London. He had missed too much work and he was unlikely to get his customers back. They had probably found someone else to do the work by now, but he did not want to stay in Somerset.

They were driving along a narrow country lane when Esther said, "Why are we going down here?"

"The motorway will be far too busy at this time of year."

He drove round more narrow roads and through villages with strange sounding names. When they had been driving for about ten minutes and the sun had been in her eyes all the time, she knew they were going the wrong way.

"We're heading East, aren't we?" she said. "I can tell by the sun. But Bristol's North of here."

"It's just these little roads," Edward said. "They twist and turn in all directions."

***

"Sir, we've just had an alert through," Jessica said. "Somerset are looking for the same car as we are, the one on the hospital CCTV."

Archie looked up sharply. "What's the story?"

"A man called Rolf hired Jonathan Whicher to find a woman called Angela Connors. He seems to be working for a man called Seb. When Jonathan wouldn't tell them where she was, they beat him up. He thinks they've gone after her – a picture on his phone gave her location."

"Jonathan Whicher?" Archie had not heard that name for years. Jonathan Whicher, Private Investigator, otherwise known as former DS John White.

When John's daughter had been killed by a drunk driver ten years ago, it had knocked the stuffing out of him. After being on sick leave for three months, he handed in his notice and moved to London to set himself up as a private eye. Archie smiled at the name.

Despite the problems, John had not lost his sense of humour. Jonathan Whicher was a famous Victorian detective who worked on the case of a baby that was murdered at home. Whicher announced that he thought his sister had done it, and had been vilified by the press. Years later, she confessed to having committed the murder out of anger at the way her stepmother and former housekeeper had treated her mother.

"What do we know about the car?"

"It is registered to a Rudolf Przybyszewski in Poland but no tax or insurance."

Archie wondered how long it had taken Jessica to get her tongue round the unwieldy surname. "So Rudolf, or someone driving his car, took Esther to hospital on the day of the murder," he said, "and visited for the next six days, until Esther was moved to Somerset. This Rudolf is now in Somerset looking for Angela Connors. I'm going to Somerset. It's time to visit my old friend John."

CHAPTER 27

The sun was still in Esther's eyes as Edward drove and she was certain now that they were not going to Bristol. Who was this man who had kidnapped her, Edward Thatch? The name sounded familiar, maybe a name from a film she had seen some time ago. Suddenly she had it. "Edward Thatch was the real name of Blackbeard, the pirate, wasn't it?" she said, trying not to let her voice betray her mounting fears. Anyone who used a false name was up to no good.

Edward smiled. "You have found me out," he said. The receptionist at the hotel had wanted his name and it was the first thing that came to mind. "My real name is Rolf," he said. "In this business you must have several different identities – like you. You call yourself Esther, but that's not your real name, is it?"

Esther pondered this. Had she chosen a different name because she was involved in – what? Why do people call themselves different names? Famous writer, actor, spy?

They passed a sign for Muchelney and a few miles on, Edward turned down a narrow road, pulled over and stopped in front of a modest semidetached house. It was a picture of happy family life with children's toys scattered on the front lawn and a bicycle was propped up against the garage door. Edward said, "I just want to say hello to my sister while I'm here. I don't see her very often. She would love to meet you. I promise it won't take long."

"I'd rather stay in the car."

213

"You must come with me so I can keep you safe." He got out, went round to the passenger side, opened the door and took hold of her arm firmly.

He kept hold of her arm, herding her towards to front door, taking a bunch of keys from his pocket.

"You've got your own key?" Esther said.

"Yes, I often look after the place while the family's away."

He opened the door. Esther hesitated. There was something wrong. There were no sounds of children playing, no TV or radio, no smells of cooking. Rolf gave her back a gentle push and followed her inside, locking the door behind him. Esther whirled round. "What are you doing? Why are you locking the door?"

Someone came out of the living room behind her. "Hello Angela."

The voice seemed familiar, but she did not recognise the face.

"I'm not Angela, I'm Esther."

"Rolf's a good friend," Seb said, laughing. "He went along with my little charade, pretending to be searching for his girlfriend, so I could be reunited with my wife. Rolf knows the value of family, don't you, Rolf."

"We have all the time been searching for Angela, but this lady says she is Esther."

"Don't you think I know my own wife when I see her?"

"But how is it that she does not know you?"

"She's just pretending."

"I don't know you," Esther said.

"I'm sorry I tell you lie," Rolf said. "My sister is on holiday with her husband and the children."

"Why did you tell me she was here?"

"I must get you inside. You really not know Seb? He had a picture of you I give to Mr Whicher when we look for you."

"I don't know him, or this Mr Whicher."

"We're wasting time," Seb said, pulling Esther into the front room. Afterwards, she could remember nothing about the room except the plate of Garibaldi biscuits on a low table. There was something in the back of her mind about these biscuits, but she couldn't quite catch at the memory.

"So where have you been, Angela?" Seb asked. "I've missed you. Come and sit beside me."

"I told you, I'm not Angela. I don't know who you are."

"Maybe we let her go if she doesn't know you," Rolf said, feeling uneasy now. This woman looked like the one in the picture, but she clearly didn't know Seb.

Seb thumped the arm of the chair. "If you know what's good for you, you'll shut up," he said. "She knows me. She's just pretending she doesn't, but it's not going to work." He turned back to Esther. "You can call yourself what you like, but I'm still your husband."

"I'm not married to you, I'm married to Ray," Esther said. She didn't think this was true, but she was confused. What was it Ray had said?

"Who's Ray?"

"I've lost my memory. I don't remember anything."

"Oh, I see. He's the one you went off with, your lover."

Esther put her head in her hands. It was aching again and she couldn't think straight.

"I was taken to a house near Portlake. Ray was there. I thought he must be my husband, or brother perhaps, but maybe he's not. I don't where I was before that."

"Rolf tells me you want to go to Bristol. Something about treasure."

"Yes."

Seb laughed.

Esther turned to Rolf. "You understand, don't you?" she said. "You were talking to me about it, you knew all about the treasure."

"Sorry, I read your notebook," Rolf said. "That's how I know you want to find treasure. I want you to trust me after I take you from the garden."

Esther looked deflated and Rolf said, "I'm sorry." He regretted ever having agreed to look for Angela. This was turning out to be unpleasant. Seb must let this girl go. She wasn't the right one.

"Why are you saying sorry?" Seb asked. "You've reunited husband and wife. That's a good thing, isn't it, Angela."

She remained silent and Seb went on. "You always did live in a fantasy world." He turned to Rolf. "You don't know what I had to put up with. Years of her making up stories about the terrible way I treated her. Do you know, she even accused me of having an affair with a waitress in a Chinese restaurant."

Esther's head was spinning. *It's true!* Esther wanted to shout. Not about the affair, she had never claimed that, but the horrible way he had flirted with the woman, making disgusting suggestions. But if he knew the story, then he must be her husband, mustn't he? But why did he keep calling her Angela?

"Have a squashed fly biscuit," Seb said, pushing the plate towards her. Esther took a bite and spat it out. Seb laughed. "She never liked Garibaldi biscuits," he told Rolf. He turned back to Esther, his smile reduced to a cruel smile. "I was testing you, see if you remembered you didn't like them, although you could have been playing a trick of course. I wouldn't put it past you."

"What do you want, Seb?" Esther asked, retreating inwards, cloaking herself in a protective covering, going to a place where neither Seb nor Rolf could hurt her. It felt familiar. She was tired of the games and just wanted to get this one over with.

Seb turned to Rolf with mock anger. "After all this time, she asks me what I want. What I want, little wife, is to be with my family again." He stared at her. "Now, *Angela*, where is our child, what have you done with her?

Esther sighed. "I told you, I'm not Angela and I don't have a child." That was not true, she *did* have a child, she was sure of it, but she wasn't going to tell this man. There was no knowing what he might do.

Rolf said, "I never saw her with child." He handed Esther's phone to Seb. He had been flicking through it as they spoke. "There's no messages on there about a child, no pictures."

"There wouldn't be. It's a new phone. I never let her have a phone when we were together. She would have used it to tell everyone how terrible I was, more lies."

Esther knew that there was no hope for her. She had trusted Rolf, but he had deceived her, taken her phone and now she had no way to get help.

217

Suddenly Seb jumped up from his chair and slapped Esther round the face. "You'll tell me where she is," he said.

Esther broke down, her anguished sobs filling the room. Rolf moved towards her but Seb said, "Leave her alone. She always was a drama queen." To Esther, he said, "Don't think you've got away with this. I'll get it out of you sooner or later."

Seb motioned to Rolf and they left the room. Esther could hear them talking in the kitchen, but she knew there was no point in trying to escape. There *was* no escape. After a while Seb came back into the room smelling of drink. Esther picked up a cushion and held it in front of her, although she knew it offered scant protection from his fists.

"Rolf's been telling me what a slut you are," he said, "going off with that Tom. I should have known. You were always trying it on with men, you used to make a right fool of yourself. What I had to put up with!" When she didn't say anything, he went on, "You'd better start telling me what I want to know soon or I'm going to get angry. Very, very angry."

He went out into the hallway and called out to Rolf, "Give me the car keys."

Rolf came out of the kitchen. "Why? I want to go home now. I've done what you asked and found Angela for you. No more touring around Somerset."

"Give me the keys, I've got one more errand and then you're free to go." He planted his feet firmly a little way apart and held out his hand.

When Seb had gone, Rolf said, "I am sorry I deceive you, but Seb tell me you are Angela."

218

"What does he want with this Angela?"

"He say she is his wife, he want to find her. Now I do not know."

"It's true that I can't remember anything," she said, "although wouldn't I have recognised Seb if he was my husband?"

"I don't know. When Seb come back, I go to London, to my work."

"How did you get mixed up with Seb?"

"He's my boss. I work for him. He tell me that his wife has left him gone to live with someone else."

Seeing the way Seb was with Esther/Angela and the anger that threatened to spill over into violence, Rolf wished he had not gone along with Seb's plan. He wasn't certain how everything worked in this country, but was fairly sure he'd be in trouble for kidnapping her, even though he was doing it under Seb's orders. The sooner he could get back in London, the sooner he could forget all about Seb. In fact, he would be glad if he never had to have anything to do with the man again. He was going to set himself up as a builder and work for himself.

Rolf retreated to the kitchen. It sounded as if he was cooking a meal. Esther curled her feet under her on the settee, leant against the cushions and thought about the last journey she had made to the medieval castle. Estrila had, at last, one surviving baby. Thinking about it brought a memory of her own to the surface. She was reluctant to let it in, but it gave her no choice.

She was in the early days of pregnancy. She still worked and on one this occasion, she arrived home feeling really ill. She lay down on the bed for a rest. When her husband came in, she asked him if he would make a start on the meal. "Get up, you slut. I've been working all day. It's your job to get me my food," he said. She tried, but just couldn't get out of bed. He had lashed out at her, punching her in the stomach. Later she had started bleeding and knew she had lost the baby.

Could that man who had punched her be Seb? Try as she might, his face remained out of focus, a blur.

She heard the front door bang. Seb was back. She saw from his red face, his puckered eyebrows and his thin, down-turned mouth that whatever he had been doing, it had not gone well. Rolf asked for his keys, but Seb just glared at him put them in his pocket.

Rolf said, "My sister's coming back tomorrow afternoon. You must be gone in the morning."

A vein stood out in Seb's neck. "She'll tell me what I want to know first."

"She has lost her memory," Rolf said.

"She knows all right and she'll have to tell me."

"You know what women are like, be nice to her then perhaps she tell you."

"Oh, I might have known you'd be on her side," Seb said.

Seb's attempt at a smile was more like a grimace. Esther winced as he put his arm around her. "It's all right, I'm not going to hurt you," he said in a mocking, sing-song voice. "You've had a hard time recently and you don't know what you're doing, what you're saying. If you don't want to be with me, I accept it, but don't keep me away from my child."

Esther knew the pain of missing your child, but there was nothing she could tell this stranger.

When she said nothing, Seb went on, "Rather convenient isn't it, losing your memory?"

"No, Seb, it really isn't. I don't know who I am, where I live, what I did before I came here."

"So you admit it, you could be Angela."

"I only know that I am Esther."

"And you've got a child?"

Esther shook her head. "All I remember is my name," she said.

Seb thumped his fist in his hand and went out of the room. Later, Rolf brought her some slices of pizza on a tray and left her alone to eat. She could hear him talking to Seb in the kitchen.

When she had eaten as much as she wanted, Rolf showed her to the place where she would sleep, a little girl's bedroom. "Maybe it help you remember something," he said, indicating the pink walls, pink bed cover and delicate butterflies on the wall. "Tomorrow you must go," he said. "My sister come back from holiday."

"He hasn't given you your car keys back, has he?" Esther said. "You're as much a prisoner as I am."

CHAPTER 28

Archie sat on one side of Jonathan's bed and Silvie on the other. He had only met John's wife on the odd occasion, at a Christmas party or when she'd popped in to the station. Her hair was in a different style, shorter but otherwise she was the same Silvie who had surprised everybody with an energetic Salsa dance at the Christmas party. She had danced with one of the young constables while John had looked on, bemused.

"Well look what the cat dragged in," she said. "After all this time. I never expected to see you here. What are you doing in Somerset?"

"Catching up with an old friend," he said. "I've come down from London. I'm living there now. I was offered a big promotion."

"You must miss the moors," Jonathan said, "but at least we can meet up when I'm out of here, catch up with old times. What really brings you here, though?"

"I'm investigating the disappearance of a young lady who has lost her memory. We were looking for a particular car, the same one that was used to take you to the bird hide."

Jonathan raised his eyebrows. "They're a nasty couple – at least, the one called Seb is."

"What do you know?"

"The other one's called Rolf, he had a foreign accent. He came to me saying he was looking for his girlfriend, Angela Connors. I traced her down here, but I had a feeling

Rolf wasn't telling me the truth. When I wouldn't say where she was, they beat me up."

Archie took out a picture of the man who had visited Esther in hospital. "I know you can't see the whole of the face, but do you think this could him?"

Jonathan peered at the picture then handed in to Silvie. They both agreed that it was possible, but the picture was too fuzzy to be able to say with certainty. Next, Archie took out a picture of Malcolm Dayton. Jonathan took one look at it and said, "Yes, that's him, that's Seb."

"We know him by another name, but you're sure it's one of the men who beat you up?"

"Yes, definitely. I won't forget that face. That's the one I know as Seb."

"So, there is a connection between the Esther we are looking for the Angela Connors you were asked to find," Archie said.

"Do you have a picture of her?" Jonathan asked.

Archie took the picture of Esther out of his file and handed it over.

"That's her," Jonathan said. "That's the one we're looking for. Seb told me she was his wife, Angela Connors."

"Esther turned up at the hospital saying she had fallen and hurt herself and could not remember anything. She was transferred to Somerset after a week."

"And that's when Rolf came to see me, looking for her. Do you think it could be true?"

Archie thought. "If Seb really was married to Esther, there was no need for a private investigator. He just needed to come forward and tell us his wife was missing. There was no need for secrecy. The hospital would have

223

told him where she had gone. No, there is more to this than a husband looking for his wife." He paused while Silvie helped Jonathan to drink.

"Why would he be looking for her?" Archie said, thinking out loud.

"She knows something that he wants to keep secret?" Jonathan said. "She has some information he wants?"

Silvie said, "I went round to the address Rolf gave us. It was a rented house. I spoke to one of the tenants and he suggested I talked to the landlord. He gave me an address in Hampstead."

"Red Lexus outside?" Archie asked.

"Yes, that's right."

"Dayton's house."

"He wasn't there, but the next door neighbour said he and his wife had gone away. She asked me if I was looking for the cup."

"What cup was that?"

"All she said was the husband, Malcolm, had asked her to look after it for her. I got the impression it was something fairly valuable. I didn't take much notice. I couldn't see how it would help."

"That doesn't get us any closer to knowing why he is looking for Esther, or where they are now," Archie said. "What does this Rolf look like?"

"About five foot eight, light brown hair, brown eyes, about thirty years old, weather beaten face, poor skin, possibly a heaver smoker when he was younger, long nose, pointed chin."

"I need to find Esther before he does," Archie said.

He left the ward and phoned Jessica to ask her to go round to Mrs Williams' house, collect the cup and report

224

back to him. An hour later, she sent him a picture of a beautiful silver cup with a gold lining, engraved with a pattern of leaves. There was no report of a cup of that description having been stolen. A photograph and a description of the cup was being circulated to all insurance firms and the team were visiting jewellers in the area to see if they knew anything about it.

***

When she woke the next morning, Esther knew something was different. It was as if a malign presence had left the house. Downstairs, she found Rolf in the kitchen, frying bacon. "Where's Seb?" she asked.

"He had to leave. You go after breakfast too." Rolf was furious. Seb had gone off early, before he was awake, and taken the car. Now he had no way of getting back to London.

"I'm free to go?"

"Yes, where you want, but have some breakfast first." He threw a phone on the table and a few notes. "Here, have your phone back." The last thing Seb had asked him to do was make sure she had enough money. He didn't want her going to the police, claiming she was destitute. She grabbed the phone and the money and rushed upstairs to ring Tom. As her finger hovered over the keypad, she realised that this was exactly what they wanted her to do. She was certain that Seb would be watching her from somewhere just outside the house and would follow her when she left. Maybe he was able to listen into her phone calls too. She couldn't risk it.

She went slowly downstairs. "I'm free to go anywhere I like?" she asked.

225

"Yes, anywhere you like," Rolf said. The sooner she led Seb to the child, the quicker he would get his car back.

***

Archie sat in Yeovil police station looking through the file, trying to find something they'd missed. The people who lived in the small hamlet where Tom had taken Esther had all been interviewed, and a house to house enquiry had been conducted over a wider area. Posters had been placed in prominent positions, but nobody had come forward with any information that helped.

Most of the people who lived there had been at work when the kidnap had occurred. Because the village was only twenty minutes' drive from the town (no buses, there hadn't been any for a long time), young working couples snapped up the houses. Unfortunately, there was no Mrs Williams to tell them what the whole neighbourhood was up to. It was hard to credit it: a grown woman had been abducted, but nobody had seen anything.

It was the next day before PC Wilkinson visited a remote farmyard and learnt that a red Fiesta had passed through there a couple of days ago. That was old news. They knew where Esther had gone with Tom. Of more interest was the car that came later, making enquiries about a red car. The man was driving a Skoda, the farmer said. He had not written down the registration number, but he could remember part of it, numbers and letters that matched Rolf's car registration plate. That definitely put Rolf in the frame for the kidnap.

***

Esther left the house and turned right, looking for clues to where she was. The place was deserted. Children were back at school and their mothers indoors or at the shops.

Apart from a dog watching her from the safety of its own garden, she saw no living creature. She wandered down to the main road, and after a while, came to a bus stop. Someone had scribbled all over the timetable, making the destinations and times of the buses indecipherable.

A man was heading her way, a big man with tattoos on his arms, long hair tied back and a cigarette dangling from his mouth. He was leading a strange looking dog, small and hairless except for a few hairs around its face. They looked like Laurel and hardy. As he drew level, Esther asked the man how she could get to Bristol. He looked at her, took a puff of his cigarette, blew smoke in her face and said something that Esther didn't catch. "Sorry, what did you say?" she asked.

Through the fog of his West Country accent, she managed to work out that he was saying that there were no buses that day. "I could take 'ee some of the way on my bike," he went on. "I be going that way." It seemed the only option open to Esther. She had to get away before Seb came back. She wasn't convinced that he had agreed to let her go.

"I be Tank," he said, offering her an oily hand, with dirt beneath the fingernails. "Sorry," he apologised, "I've been working on 'er this morning, sweet as a nut she be now."

She followed him as he took the dog home and looked out a second crash helmet. He revved up as she climbed on the back of his bike and set off along the country lanes at a breath-taking speed, flying round narrow bends and overtaking in front of oncoming traffic. Esther clung on tight, secure in the knowledge that Seb would not be able to

227

follow them. Rolf's car was incapable of going at such speeds, and they would have left him behind long ago.

After a while, Esther noticed pale yellow and green signs for a beer festival on the side of the road, and after another mile or two, a pub decked out in livery that matched, with its pale yellow walls and green paint around the windows and doors. Hanging baskets full of petunias, geraniums, lobelia, begonias and busy lizzies made a bright display, a coloured fountain flowing down the walls. A group of bikers had congregated outside, sitting aside stationary bikes or leaning against the wooden benches and tables.

Inside the function room, thirty large metal barrels had been placed on tables against the walls with names such as Pitchfork, Viking, Betty Stoge, Golden Thread and Corby Fox. The breweries were doing a brisk trade. Tank took a small taster cup that was offered to him and handed it to Esther, "Where you be sleeping tonight?" he said, nodding towards the pub. "She be booked up, you won't get in there."

"Don't worry about me, I'll find something," Esther said, sipping the beer and finding it too bitter for her taste. She had no idea where she would sleep, but after the last few days, it was the least of her troubles. Tank decided against the beer he had just tasted and moved on the next one.

"Would you like a glass of that?" the seller asked Esther hopefully and she shook her head. Leaving the other bikers to choose their beers, she went into the bar to buy a fruit juice. She needed to keep a clear head. Tomorrow she was going to Bristol, even if she had to walk all the way.

She hung around at the edges of the conversation, sipping her drink and trying to join in the banter, but really, she had nothing to say. Nobody minded and nobody asked about her past, which was a great relief. Other people turned up for the festival, mainly men, but after a while an old Volkswagen pulling a caravan drew into the car park, its tyres and sides covered in mud as if it had driven through a field. There was a dent in rear passenger door and the bumper was tied on with a piece of string. The caravan was small and its original white paintwork had long ago turned into a dingy yellow.

All eyes were on the car as two women got out, to a chorus of wolf whistles. The two were a complete contrast. One was tiny, about four foot six inches tall, with short hair dyed blonde and the other was average height, dark, with long black locks. They were both heavily made up, with black lines around their eyes and bright red lipstick. They wore cowboy hats, short leather skirts and knee high boots and had elaborate tattoos on their arms – the blonde had a series of flowers in pale green climbing up her arm, and the raven haired beauty had a lizard climbing down.

The men whistled again and the girls waved, taking in the men in one glance, sizing them up. They spotted Esther and gave her a special wave before disappearing inside, emerging a few minutes later with pints of golden, frothy liquid and making their way through the admiring crowd, pushing away arms that tried to touch them, and giving a caustic reply to saucy comments. When they reached Esther, they introduced themselves as Razor (the dark one) and Babydoll (the blonde one). "You don't look like the usual type who comes here," Razor said.

"No, I'm not," Esther said. "Tank gave me a lift on his motorbike. I'm trying to get to Bristol."

"We can't call you Esther," Razor said. They whispered together then said, "If you came here with Tank, you must have travelled faster than a bullet, so that's what we're going to call you, Bullet!"

"You can bunk up with us tonight, and we'll take you there tomorrow, we're going that way," Babydoll said.

"You're so kind," Esther said. Razor linked her arm in Esther's and said, "Come and meet the boys, they don't bite – not often, anyway!"

Esther felt happy and relaxed in the company of the bikers. Really, they were just ordinary people. On Monday, no doubt as they put away their leather biking clothes and became office workers or teachers.

Esther would not have been so carefree had she known that Seb was not far behind her. He had followed her at a leisurely pace. When she stopped at the pub, he drove to the nearest village and found a b & b place that had a sign in the window, "No Bikers." He would follow her until she led him to Abigail, then he would have no further use for her.

Esther searched her pockets for money and found the bunch of £10 notes Rolf had given her. She bought the girls a drink and ordered fish and chips for herself and Babydoll. Razor wanted "something to get my teeth into" and chose a beef and ale pie with roast potatoes, carrots and peas.

Later on, a band arrived. Esther watched them unloading their heavy amplifiers from a van and thought about Tom. Sometime later, the first guitar chord sounded and the bikers wandered back into the pub to listen. The music was loud, harsh, and hurt the ears. It was nothing like the music Esther used to listening to – at least, she didn't think so. It sounded like something from a horror movie.

"It's gothic metal music – great isn't it," Razor shouted, but Esther could not hear her. Esther tried to enjoy the experience, copying the girls' dance moves and flinging herself about. There was a wonderful freedom to it all, as if she was shaking off all the recent past events and was being born again. By the time the first set finished, her ears were ringing, but she was looking forward to the second half.

"I never took you for a goth fan," Babydoll said.

"I don't know if I am," Esther said. "I've lost my memory." The girls were intrigued and wanted to hear all about it, but there wasn't much to say, and soon the band were back. She felt liberated, as if there was nothing she couldn't do.

The music finished at midnight. People began drifting home, car doors slamming and engines roaring. Esther lay in the garden at the back of the pub with Babydoll, Razor and Tank, looking up at the stars, until the landlord called out that he was locking the door now. Tank went inside and a few minutes later, all the lights went off.

The caravan seemed even smaller inside than out. There was hardly room to stand. The settee pulled down into a double bed at one end and there was a tiny toilet, so small you could hardly shut the door when you were inside. The wallpaper was stained over the tiny cooking area and the colourful ethnic throws did not disguise the dirty upholstery. The faded curtains drooped and the windows were dirty and scratched.

"Not the Ritz, I'm afraid," said Babydoll, but Esther was just grateful to have somewhere to put her head.

Babydoll and Razor lay on the bed. Esther took the floor, lying on some stale smelling cushions, covering herself with a thin blanket and declining the thin cigarettes the girls rolled up for themselves. They talked long into the night.

Esther began to open up, telling the girls how she had found herself in a house with someone called Ray, how she had no idea how she got there, the trips to the castle to see Estrila and the search for treasure. When she paused for breath, she realised the girls were asleep. Esther took one of the colourful throws from the chair and wrapped it round herself. Before she went to sleep, she took the rest of the money from her pocket, put it inside her bra and pulled the zip up tight on her track suit top. If anyone tried to take her money, she would know about it.

She was woken by the sound of a brewery delivery lorry. Her watch said 6.30 a.m. The girls were still asleep. She ate a chocolate bar she found in one of the cupboards and went outside where the air was fresh. There was quite a fug inside. When the lorry had gone, it was peaceful once more, with only the occasional bird call or dog barking. She sat on the wall of the garden, kicking her heels, enjoying the peace and quiet. A little later, the landlady of the pub came out and invited her to come inside for breakfast.

"The bikers aren't awake yet," she said. "I could do with the company." Esther sat by the window in the bar, looking out of the window at a blackbird rooting among the leaf litter.

It was some time before the girls appeared. With heavy eyelids, blood shot eyes and no make-up, they no longer looked like the girls of yesterday. "Just call me Ruby," said Razor. "And I'm Barbara," said Babydoll. By

232

the time they had drunk several coffees each and had eaten the breakfast Esther bought for them and were ready to set off, it was nearly noon.

Half a mile along the road, Seb was getting increasingly impatient. He sat in his car waiting for some action. He hadn't slept very well. The noise from the pub had kept him awake until the early hours. The b & b landlady expected him to leave after breakfast and he had sat in the car dozing, waiting for Angela to move.

He laughed at her naivety. She had taken the phone gratefully, unaware of the tracking app he had installed. She'd been cautious enough not to ring Tom, but didn't know that he could follow wherever she went. He cared nothing about this Tom. He wanted Abigail. Once he had her, he could get rid of his wife and take Abigail a long way away where nobody knew them. Angela had lost all rights to the child when she'd started that affair.

He woke from his nap as he heard the caravan moving off. Wherever Angela was, he would not be far behind. He would take as much time as it needed. Now she felt safe, she would not be able to stop herself from going to Abigail.

Following the route she was taking on his phone app, he had a good idea of just where she was headed now: Bristol. She was travelling slowly, but he was in no doubt of her destination. She had said she was going to look for treasure in Bristol and he now realised that the 'treasure' was Abigail. He laughed. Did she really think he couldn't work that one out?

He needed to fill the car up with petrol but was running low on cash. He didn't want to use his credit card, which could be traced. Rolf should still have enough cash left, but he had refused to come this morning, and Seb had let him stay at the house, thinking he didn't need him anymore.

Seb pulled over to the side of the road and called Rolf's number. When he answered, Seb told him to get on a train to Bristol and meet him there.

"I told you, I'm not coming," Rolf said. "I don't get to see my sister very often and they've invited me to stay for a few days. Seb, I want my car back, I need it. You could hire one, couldn't you?"

"No, I'm not hiring one," Seb said. "Why do you think I brought you? I don't want there to be any trace of me. I'm nearly there now, I am certain she has Abigail somewhere in Bristol. I have to keep one step ahead of her, I can't risk -." He had been about to mention the police, but that would only make Rolf determined to stay out of sight.

CHAPTER 29

Rolf had had reservations about this job from the very start. There had been something strange from the beginning. Seb had made a weak excuse as to why he couldn't visit the private eye himself but needed Rolf to go. Then Seb had wanted to drive, but not use his own car. He did not believe, any longer, that Seb's car had been in the garage. It was a new car, less than one year old.

Angela had been afraid of Seb. He thought at the time that it might be because she was hiding the child and wouldn't let her father see her, but now he began to wonder whether Seb had been telling him the truth. Seb never liked it when he couldn't get his own way and it wasn't hard to imagine him getting rough.

"So, you'll get your sister to drive you to the station?" Seb said, putting on his most charming voice, despite the anger that was boiling up inside him.

"No. I want my car. I want to go back to London at the end of the week. I'll lose all my customers if I don't."

"If you don't get here in the next hour, you can forget about your job. You'll never work for me again. And if you want the car, you'll have to come and get it." The suppressed anger in his voice put Rolf on alert. He was even more sure now that he should have kept Angela away from him.

Seb rang off and smashed his fist on the dashboard. When he had finished with the car, he would have it crushed and delivered to Rolf's house to teach him a lesson.

Rolf resented the way Seb had treated him. He needed his car. Without it, he would not be able to work. The few tools he had were in the boot too. On the spur of the moment, he took his phone from his pocket, punched in a number and reported his car stolen.

Seb stopped briefly in Bath and took £500 - the most he could get - from the ATM using his credit card. If he was careful, it should keep him going until he got back to London. He put the money in his wallet and drove quickly away from the area.

As soon as the transaction went through, an alert came up on the police computer back in London. Jessica rang Archie to let him know. "The credit card you wanted to trace, the one belonging to Dayton, has just been used. £500 has been taken from an ATM in Bath. There's also been an anonymous phone call to say that a car was stolen near Muchelney this morning. It's the same registration as the one we're looking for, Rolf's car."

***

Ten miles away, Esther's excitement mounted as they reached the outskirts of Bristol. "We won't be able to park in the centre," Ruby said, "but there's a caravan site not far from there with a riverside walk. Where is it you want to go?"

Barbara looked the address up on her phone. "Oh yes, it's not far from the site, we can get to it easily."

It was getting on for the rush hour and the traffic was heavy. The tight turn to get into the caravan park was difficult but she just managed it without scraping the wooden gate posts. They parked on a small gravel strip. Esther was keen to get going.

"We'll come with you, we could do with a walk," Ruby said.

"It will take too long to walk," Esther said. "I must get there as quick as I can to have as much time as I need looking through the papers."

"OK. We can take a water taxi."

They went out of the back gate, which bordered onto the river, and boarded a blue and yellow boat. It navigated past a small sailing boat before setting off towards the city centre, accompanied by the shriek of the seagulls circling above.

The boat stopped at the harbour, the vibrant entertainment centre of the city, close to its commercial centre with its numerous cafés facing the river. As they passed the Grain Barge, Ruby stopped to read a poster. "Oh look, one of our favourite bands is on tonight," she said. "You coming with us Esther?"

Esther had been so anxious to get to Bristol, she hadn't given much thought to what she was going to do afterwards. *If* she was able to look at the newspaper for the right date, and *if* she found details of the treasure, she would need to get back to Estrila, although she had no idea how she would do that.

They left the harbourside and made their way through the streets and into the commercial centre with its tall buildings in classical and gothic style side by side with all-glass modern offices. The newspaper office was directly up ahead. They just needed to cross the busy main road and they would be almost there. As they waited at the traffic lights, a figure standing on the steps of the offices waved. Esther recognised the man. It was Tom. She moved back and stood behind Ruby.

237

"What is it?" Barbara said.

"That man – I don't know. Edward – Rolf – told me he was part of a gang that was after me. I didn't believe him at the time, but now I'm not sure. Can we wait here a minute?"

The lights turned red and people began to cross, but three figures remained standing where they were while Esther deliberated.

The lights turned green. Another figure came into view on the other side of the road. Seb. What was he doing here? Esther was certain she had evaded him, but here he was, dodging behind a tree, hoping she hadn't seen him. She had only seconds to decide what to do. A steady stream of traffic prevented him reaching her, but very soon the lights would turn red again.

Seb chided himself for his impatience. He had not wanted Esther to see him. He had intended to follow, unseen, at a distance.

Tom faltered as Esther stayed on the other side of the road, realising she was afraid of him again. He followed the line of her gaze and saw a man he didn't recognise, but who didn't look friendly. The lights turned red. He began running towards Esther, pushing his way through the crowds, hoping to sprint across the road before the lights changed and the other man could reach her. Esther saw him, looked back at Seb, made a decision, turned and ran. As she ran as fast as she could away from him, two policemen approached Seb.

Tom was across the road now. Esther was running, following signs for the railway station. Barbara and Ruby, still with a slight hangover from all the beer they had drunk the previous night, ran a few yards, then gave up.

238

Esther had no time to admire the gothic architecture of the station with its clock tower resembling a church, or the stunning curved cast iron and glass roof. With hardly a pause, she scanned the destination board and saw that a train was about the leave from platform seven. She leapt into the first compartment as it drew away.

Pushing her way through the people standing in the aisle, she stepped into the next compartment. A sudden swoosh alerted her to the fact that someone had entered behind her. She turned, her shoulders hunched, her expression guarded, ready to scream if she had to.

"Esther! Oh, I'm so glad to see you."

It was Tom, red of face and out of breath. When he was breathing normally again, he tried to take Esther's hand, but she shrank from his touch.

"Esther, you're safe. That man who was waiting for you – I don't know who he was, but he's been arrested."

She watched him as a cornered fox watches the hunt saboteur: unsure whether death or a saviour had come to visit. "You're sure?"

"Yes. I saw two policemen go after him. Who was he, Esther?"

"My husband," she said dully, and added, "Or so he said."

"Why were you running away?"

Instead of answering, Esther said, "What were you doing in Bristol?"

"I knew you would go to the newspaper office. I've waited there every day since you were kidnapped."

"Seb said we were married, with a child. I don't know if that's true. How did he know where I was?"

"Tell me what happened. I left you in the garden and when I looked, you were gone. I was frantic."

Esther recounted her kidnapping and how they had let her go. "Seb wasn't there when I left so how did he manage to follow me? Tank gave me a lift on his motorbike and no car was following."

"Did he give you a phone?"

"Yes," she took it out of her pocket. "It's my phone. There were lots of messages from you but I wasn't sure if I should ring you. I didn't want to put you in danger."

Tom took the phone and studied it. "There's a tracking device on here," he said. "He would have known your every move."

"Can he do that?"

"It's very easy."

"So he'll know where I am now?"

"He's been arrested, he won't be able to follow you."

Esther opened the window, threw the phone out and closed the window with a satisfying thud. "Nobody will be able to find me now." Esther twirled her hair around her fingers. "Tom, I need to remember everything. If I am married to Seb, if I've got a child."

"We should call the police."

Esther shook her head. "No," she said. "I have flashbacks sometimes to a building. I don't know where it is. I can't remember anything, but every time I think of it, I am filled with fear. I sometimes see a room, they've taken me to a room, and there's so much pain. I think they were torturing me, trying to get some information from me. I don't want to go back there. I don't know what I've done, but I'm afraid of the police."

240

The train pulled into a station. "Don't worry, I won't do anything you don't want to do. It's a promise I made you once before and I don't ever intend to break it," Tom said.

"I've been thinking – of a lady. It's foolish. I don't know who she is." Esther took a card from her jeans pocket. "She gave me this when I was at the medieval festival and said I could ring any time. I've been carrying it around, but …"

"You think she might be able to help?"

"I know I'm being silly, but there was something about her. Tom, she looked just like Estrila."

"The lady in the castle?"

Esther nodded. Tom said, "Esther, you need to be careful. It could be a trick."

"I've got to do something."

"How about if I ring her first, get some idea about her?"

Esther nodded, relieved.

Eloise answered on the first ring. "Hello, my name's Tom. I have a friend with me that you met at the medieval festival."

"Oh yes, Esther. Is she all right?" Her soft voice soothed him like trees gently rustling in the wind, or a stream bubbling over stones.

"She is, but – I know this might sound strange, but she's lost her memory and thought you might be able to help."

"I'm so glad you rang me. I knew that day at the festival that she was in trouble. A man pushed between us and I was afraid he was going to take her, but she seemed to know him. I saw her later with the man and a woman and they were looking after her, but I was still worried. Can I speak to Esther?"

Tom handed the phone over.

"Esther, are you all right? I've been worried about you. Where are you?"

The voice calmed her. It was as if she had known and trusted Eloise all her life.

"We're on a train, somewhere outside Bristol."

"Oh, you're not far away. We're at Stonehenge – we've been here for the ceremony – Midsummer's Day, you know."

"Oh yes. I thought that was just for Druids," Esther said. Sensing a movement from Tom, she glanced at him. He was leaning forward, alert.

There was a slight hesitation before Eloise said, "We are Druids."

"Oh!" exclaimed Esther. "I've never met a Druid before. I didn't know there were any these days."

"You might well have met a druid and not realised," Eloise said. "At the last census, more than four thousand people said they were druids, but there will be more than that. Many people don't let on, as people can react in strange ways."

"I have to find the cup," Esther said. "It belonged to the Druids. I have to tell Estrila."

"I want to hear everything. We're just packing up our tent and we'll be leaving here soon. We can drive and meet you somewhere."

"I'm not sure where this train is going, but it's come up on the display that the next stop is Westbury. Is that anywhere near?"

"Get off at the station, Esther, and we will come and pick you up. I'll ring when we get there. We'll be about half an hour."

Esther ended the call and sighed. Everything was going to be all right. She knew it was.

"She said she was a Druid," she told Tom. "That's strange."

"Grant Oh God and Goddess protection, and in protection, strength," Tom said.

"That's nice, is it a poem?" Esther asked. "Did you write it?"

"Oh no, it's part of the Druid's prayer. It's very old. It was written in the 18th century by a man called Edward Williams, better known as Iolo Morganwg.

"Oh, are you a Druid too?"

Tom nodded then went on, "Druidry is a state of mind, really. There is no church, there are no rituals that you must undertake, no book of knowledge. There are courses for those who want to study but being a Druid is more a feeling, a knowledge – that your soul belongs to nature. It is a spiritual connection to the land."

"Can anyone be a Druid? Could I be?"

"Yes, there is no restriction. You need fear nothing from Eloise. The Druids are a peace-loving people. She will help you find the treasure and reach Estrila again."

Esther asked, "That house you took me to. Whose was it?"

"It belongs to one of the Druids in my Grove. He lives there when he's over here, but he goes away a lot. He lets anyone use the house who needs it."

"Like a safe haven," Esther said.

243

CHAPTER 30

The train pulled into Westbury station and they took a taxi to the town centre, passing the white chalk horse on the hillside above. Esther said, "Let's have some lunch first, and then go shopping. I must buy some clean clothes. I've been wearing these all night."

A market was in full swing in the centre, the oldest part of the town. They bought some pasties and sat eating on a wall facing the Old Town Hall and the 14th century church.

"Do you want to go into the church?" Tom asked, inclining his head towards the magnificent structure.

"After I've bought some clothes," Esther said.

"Do you have any money?"

"Yes, lots," Esther said. "Rolf gave it to me. I wasn't going to take it, but now I'm glad I did."

Esther bought some cheap underwear and tops, promising herself that once she knew who she was and what she liked, she would buy herself some new clothes. The church was cool, a welcome drop in temperature from the heat outside. She picked up a leaflet and read aloud. 'The church was built in the second half of the 14th century, but' – Oh look, Tom, it says there was a church here in Saxon times." She paused. "What year's that?"

"From about 410 to 1066 AD," Tom said.

"There must have been a church here in Estrila's time", she said, "maybe even this one." She sat down on one of the pews. "I feel close to her here," she said. "Do you think that's silly?"

"Not at all." Tom said, admiring the rich blue stained glass window above the altar.

"Estrila got married in a church like this," Esther said, remembering her beautiful gown that day. She could almost hear the words of the Latin mass spoken by the priest reverberating around the church.

Munda cor meum ac labia mea, omnipotens Deus, ut sanctum

Evangelium tuum digne valeam nuntiare

***

Tom had been wrong when he said Seb had been arrested at the traffic lights. There was no way the two policemen could have known that the man standing at the lights staring at the three women opposite was the man who had beaten up Jonathan Whicher. They had seen Esther running as if afraid, begun to follow her and lost her in the crowds.

Seb had followed Esther at a walk so that he did not draw attention to himself. He had no need to hurry. He knew where she was from the tracking device. He took the next train going in the right direction and had just passed Oldfield Station when his phone indicated that he Esther had stopped. He looked around. Even if she had got off the train, the embankment was too steep to climb down and anyway, it was covered in brambles. He tapped his phone on the edge of the table, but it still showed no movement. Was it possible that Esther had got on the same train as him and was sitting in a carriage nearby? With a grin of triumph, he got up and made his way along the train looking for her. Unable to find her, he made a second tour but she was in none of the carriages. She had either got off and was hiding somewhere along the side of the track (rather unlikely) or she had thrown the phone out of the window. He began to think she had given him the slip.

Peacefully unaware that Seb was so near, Esther relaxed in the peace of the church until the sudden sound of a ring tone tore into the silence.

"Hello, it's Eloise. We've arrived in Westbury. Where are you?"

"In the church, by the market place."

"I see it. We'll be with you in a few minutes."

"Let's go outside and wait," Tom said, thinking that if she had brought Seb or the police with her, they had more chance of escaping than in the confines of the church.

"There she is," Esther said, waving. Before Tom could suggest caution, she was running towards her and holding her in a warm embrace. Eloise was middle aged with a high forehead, long brown hair already streaked with grey, no make-up, a homely type. She was with a man a little younger, hair thinning on top. "Hello, I'm Adam," he introduced himself, holding out his hand.

"We came with a group of people, but they've gone back to London now," said Eloise. "Adam and I had already decided to spend a few days in the West Country when you rang. There's some people we know who live not too far from here. They run a retreat. I phoned them once we were on the road, and they have a couple of spare rooms. They've agreed that you can stay there as long as you like. You'll be safe there."

"But I have to go to back to Bristol, to find the treasure," Esther said. "I promised I would help Estrila."

When she had explained her journeys to the medieval castle, Adam said. "I can go to Bristol for you if you like. If

I hurry, I can get a train back from the station, look up the paper and be back at the retreat by dinner time."

Esther hesitated, then nodded. Seb could be waiting for her at the newspaper offices, knowing she would return.

The retreat was a long way from any station. "Let them know when you want picking up," Eloise said. "And I'll come and get you." Adam gave the thumbs up signal and set off towards Westbury station.

As she made her way to the car, Esther asked, "What goes on at a retreat? What is it like?"

"It's a place where you can be quiet away from life's stresses, be on your own if you want to, reflecting, meditating, taking a stroll through the garden. Time to recharge the batteries."

"It sounds heavenly," said Esther.

"The retreat we're going to has a watercolour painting course on at the moment, but the artists won't disturb you."

Adam sprinted along the road, feeling light and happy. The midsummer ceremony had left him energised, feeling connected, even though he hadn't slept all night. At the entrance to the station, he passed a sullen character who looked as if he was ready for a fight, his shoulders hunched, his muscles taut, his knee bouncing up and down impatiently. Adam gave him a wide berth.

Tom and Esther got in the back seat of the car, a silver coloured estate. There were two large rucksacks in the back, along with a tent, a dog lead, several wrapping papers for a seaweed snack and others for plantain crisps with chilli and lime, a half chewed bone and a walking stick carved with an unusual symbol. "That's a triquetra, the Celtic symbol of the Goddess," Eloise said. "It also means mind, body, soul, or earth, sea, and sky."

247

A door in Esther's mind opened a crack and a memory popped out. "There was a woman at playgroup who used to go on and on about how we were ruining the planet, how the farmers used too many chemicals which were poisoning the food. But when she moved and had a jungle for a garden, the first thing she did was douse it in weed killer."

Eloise said, "People think that their little bit of pollution won't matter, but it all counts. One of the major problems we have is that women are made to feel unhappy with their appearance, and think they have to use all sorts of products to improve themselves. Manufacturers play on their insecurity and their desire to look younger than they are, and so we use up the earth's resources on make-up and end up with mountains of bottles that take a lot more energy to recycle. I despair at the legacy we are leaving our children."

Esther froze at the mention of children. Seb had been right, she did have a child, a baby she had loved her baby so much from the moment she had seen her, even though her conception had been so violent.

Esther wrung her hands and said, "I've got to remember. I need to find my little girl." How could she have forgotten her, although perhaps that had kept her safe. If she had remembered, maybe Seb would have forced it out of her.

Memories were crowding in, terrible memories. A cruel husband who used to complain that she spent too much time looking after the baby and not enough looking after him. There was that time that her baby was ill with mumps and had woken up crying in pain an hour after going to bed. Her husband had held her down, preventing her going to her daughter, saying, "She's got to learn."

Then there was the time her father threw her across the room when she drove her little car into the skirting board and dented it.

He had been like a jealous child. What was her name? Abbey? Amber? No, Abigail. That was it. Abigail.

***

Seb was thinking hard. Angela had been standing at the lights with two girls he'd never seen before. When she ran off, they did not follow her, but a man had come from nowhere and sprinted after her. Maybe this was the man she had been chasing after, Tom. Rolf would know more.

Seb thought Rolf was not going to answer his phone, but eventually he came on the line. "Seb, what do you want?" Seb had never heard him sound so bad tempered, but that didn't bother him.

"I wanted to ask you about this man Tom. Do you know what he looks like?"

"You want me to help you," Rolf said, "When you've gone off with my car?"

"I need your help, mate. I can't do this on my own. I didn't mean what I said. I'd bring your car back now, but it's at Bristol. I had to get on a train. I'm at Westbury."

"Did you find Angela or the child?"

"Not yet. She saw me and ran off. Why don't you come here and get the keys, then we can go and pick your car up," Seb said.

"Why don't *you* get a train back to Bristol, pick up my car and drive it here," Rolf said.

"I can't. I'm being watched."

All the more reason not to help, Rolf thought.

He turned the phone off, fuming inside. As soon as he had his car back, he wanted nothing further to do with the man.

Seb had left the car on a metre in the centre of Bristol, parking near the harbour and setting off on foot. When he had seen the exorbitant prices for parking, he had bought a ticket for an hour only. He wasn't bothered if he overran the time, it would be Rolf who got the ticket.

An hour later after he had parked, a traffic warden was watching the Skoda. There was one minute left on the ticket. It looked as if he would be able to notch up another one towards his target. As soon as the time expired, he wrote out a notice.

As he finished filling out the details on the handheld device, it connected to the police system and an alert appeared that this was the car had been reported stolen and was also the car that the Metropolitan Police in London as well as the Somerset Police were looking for in connection with various crimes.

***

As Rolf finished talking to Seb, the doorbell rang. A uniformed policemen stood on the step.

"PC Booth," he said. "I have news of the car that you reported stolen."

"That I reported?" He had made the call anonymously.

"We tracked the position of your phone to here," PC Booth said. Too late, Rolf realised his mistake.

Rolf showed him in to the dining room, which at that moment looked as if it served as a laundry. Wet clothes hung from the airer to dry and an ironing board stood to attention in the corner. Rolf moved aside a pile of clean, dry clothes from one of the chairs and motioned to the policeman to sit down.

"I just want to ask you a few questions," the policeman said. "First of all, what is your name, sir?"

Rolf figured they probably already knew. There was no point in try to make something up. "Rudolf Przybyszewski. Rolf for short."

"Can you spell that please, sir." When the policeman had written down the name, he went on, "A farmer has given a statement that someone matching your description drove into his yard asking about a girl they were trying to find, a girl called Esther or Angela. That car matches the description of *your* car."

Rolf kept quiet. If the farmer had remembered the registration number of his car, he would be already under arrest.

The policeman also knew that it was this car that had been used to drive Jonathan Whicher to the nature reserve, but knew that if he revealed that fact, he would get no useful information out of the Pole. The Met had said that the top priority was to find Esther/Angela.

"I don't know anything about a girl called Esther or Angela," Rolf said.

"Do you know a man called Malcolm Dayton?" the policeman asked, watching Rolf's face closely.

Rolf shook his head. He had never heard the name.

"You were travelling with another man. Who was he?"

Rolf realised that he was in trouble. Deep trouble. Seb had been clever. He had been set up. It was time the police knew who was behind it all. "Sebastian Connors," he said.

The policeman made a note. "Connors, sir?"

251

Rolf nodded.

"We are investigating a very serious matter," the policeman said. "I suggest you tell us everything you know."

Rolf stared at the policeman, wondering if the old man died in the bird hide and he was going to be arrested for murder. He knew they should have rung for an ambulance.

"Is Mr Whicher all right?" he asked.

"What do you know about that?" the policeman said.

"Seb told me his wife leave him and would not let him see his little girl. Jonathan try to find her."

Rolf's sister popped her head round the door and asked, "Shall I make some tea?"

She saw from her brother's expression that he was in trouble. PC Booth was saying, "If you know anything, I advise you to tell me now."

"Seb took my car," Rolf said. "I report it stolen because he would not give it back. So, it is the truth, he took it without my permission."

"Did you kidnap a woman called Esther or Angela?"

"I work for Seb," he began. "He is builder, he give me work and a place to live. One day he say to me his wife Angela has left him for another man. He want to find her because she won't let him see his child." He stopped and the policeman waited.

"You must tell him everything you know," his sister said. "If you cooperate – "

"He trace her to an address and he ask me to bring him to her."

"Where is Angela now?"

"I do not know. Seb told her she could go. She say she wants to go to Bristol to find some treasure."

"And Seb. Where is he?"

Rolf realised that Seb had thought everything through thoroughly from the start. It had been him, Rolf, who went to the private investigator. It had been his, Rolf's, car that they had driven, it was him, Rolf, who had kidnapped Esther. Sebastian had kept out of the way, telling him that it was necessary, because if Esther saw him, she would go somewhere they would never find her.

Rolf had believed him, but he now saw that the truth was that Seb had made sure he was not implicated in any way. Any evidence was going to be in his, Rolf's name. The only thing he could do was to cooperate with the police and hope they believed him when he said it had not been his idea. There had even been that time when Seb had borrowed his car for an hour every day for a week. Whatever Seb had been doing, Rolf was going to get the blame.

"He is at Westbury station," he said. "He asks me to meet him there. You must hurry. When I do not come, perhaps he will leave there."

Rolf's phone rang.

"How long are you going to be?" Seb asked irritably.

"Oh, not too long now," Rolf said, trying to sound casual.

"Where are you?"

"Not too sure, but I'm on my way, maybe I will be there in ten minutes."

"OK, I'll be in the café. Ring me when you get here."

Rolf passed the information on to the waiting policeman.

Seb got himself a coffee and sat staring moodily at the trains coming and going. It was a pretty non-descript station and the coffee was expensive. He hardly glanced at a tall, bald man who entered the station and peered at the destination board. He had planned things out well and didn't intend getting caught now. When Rolf got here, they would go to Bristol, pick up the car and follow up the trail from where Angela had thrown the telephone out of the train window. He had found her once, he could find her again.

Adam was buying a ticket when he saw two policemen go into the café and approach the man he'd seen outside who looked as if he was spoiling for a fight. He saw Seb stand up and rush out. The policemen made a grab for him and missed. The man was running towards him and Adam saw a chance to cut him off.

"Get out of the way," Seb shouted. Adam went towards him and, timing his move to perfection, put out his foot and tripped him up. Seb stumbled and regained his balance, but Adam had bought enough time to allow the policemen to catch up with him, push him to the ground and handcuff his hands behind his back.

CHAPTER 31

Eloise, Tom and Esther arrived at the retreat, a large, rambling house surrounded by ancient woodland. As they entered through the iron gates which swung shut behind them, Esther felt all the tension go out of her. She felt instinctively that she was safe here. The solid brick wall surrounding the property was at least eight feet high, but it was not that so much as the air of tranquillity about the place, as if nothing could disturb its peace. Before they got to the house, hidden from view around a bend in the drive, there was the view to enjoy through the trees of a large lake on one side and an extensive wood on the other.

"There are some cabins in the woods," Eloise said. "I've asked if you could have one of those. It will be more peaceful. Is that all right?"

"Yes, thank you, but aren't you and Adam staying here too?" She was now convinced that Eloise was the only person who could help her find Estrila and her lost memories.

"Yes, we'll be in the main house, not far away. You'll find it very peaceful in the cabin. There are no radios or TVs and we hand our phones in at reception."

"I haven't got mine any more. Seb was using it to follow wherever I went. I threw it out of the train window."

Eloise smiled. "Good for you."

They parked and entered the building. The reception area was attractively decorated with blue floor tiles and blue curtains, with a wooden staircase rising to the upper floor. They signed in, collected their keys and made their way to their rooms. Esther and Tom's cabin was reached by a bark path which wound through the woods.

Neither of them had a suitcase. Esther had dashed out of the house quickly, with no time to pack anything. She had only what she had already put in the boot of the car and what she had bought in Westbury. Tom had gone to Bristol that morning, expecting to return home the same day.

They walked slowly, shoulders touching, enjoying the silence. The cabin was spacious inside, with two en-suite bedrooms and a lounge with a small kitchen area in one corner which contained a kettle, a refrigerator and microwave oven. Esther took the bedroom at the back with its view of a large Yew tree with gnarled bark which, she felt, would stand guard and make sure no harm came to her. Tom's bedroom was at the front, with a view of the house and the lake through the trees.

Esther tipped her clothes out of her carrier bag. She could not remember when she had last worn her own clothes or even where they were, another reminder that she had forgotten everything. She picked up one of the fluffy towels and called out to Tom that she was going to have a shower. It felt wonderful to wash off all the grime and dirt of the last few days, as if she was washing off all the bad things that had happened to her: the house with Ray, the kidnap, meeting Seb. I must remember, I must know what happened to me, she thought, but the anxiety was not there, just a certainly that the peace of this place would help her get her memory back.

When she emerged, clean, in her new cropped jeans and cerise T-shirt which hugged her figure, Tom looked at her approvingly. They had grown close over the past few days, but he was not about to complicate her life by making a move on her. She wasn't ready for that. "It's nearly dinner time, we'd better go over to the main building. We can explore later," he said.

As they walked back along the bark path, their hands touched, fingers reaching out to each other.

"Esther," Tom said, his voice husky. "You know how I feel about you, but it wouldn't be fair – you need to remember who you are first."

Esther knew it was true. When her memory came back, everything might change. She wouldn't be the same person, but someone with a past, a history, someone with likes and dislikes, hopes and ambitions, all informing her choices. She squeezed his hand and he held on to it. It felt good.

Dinner was served in a large room with slate floor tiles and two long, oak tables and wooden chairs and a wood burning stove to heat the place in winter. Eloise had saved seats for them all. There were ten or so other guests, artists on the watercolour course.

The food was laid out buffet style on a side table: steaming baked potatoes stuffed with cheese, sweetcorn and peppers; tomato, basil and parmesan quiche, wild mushroom tarts, various dips and salads. Esther suddenly felt ravenous. She had never been very hungry at the house, Ray's cooking had not appealed to her, but here was a delicious vegetarian supper. She filled her plate and sat down.

"You look so much better already," Eloise said, "more relaxed. "How is the cabin?"

"Nice," was all Esther could manage between mouthfuls. "Peaceful."

The receptionist, who it later transpired was one of the owners of the retreat, came in and spoke to Eloise. "I've just had a phone call from Adam. He says, can you collect him from the station?"

Eloise drank up her glass of carrot juice and stood up. "I'll see you in about half an hour," she said. "Enjoy your meal."

When they had finished eating, Tom and Esther wandered towards the lake.

"Adam and Eloise won't know where to find us," Esther said.

"They'll find us," Tom said firmly.

Nature was settling down for the night. A few ducks glided sedately across the pond and a flock of Canada geese in V-shaped formation flew in, skidding to a halt on the water. There was still some light in the sky as the bats began to fly, catching insects in the air. Tom put his arm around Esther and she laid her head on his shoulders.

They lost track of the time and did not know how long they had been sitting there when Adam and Eloise came up behind them. "I knew you'd be here," Adam said. "It's the best view in the whole place." The sun was just above the horizon, the sky streaked with red and purple in a cloudless sky. "I've got what you were looking for."

"Really?" said Esther, jumping up. "I didn't think it was possible. Was it true about the treasure then?" After seeing Seb, she had begun to wonder if, after all, she had made everything up.

"Yes, it wasn't difficult. You gave me the date. I started looking at the papers from the day after. They didn't have those ones on the computer, they gave me the actual newspapers. There were no pictures in those days, just columns and columns of print. I kept searching, and a week after the dig, I found a small report at the bottom of a column. It mentioned several items, including a valuable cup."

"That's it," cried Esther joyfully. "Did it say where the dig was? Were there any details? Was it in the hillside like Estrila said?"

"They've been looking in the wrong place. The treasure was found in the Abbey cloister, not on the Tor. The article described a number of items that were dug up, as well as a silver cup with gold lining, believed to be a Druid ceremonial bowl."

"Oh, no wonder they didn't find it, they've been excavating the hill. They didn't find the thief either. I suppose he must have got out of the tunnels. They thought he'd been buried alive, because of the rock fall, but he must have escaped and buried the treasure in the Abbey."

"It's thought there are hundreds of tunnels under the Tor. He was probably familiar with them. You could easily get lost if you didn't know them and never find your way out."

Esther clapped her hands in delight. "Oh, I must go back and see Estrila and tell her. She will be so pleased. When she has found it, she will be able to escape with Ranuulf. Oh, but how am I going to get back there? How can I see her again?"

Eloise had been quietly enjoying the sunset, listening to the conversation that buzzed between the others. Now she spoke. "I can help you," she said.

"Really? How? I never knew how it was done, there was just a voice in my ear."

"There's a very simple technique," said Eloise. She stood up. "We can go now if you want. One of the treatment rooms is free this evening, I checked. I thought you would want to find Estrila as soon as Adam got back. We can use that."

As they made their way back to the house, bats flying low over the lake, Tom asked, "Where is the cup now?"

"The newspaper article mentions that the find was taken to the British Museum."

"I shall go and have a look as soon as I get back to London," Adam said. "See if I can find it."

They parted as they came into the house. Tom and Adam went off towards the music that was coming from a room further along the corridor.

Esther followed Eloise along a number of corridors until she wasn't quite sure where she was. From time to time, she caught glimpses of the garden. It was almost dark and the moon shone half full in the sky.

She expected a room like the one in Pilbury, a dark room furnished with the couch and nothing else. This one held a couch too, but the room was bigger and much brighter. The last of the sun shone through the window at an angle and an oil burner was lit, filling the room with the smell of sandalwood and bergamot.

Esther lay on the couch facing the window. The trees were now silhouettes in the purple sky, sentinels guarding every living creature as they slept. As she listened to Eloise's calm voice, she felt herself drifting through the window. The sky was purple with storm clouds. The retreat buildings had lost their modern extension, the cars had gone, and it had returned to being an old Manor House with the village nearby. The water wheel was there and the blacksmith's forge, silent now.

Esther saw a man's figure on a path that skirted the manor house. He was climbing to a high position, away from the village where there was a tree with a hollow trunk where he could wait. As it grew dark, he left the shelter of the tree and climbed cautiously down to the village looking for food. Esther watched as he stole apples from the orchard and searched the pig pens for leftovers.

She saw Estrila leave the Manor House, the richly embroidered cloth of her dress shimmering in the last rays of the sun. She walked slowly. Her once golden hair had turned grey with the years.

The man hesitated, then drew near, calling out "Good evening, good mistress." At the sound of his voice, she looked up.

Seeing the dirty cloak and worn leather shoes, she pulled herself up. "Who are you?" she asked. "What are you doing here? This land belongs to Lord Goran's son." He said nothing and she asked again. "Who are you

He stared at her. "You know who I am, Estrila", he said quietly.

She started at the sound of her name. He fixed his gaze on a buzzard plummeting to earth while she searched his features, looking beyond the lank curls and weather beaten face for something she recognised. Those eyes – yes, surely it could not be him? Not after all this time. She looked again. "Is it you Ranuulf, is it really you?"

"Yes, it is I."

From her position on the hill, Esther saw the indecision in Estrila's eyes. She longed to run to him, to encircle him in her arms, but she remained a dignified distance from him, as the Lady of the Manor must.

"Ranuulf, what happened to you?"

He remained silent, then finally said, "You know, my lady."

A blush rose to her cheeks. She looked back at the Manor House below, in shadow now.

"The day of the hunt," she said. "I saw you riding away on the black stallion. That is the last I saw of you. I knew that Goran had sent you to your death. I do not know who betrayed us."

"We were so careful," Ranuulf said. "We had our secret place, well away from the herdsmen tending their pigs. I don't know how he found out."

"We were so careful," Estrila repeated. "Nobody saw us enter or leave the wood together, but someone betrayed us."

"I received a message on the day of the hunt that I was to ride out to a place far from here, to tend to a sick peasant," Ranuulf said. "I thought it strange that Goran should be so concerned about this man. He did not usually require me to treat peasants. When I went to the manor house to fetch my mount, I was told that it had been injured and I was to ride the black stallion instead. I did not want to, but I had no choice."

Estrila took up the story. "When the Master returned from the hunt, leading the riderless stallion, he told me that you were thrown from the horse and were dead. I believed them. I watched the funeral procession bringing you to church and after the service, they buried you."

"I lost control of the horse and was thrown, but I was not killed," Ranuulf said. "Goran had sent one of the men to follow me. He watched me as I fell and when I tried to get up, he attacked me. He tried to kill me but I escaped and went to the house of the peasant who lives in the wood. He hid me, fed me and sheltered me. He told everyone that I was dead. When it was dark, I left the village and fled abroad where nobody knew me."

Estrila could hear the voice of Lord Goran mocking her, as it had done for twenty years. *It's your fault he's dead,* he had said. *You thought I didn't know. He died because of you.* For years he had taunted her and she had known no peace from the terrible burden of guilt.

"But your funeral?"

"Not mine, my lady. A poor peasant was given a funeral far above his station."

Ranuulf's eyes darkened as he opened his cloak and tunic, revealing an angry red scar from his chest to his navel. Estrila trembled violently at the sight of it. "Can you forgive me?" she asked, her eyes pleading for absolution.

He saw the pain in her eyes. It was his pain too, but when he spoke, he did so with a calm voice. "I heard Goran was dead," he said.

"Yes, Goran is dead". Her voice was a hoarse whisper. "They are all dead".

Ranuulf remembered how Goran's man had mocked him, saying, 'She could have saved you, but she wants you dead too.' He had waited twenty years to find out the truth.

"Can you ever forgive me?" Estrila said.

"There is nothing to forgive. You were young and afraid," he said, taking her arm and helping her up from the fallen log.

His hand trembled. He was safe at last. He took a deep breath and asked the question he had been waiting to ask. "You have married again?"

"When Lord Goran died, I did not remarry. I live here with my son, Eluard."

A smile flickered over Ranuulf's mouth at knowing she was free. "Should I fear Eluard too?"

"No, he will not harm you when he knows who you are."

Ranuulf did not need to ask. Her eyes told him the truth. She took his arm and they turned back to the stables. It was time for Eluard to meet his father.

The scene faded slowly until there was only Estrila standing on the hillside. She turned to Esther.

"Lady Esther, I am glad you have come. It has been a long time."

"I have come to give you the information you wanted. I have discovered where the treasure is buried."

"Ah yes, the treasure, the druid's cup. It was all so long ago. Goran is dead now and as you see, Ranuulf has returned from the dead. I have no need to flee to France anymore. Where was the treasure buried, my lady?"

"Under the cloister of the Abbey at Pilbury."

"That is a place nobody has looked before," Estrila said. "We believed it was hidden in the Tor."

As Esther watched, Estrila's image began to fade. "Thank you, lady Esther, for all you have done for me," Estrila said. "One day we will meet again, many years hence and I will repay your kindness."

"Don't go," said Esther, the wind of desolation passing over her.

"I must, my lady," Estrila said. "It is time." Esther took one last, long look at the fading image and then it was gone, leaving Esther with a deep sense of loss.

She heard a familiar voice. "Esther, you are back in the 21st century. Open your eyes when you are ready."

The voice counted downwards from ten. Esther was sad that it is time to say goodbye to Estrila, but happy at the thought of the life that was to come. She slowly opened her eyes, blinking a few times at the sight of the twenty-first century. It was almost dark now. Eloise's long hair looked golden in the fading sunlight and her blue eyes had deepened to violet.

"Estrila?" Esther said.

"It is Eloise. Do you remember where you are?"

Suddenly, a dam burst in her mind and memories flooded in to consciousness, jostling for position. Loud, desperate sobs filled the room and Esther realised they were coming from her. She rocked to and fro as the full horror of her past came to her. Like a film fast forwarding, images flashed in front of her eyes, her life story, all the pain and horror of it.

As she watched, a small figure began to emerge, a little girl. As she came nearer, she held up her arms. "Mummy," she said.

Abigail. Her baby. She remembered it all now. "Abigail, stay where you are, Mummy's coming to get you," she said.

CHAPTER 32

Archie was sitting on a train going to Bristol. That morning, the DI had told him that Malcolm Dayton, otherwise known as Seb had been arrested, along with Rolf. Rolf had told them everything he knew, but there was much that was still unanswered.

Archie was looking forward to meeting the elusive Pole. He could not rest on his laurels, though. There was still Esther/Angela and the child to find and so far, he did not have a clue where they were.

When he reached Bristol, a police car was waiting to take him to the station. He asked to see Rolf first. He looked a sorry sight when they brought him in to the interview room. He had bags under his eyes and it looked as if he had been crying.

Rolf was very anxious that he should know he had been working for Seb; that Seb had told him he needed to help look for his wife, who had gone off with another man. Rolf told his tale with tears in his eyes. "Don't send me back, please. I have family that needs me. I was made a fool by Seb."

"Why did you kidnap Angela?" Archie asked, unmoved, as ever, by displays of emotion in the criminal.

"Seb asked me to," he said.

"You didn't think it was wrong?"

Rolf paused. "Not at first. Seb tells me she left him and took the child and would not let him see his daughter. I have child, I would be upset too if my wife did not let me see her. But when Angela was at the house, there was something wrong. She said she could remember nothing and I believe her. I want to go back to London but Seb have my car. My tools are in the back, I cannot work if I do not have my tools."

Rolf took a sip of water from the glass in front of him. "I try to be kind to her," Rolf said. "When Seb let her go – my sister is coming back from holiday in Poland, Seb could not stay in the house – he ask me to follow her but I refuse. Then he took my car."

"Is that when you reported it stolen?"

"Yes. I just want my car back so that I can go back to London."

"What do you know about the murder of Fergus Cormac?"

"I do not know this name. I know nothing. I have never heard of this man before."

"Did Seb ever mention him?"

"No, sir, I never heard him speak of this man. Seb is a bad man, yes?" Rolf said.

Archie did not reply, but he had to agree.

Sebastian Connors, otherwise known as Malcolm Dayton, sat in the interview room, his arms folded. He had refused the offer of a solicitor, saying, "I haven't done anything wrong". In the flesh, Archie could see just how attractive he would be to women with his brooding dark looks, but he didn't impress Archie.

He started with a question he did not think Dayton would be expecting, to knock him off balance.

"How old were you when you married Angela?"

Dayton stared at him and said, "What's that got to do with anything?"

"I have a copy of your marriage certificate here," he said, producing a piece of paper from the file. You were thirty eight and Angela was sixteen."

Seb leaned forward. "So? It's not illegal, is it?"

"You like your women young, do you? Where is your daughter, Mr Dayton?"

Seb sneered. "I don't know what you're implying but the answer to your question is, I don't know. Why do you think I was chasing Angela all over Somerset? I was trying to find out."

"Did you find her?"

"No." Archie was inclined to believe him. If it was true, it would be a weight off his mind.

"Tell me about Rolf."

"Rolf?" Seb said, playing for time, wondering how much the detective knew. "He works for me."

"Have you ever driven his car?" Seb thought quickly. He had left the car at a meter in Bristol. The police had probably towed it away by now and were dusting it for fingerprints.

"I used to drive his car sometimes when we were going on a job together."

"Can you explain why Rolf reported his car stolen by you?"

Seb was silent for a while. So Rolf had turned traitor. He would never work in this country again. "Rolf is lying to save his skin," he said at last.

"Why did you go to Rolf's sister's house?"

His fingerprints would be all over there too. "Rolf was looking after the house for a few days and he invited me to stay."

"Did you see your wife at the house?"

268

Seb fell silent again. He wondered whether they had Angela. She would tell a load of lies, of course, to make sure he never saw his child again – like the way she'd changed her name, to avoid being found. He wouldn't be surprised if she and Rolf had decided to stitch him up together. Her prints would be all over the house, so he decided to admit to seeing her there.

"Yes," he said. "I asked Rolf to collect her from an address and bring me there. He told me she came willingly."

Archie tried a different line of questioning. The cup that Seb had given to his neighbour to look after contained a single hair from Fergus Cormac's head sticking to the bottom. Once forensics got to work, they confirmed that Fergus had been hit over the head with the cup, although it had not been the blow had killed him, but the kicking that ruptured his spleen.

"You gave your neighbour a valuable silver and gold cup to look after. Where did you get it?"

Seb had his answer ready. "Angela gave it to me."

"Where did she get it from?"

"I don't know."

"When did she give it to you?"

"A few weeks before she disappeared."

"How do you know Fergus Cormac?"

Seb frowned. He didn't know that name, but the detective presumably had information to connect him to the man. He said cautiously, "I've not heard of him. I don't know him."

"We have matched your fingerprints with some found inside his house."

"I still don't know what you're talking about."

"He lives at 41 Primrose Hill Avenue. What were you doing there?"

Seb knew who he meant now. "I didn't know the name of the guy who lived there. Angela asked me to pick her up from there a few weeks before she disappeared."

"What was she doing there?"

"She was his cleaner." Archie wondered whether that could be true. It was a trick criminals had, to scatter some truth among the lies to try to outwit the detectives. If she was a cleaner, maybe she worked for a cleaning company who might know something about her whereabouts. It was a long shot, but he made a note anyway to investigate that possibility.

"Why were you searching for Angela Connors when your name is Dayton?"

"That's the surname of the man she went off with, her lover. I assumed she was using his name."

"Did you keep the note from Angela saying that she had left with another man?"

"I threw it away. Why would I keep it?"

Archie paused to look through the file. While he was thinking of his next question, a constable entered the room and passed a note to him. He suspended the interview, told the constable to stay in the room and hurried outside to the front desk. "She's on the phone?" he asked.

"No, she's in the interview room."

Archie hurried along the corridor. Someone calling herself Esther was here. He opened the door to the interview room and saw that it was unmistakably her. Her face was carefully made up, her hair brushed so that it shone and she was smiling, relaxed, a very different woman from the one who had been photographed in the hospital.

270

In any case, he had expected a nervous, scared woman but that was not the case. She had come a man who he guessed would turn out to be Tom.

Archie felt relieved that she was safe, but he must not allow his emotions to cloud his judgement. He could be looking at the murderer.

"We've been looking for you," Archie said. "We were concerned for you when you disappeared from the house."

"I've remembered everything now," Esther said, "with the help of Eloise. I thought my name was Esther, but it's not, it's Angela, Angela Connors."

That cleared up one matter at least. Archie said, "I'm in the middle of an interview, but the desk sergeant will make you a cup of tea. I'll be with you as soon as I can."

It was late when Archie finished interviewing Dayton. He'd denied having anything to do with Esther's kidnap, the cup or the murder, and they had no evidence to prove otherwise. Rolf's statement implicated Dayton. His evidence implicated Rolf. Esther's statement would, hopefully, clarify everything. It was too late to interview her now, it would have to wait until morning.

Esther (he continued to think of her as Esther instead of Angela) looked disappointed and asked if she could come first thing as they were setting off for London the next day to see her little girl.

"You know where your daughter is?" he said.

"Yes, I've remembered everything."

That was a weight off Archie's mind. As long as the girl was safe. "I'll see you tomorrow then."

Angela felt deflated. They had hoped to make a statement that evening and set off for London straight away so they could avoid the worst of the traffic. "The traffic can

271

be heavy in the daytime," Adam had said, "especially the single lane traffic over Salisbury Plain. I've known it take up to four hours to get to London from there during summer."

"I really wanted to see Abigail tonight," Angela said, "but I suppose she would be in bed by the time we got back. I can't wait to see her again."

She and Tom returned to the retreat and followed the sound of music and singing to the communal room.

"I don't really feel like it," Angela said. "I think I'll go to bed."

"I'll come back with you, make sure you're safe," Tom said, looking disappointed.

"I'll be all right," Angela said. "There's nothing that can harm me here. Rolf and Seb are locked up."

Tom hesitated. He had said he would not make her do anything she didn't want to do, but he hated leaving her alone. The last time he'd done that, Rolf had taken her from the garden, even though he'd thought it was impossible.

Angela thought of the way Tom had looked after her from the beginning. He had watched over her, been there to help. It was time to do something for him. She took hold of his arm. "Come on, then, or we'll miss it all," she said, smiling at the sight of Tom's boyish grin.

The communal room was a lovely, light room with high ceilings and windows along one wall which looked out onto the garden. Some of the art group were stretched out on the floor on large cushions and others had made themselves comfortable on the soft chairs. A lady in a long skirt, a colourful silk scarf at her neck, was singing Scarborough Fair while a man in black jeans and a black baseball cap played the guitar. He reminded Angela of the man she had seen in Pilbury. It seemed a very long time ago. She had been so scared then, not knowing what had happened to her and why she was in Somerset.

The rest of the group were humming or singing along and someone in the corner was playing an Irish drum or bodhran. It reminded Angela of the folk club she had gone to with the girls.

Love imposes impossible tasks
Parsley, sage, rosemary and thyme
Though not more than any heart asks
And I must know she's a true love of mine

"One more impossible task," said Angela, "and then I can go home."

CHAPTER 33

The next day, Archie arrived at the station early to find Angela and Tom sitting on the steps waiting for him. He took them into the interview room, ordered three coffees and began.

"Has your memory returned?" he asked.

Angela nodded. "I can remember everything." She plunged into her story. "I was working as a cleaner."

"Were you working for a company?"

"No, just myself. I started with Fergus, then he recommended me to some other people." At the mention of the name Fergus, she looked sad. "What happened to Fergus? Did he recover?" she asked.

"Just tell me the story in your own way," Archie said.

"When I got to Fergus' house one day, there was a cup on the table, a silver cup lined with gold, engraved with leaves on the side. It was beautiful and I thought it must be very valuable. He told me he'd been sorting out his parents' house – his father recently died - and found this cup. His mother's been in a nursing home for years – she has dementia. Fergus had just begun to clear the house so he could sell it. He wanted me to help him, it was a big job. He had no idea his parents had anything like the cup. He brought it home and he was going to take it to the jewellers to have it valued.

"There was a knock on the door and when Fergus opened it, it was Seb. He burst in, he looked awful, really angry. I don't know how he knew I was there. The only thing I can think of is that he looked at my diary. Yes, that's

274

it, that's how he must have found me. I'd written the address in there so I didn't forget. Anyway, he started accusing me of having an affair. He always was very jealous. Not that he ever had any reason to be. I tried to explain that I was just cleaning the house, but he wouldn't listen, he just got angrier and angrier. He picked up the cup and was going to throw it against the wall. Fergus tried to stop him and there was a fight. In the struggle, I grabbed the cup from Seb and accidentally hit Fergus on the head with it."

Angela had gone very pale. In a tiny voice, she said, "Did I kill him?"

"No, the hit on the head was minor, you did not kill him."

"I didn't mean to hurt him, it just happened in the fight."

Tom put his arm around Angela and said, "It's all right, you haven't done anything wrong."

Archie said, "Go on with the story. What happened next?"

"The cup fell on the floor and I thought it would get crushed, so I picked it up and put it back on the table. That's when Seb started …" She came to a halt.

"It's all right, take your time," Archie said.

Angela turned to Tom. "It was so awful. He punched Fergus. He collapsed on the floor, but Seb kept on kicking him, over and over again."

Tom held her tighter and Archie said, "I know it's difficult."

Tears ran down Angela's face. She drew a clean handkerchief from her pocket and wiped her eyes. "Then he started on me, punching and hitting. I was trying to get

275

out of his way when I tripped and banged my head on the table. What happened to Fergus?" She peered into Archie's eyes and saw the truth. "Oh, he's dead, isn't he?"

"Yes, I'm afraid so," said Archie. "Ruptured spleen."

"It's all my fault."

"How is it your fault?"

"I knew what Seb was like, I shouldn't have gone there, I shouldn't have tried to escape. Seb didn't like anyone coming to the house, he didn't like me having friends. I wasn't allowed a phone – he said he didn't want me wasting my time talking to other people. He said I shouldn't need anyone but him."

Angela put her face in her hands and sobbed. "I was doing the cleaning so I could get a bit of money together and leave him," she said in a broken voice. "I wanted to get Abigail away from him too."

"Would you like some water?" Archie asked. Angela nodded.

"Did he hurt Abigail?"

Angela nodded but said nothing further. She clearly did not want to talk about it at the moment so Archie said instead, "You walked into Accident and Emergency. Do you remember how you got there?"

Angela nodded slowly. "I got up after I fell, but I was dizzy. I felt ill. Seb took me outside and put me in his car." She frowned.

"Take your time," said Archie.

"It can't be right, I can't be remembering correctly."

"What is it?

"We drove somewhere, then I remember getting in another car. I don't know whose it was, it was old and

276

battered. Seb drove me to the hospital. Why would he do that, change cars?"

"I expect he had a reason," Archie said. "It's nothing to worry about."

"You know, don't you? Oh, I see. They have cameras at the hospital. He didn't want the camera to pick up his car." Archie nodded. "I remember being in the hospital. Then I was taken to a large house with a man called Ray. I was kept prisoner there, but I managed to escape."

"You felt you were a prisoner there?" Archie asked. He was very sad to hear that.

Angela nodded. "It was awful."

"I'm sorry about that," Archie said. "We took you there for your own safety. As you were found in the hospital car park just a short time after the murder, we thought there could be a connection, although we had no evidence. We suspected you had important information, perhaps you were the sole witness."

Angela pondered for a while. "He could have killed me easily enough at Fergus' house," she said, "but he didn't. I suppose he loves me in his own, strange way."

Archie had had a lot of dealings with the perpetrators of domestic violence. They had all claimed they loved their wives. He didn't call that love.

"Ray was like Seb – no, not so bad as that, but he had all these rules and used to get angry if I didn't do everything right."

"I'm so sorry," Archie said again. "There were rules to keep you safe, but someone should have explained things to you."

"One day, Ray said I was to be transferred. I didn't want to go back there."

277

"Back where?"

"It wasn't very clear at the time. I just remember pain, terrible pain."

"Perhaps you were remembering the hospital, or what happened with your husband at the house."

"Maybe. I got away and Tom kept me safe, but then I was kidnapped by a man with a foreign accent called Rolf. I knew someone was after me, a man called Jonathan Whicher warned me about it. Tom took me to a house. Seb was there. I didn't know he was my husband at first. He said we had a child, I had left him for another man and refused to let him see his daughter."

"Was it Seb who took you from the garden in Tom's house?"

"No, that was Rolf. He was quite nice to me actually. I don't think he realised what he was getting into when he started."

"We have both men in custody," Archie said.

"You've got Seb? So he won't be able to follow me anymore?" Her smile faded. "When he gets out, he'll kill me.".

Archie said, "I will oppose any bail application that he makes. I am going to make sure he does not get out for a very long time."

Archie paused before he said, "Angela, we have not been able to find where your daughter is. But you said you were going to see her. I assume you know where she is?"

"Yes. I need to get back to her. That day when I went round to Fergus' house – I know now that I left Abigail with a friend."

"Does she still have her?"

Esther frowned. "Oh, I hope so, I do so hope so."

Archie did not want to give Esther false hope, but surely there was only one missing toddler called Abigail. They'd had a lot of cranks claiming that they'd seen the girl, or they were looking after them, but none of the stories had stacked up except this one.

"Angela, a couple of days ago, Crimestoppers got an anonymous phone call from a lady who would not give her name. She said she has Abigail, she's been looking after her all this time, keeping her safe. She claimed that on the day of the murder, you dropped Abigail off at her house in the morning and said you would be back after lunch. When you didn't return, she knew something was wrong, but she couldn't ring you as you don't have a phone. When you were kidnapped, we notified the media and she saw your face on the news. We asked her why she hadn't rung the police before and she said she knew you were afraid of your husband and was trying to get away from him. She thought that if she rang the police, we would give Abigail back to him. Either that or take Abigail away. Her body was still covered in bruises. She said that she still has Abigail."

"Oh, thank goodness," said Angela.

Archie said, "If you tell me where she lives, we'll send a PC round there to make sure everything's all right."

Angela thought. "I don't know her address. I can't remember. But I know how to get there."

"Don't worry. I am sure everything will be fine, but if you need me, here is my number. I shall be returning to London myself later." He handed over his card.

"Have I told you enough?" Esther asked. "I want to go and get Abigail. She must be wondering where her Mummy is. We've got a long journey ahead."

279

"Just one more thing. All the records we found at the house were in the name Malcolm Dayton, and yet you and Rolf call him Seb."

"Yes, that's right. He uses the name Malcolm Dayton for his business records, but his name is really Seb, Sebastian."

"And the name Connors?"

"That's his proper surname. He likes to keep the business separate from the rest of his life, which is why he has two different names. He explained it to me once."

So he could not be contacted by disgruntled customers or the tax man, Archie thought but said nothing. He looked at the clock. "Just one more mystery to clear up. I spoke to your neighbour, Mrs Williams. I showed her a picture and asked if it was Esther, and she agreed it was. Why didn't she tell me I'd got her name wrong?"

"She's very forgetful. I suppose she thought that if you were calling me Esther, that must be my name. I've got a question for you. Who were those four girls in the house? I never understood who they were."

"They were victims of abuse. Leanne was a child when her uncle started abusing her. She was kept a virtual prisoner, but the family all denied it was happening. Then she began refusing to eat. We got her out, but every time she felt unhappy, she would stop eating."

"Oh, is that why Ray let her do what she liked?"

"I expect so, but he should have treated you all the same. Yasmeen was a refugee – all her family had been murdered back home in Syria. She was spared because she is an attractive girl – if you understand my meaning. She suffered badly at the hands of soldiers. Rachel's father wanted to stop her from marrying outside her faith. Her body was covered in cigarette burns, but she refused to implicate her family. She said she'd done it to herself, but we didn't believe her."

"Oh, if only I had known! What about Fiona?"

"Domestic violence."

"Like me. We could have been of comfort to each other if we'd only known."

"We could not betray a confidence. We were hoping you would all talk to each other, but it doesn't sound as if that happened."

"I didn't say much to the girls because I was so confused. I couldn't remember anything, so I had very little to say."

"If there are no more questions, there are some people I want you to meet. I think it will help you come to terms with what's happened to you." Archie stood up and led the way to a small conference room. When Angela saw who was there, she backed away and said, "I don't want to see them."

Archie addressed Tom. "Angela really would benefit by hearing what they have to say."

Tom said, "You know I would never make you do something you don't want to do, but how about if Eloise came in with you too?"

"If I'm going in, I want you all to be there," Esther said.

"They're in the park," Tom said. "We'll have to ring them and ask them to come back."

"Let's have a break for, say, half an hour," Archie suggested, "and we'll resume at eleven o'clock."

"Don't worry," Tom said as he and Angela went out of the police station into the fresh air, "we'll get you home in time to see Abigail today."

They went to a little café near the station for a drink and a few minutes later, were joined by Eloise and Adam. "We'll have to get used to calling Esther Angela," Tom explained. Easier said than done.

Just before eleven o'clock, they returned to the station and waited in reception for Archie. When Eloise and Adam saw him, they looked surprised.

Adam said, "Oh, it's you."

"You've met before?" Angela asked.

Eloise nodded. "I will tell you later."

They sat down in the spare seats at the round conference table looking at the two people waiting to speak to them. Ray was there, and a woman Angela had never met, in her thirties, hair tied back in a bun, dressed in a Jacques Vert suit. Angela instinctively disliked her. The woman shook hands and said, "How are you, Angela?" Angela took her hand back sharply. She knew who she was now.

"You're The Voice," she said.

The woman nodded. "Mrs Underhill," she said.

"We will explain everything," Archie said, taking a seat at the head of the table. As I told you, we took you to a refuge where we could keep you safe until your memory returned. Ray was there to supervise you."

Ray's eyes were still too close together, his eyebrows still thick and wayward and there was still a gap between his front teeth, but he looked worried rather than scary. He had been told by his supervisor at the security company that the job had come to an end and he wasn't certain they were going to give him any more assignments, not after he'd messed this one up.

282

He looked out from under his eyebrows and said to Angela, "I want to apologise if you thought I was being rather heavy handed with you at times or trying to control you. I was just trying to keep you safe."

She looked at him and narrowed her eyes. She didn't believe him. He had made life miserable for her, and he was just worried that his employer, whoever that was, would give him the sack.

"You let the others do things you wouldn't let me do," she said.

"I had to keep you safe. We didn't know what had happened to you, and anyway you might have been the only witness to a brutal murder. We were worried for your safety."

"And you weren't worried about the others?" she said.

Archie put his hand on Ray's arm. "I don't think Angela wants to hear about what happened to Fergus," he said. "It's been a difficult day for her."

"Perhaps I could say a few words," said The Voice. "Angela, when you first came to me, you could remember nothing about the past. The world was a confusing place for you. We have found that putting patients into a hypnotic state will often release the memories that lay hidden. In your case, you were so traumatised by those memories, that your mind presented them to you in the form of a story of medieval times."

Angela shook her head. "No, I met them, Estrila and Ranuulf, it was all real."

"I know it seemed real," said Mrs Underhill. "That is because the *memories* were real. For instance, the way Estrila was treated by Goran told us of the abuse you had suffered at the hands of your husband. And when you spoke of finding a druid's cup, we knew that we needed to find a valuable cup or other valuable item. We were right. We found it at your house."

"That doesn't prove anything," Angela said. "That wasn't The Druid's Cup, was it?"

"No. What I am saying is that your memory of what happened at Fergus' house was so traumatic, you buried it. Your mind had to find another way of telling us what had happened. It worked. DNA evidence proved that Fergus had handled it."

Angela looked at Archie who said, "It's true that the evidence of the cup is crucial in making a case against Mr Dayton, or Connors."

Angela turned to Eloise with tears in her eyes. "It's not true what that woman says. I *was* there, Estrila and Ranuulf were *real*. You know that, don't you?"

Eloise fixed her eyes on Mrs Underhill. "Angela was given a date by Estrila, July 19th 1893, a date when treasure would be dug up."

"Yes, and I went to the newspaper offices and asked to see the papers for that time," Adam said. "I found the report a week later. It was there in black and white. How do you explain that?"

Mrs Underhill turned to Archie and whispered something. "What?" said Adam. "You think I made it up?"

"We are sure you thought you were doing what was best for Angela," The Voice said.

Esther felt cold all over. The Voice had, according to her, manipulated her without her consent. She had never given them permission to hypnotise her. She thought Archie was on her side, but now she saw she was wrong. He probably didn't believe it was real either.

Eloise touched her arm and said in a clear, authoritative voice, "Angela, it doesn't matter what these people think, Adam and I and Tom -". She looked at Tom who nodded. "Know that you are speaking the truth. A particular technique can take you back into another world, another time. We call this Past Life Regression. This is how I helped you on your final trip to see Estrila. *I* did not hypnotise you. I simply helped you to go back to the castle."

Mrs Underhill bridled and said, "I am qualified to practise hypnosis for medical reasons, not some sort of - ." She had been about to say "quack", but thought better of it.

Adam was fiddling with his phone. "Here," he said. "You can't accuse me of lying now." He handed it round. It showed the image of the newspaper with the date clearly shown – July 26, 1893, and at the bottom of the column, the story of the treasure which was dug up from beneath Pilbury Abbey a week earlier.

Ray and The Voice shook their heads, opened their mouths to speak and closed them again. Archie turned to Mrs Underhill and said, "You yourself recorded the date of 1893 when Angela mentioned it in her sessions with you. How do you account for her knowing the date the treasure was found? The evidence of the newspaper is solid. Angela could not have made it up." He looked at Mrs Underhill and Ray with a fixed stare. "You may not understand how this happened, but that does not mean that it is a lie. It merely means that you do not understand."

Angela looked at Archie in awe. How she wished she had come up with that. Mrs Underhill blushed and Ray fiddled with some papers in a file.

Archie spoke to Esther. "I hope you have found this meeting helpful. I thought it would be a good idea for you to meet the face behind the voice and I apologise for Mrs Underhill's remarks."

Mrs Underhill shifted in her chair and pursed her lips.

"It *has* been useful," Angela said, thinking of the way Archie had defended her. She had never had that experience before. She had been with Seb since she was thirteen. He would have told her she was mad, crazy and needed psychiatric help. He had certainly never defended her to other people. She was even ready to forgive Archie or whoever ordered the hypnosis. She had wonderful memories of her time with Estrila.

As they left the police station, Eloise said, "I got a surprise when I saw Archie. We met him at Stonehenge. It was he who opened the ceremony at sunrise."

Angela's mouth fell open. "You mean the Inspector is a Druid? How is that possible?"

"Don't sound so surprised," said Adam, smiling. "You can find Druids in all walks of life. We've been around a long time. In Estrila's time, there were three types of Druid, the bards who sang and wrote poems, the Ovates who studied healing and divination and the Druid priests who were leaders and judges, solving disputes. So you see, working as a Police Detective is completely in step with being a Druid."

"Maybe you'll become a Druid one day, Angela." Eloise said.

Angela smiled. She had been thinking the same thing, ever since she had returned from her last visit to Estrila.

CHAPTER 34

Angela and Tom settled into the back of the estate car as Eloise and Adam took turns with the driving. As they crossed Salisbury Plain, Eloise said, "Maybe you and Tom will come here for the ceremony next year."

Tom looked at Angela quizzically. "What do you think?"

"Oh yes," said Angela. "I would like that."

"Bring Abigail too," Eloise said. "She could sleep under the stars, join in the ceremony. I think she would like it."

"What exactly happens?" Angela asked.

"We have certain rituals – holding hands, drinking from a special chalice."

"The Druid's Cup," Angela said.

"Yes," said Adam. "The same ceremonies have been carried out for thousands of years."

"We honour the God and Goddess and the Spirit of the Land and ask for blessings and healing for the Earth," Eloise went on. "We bring gifts which we leave within the circle – a flower or a poem perhaps. Stonehenge is the most sacred space in this country, a place where we come to meet the divine and be reminded to live our lives with love and respect for all things."

"It sounds wonderful. Didn't you want to go, Tom?" Angela asked.

"I was looking for you," he replied. "That was more important."

Angela leant her head on his shoulder.

They stopped briefly at the Fleet Services for a snack, sitting at a picnic table among the tall pine trees.

"How long have you known your friend – what's her name, by the way?" Eloise asked.

"It's Esther. The one name I remembered." Angela smiled. "More important than my own name – the person who had my Abigail. It's a pity I couldn't remember *why* it was so important, I could have seen her weeks ago."

"Never mind, not long now. How long have you known Esther?"

"Only a few months. We met at playgroup and we got on straight away. Seb didn't like me having people round, but I took Abigail to her place to play with her Ethan. I was terrified Abigail would mention the visit to her father. I told Esther I had better not go round again and I could see she understood the reasons without saying. Other people look at me as if I'm a bad mother when I say Abigail can't go to a birthday party, or I won't go to their place for a coffee. I was too ashamed to tell them the truth, but Esther never asked any questions, just went on being my friend."

"She sounds a very good friend," Eloise said.

"Yes, she kept my Abigail safe all this time and didn't let the Social Services have her. She knew I'd be back."

"Have you rung her?"

"No, I don't know her telephone number. Seb never let me have a phone."

They continued on their journey, making slow progress around the M25. Eventually they drew up outside a large, detached Art Deco style house in Hampstead with its sleek, simple lines and pale green decorative features. Now that the time had arrived, Angela felt nervous. "I'm so worried she won't know me, or she'll be upset with me."

"It will be fine," Tom said, squeezing Angela's hand. "Go and find your little girl."

As she walked up the path, the door opened and Esther stood there with her arms out. She drew Angela to her and they embraced. When they pulled apart, their cheeks were wet with tears. "I am so grateful that you kept Abigail safe," said Angela.

"I knew you'd be back. I told her you were coming, but she got so excited, she wore herself out. She's fallen asleep on the sofa."

Angela followed her into the front room and caught a glimpse of Tom watching from the car. Abigail lay asleep on a chair, looking like an angel in a pink organza dress and a ribbon in her hair. Angela watched her for a moment before she gently touched Abigail's arm. She opened her eyes sleepily. "Mummy!" she was awake in an instant, reaching up with her chubby little arms. Esther swept her up and hugged her to her chest, smelling the sweet smell of baby shampoo. "I will never leave you again," she said.

"Mummy, push me," Abigail said.

"She means on the swing," Esther said. We've got a new swing in the garden."

Angela followed Abigail out into the back garden as Esther said, "I'll go and get your friends. I've got a special tea ready." There were pink marshmallows and tiny fairy cakes and peanut butter sandwiches – all Abigail's favourites, as well as a grown-ups' vegetarian buffet.

It was time to go home. When Angela saw Seb's red Lexus, she thought of the way he had spent money on himself but left her so short of money, she sometimes had to go without meals. She knew what she would do. She was going to sell the car and the house and go and live somewhere Seb would never find her.

As Abigail skipped up the path, Mrs Williams came out of her house.

"You're back then. There was a policeman looking for you," she said.

"I know," said Angela.

Mrs Williams looked at Tom and said, "Where's Seb?"

"You won't be seeing him again."

Mrs Williams stood watching as they waved goodbye to Eloise and Adam as they drove off. Angela reminded herself that she would be seeing them again soon. They had invited her to their Grove's open meeting the following week.

Inside, the house was the same as she remembered it, except that everything was covered in a layer of dust. It felt strange to be home, but Abigail pounced on the toys in the corner, pulling out her favourite doll, Mirabelle. "You're safe now. Mummy's home," Abigail told the doll.

Angela remembered the medieval doll she had bought at the festival, even though she hadn't known why she wanted it. She fished in a bag and drew out the doll. Abigail hugged the two dolls and announced that they were sisters.

Abigail didn't want to go to bed, so Angela put her in her sleep suit and let her fall asleep on the settee. Tom watched over her while she went and looked at her old clothes. Most of them were from charity shops. Seb had always kept her short of money. She had intended to change, but the clothes belonged to another life, another person. She would treat herself to some new ones soon. She saw that Seb's computer was missing. Archie had explained they would return when they were finished with it. She didn't care about that. There was nothing of hers on it. Seb had forbidden her to use it.

She sat in the garden with Tom later, gently rocking on the swing seat, watching the sun go down over the tall buildings of central London in the distance.

"When are you going back to Somerset?" she asked. She didn't want him to go back, but he had given up enough work to help her and she couldn't be selfish.

"I can do my work just as easily up here," Tom said. "There are plenty of opportunities. I could move to London – if you'd like me to."

Angela took his hand in hers and smiled. At that moment, the world turned on its axis, the buildings slipped away, and there were only fields ahead. An older Angela sat in a garden with an older Tom, facing the setting sun. Their two grandchildren played on the grass in front of them, watched by their mother, a grown-up Abigail and their father, a young man whose face Angela was yet to see.

"Yes, I'd like that," said Angela. "I'd like that very much."

SECOND GENESIS

Gerald is frozen in the 20th century and wakes two thousand years later to find himself a prisoner in a strange and violent world. He escapes, only to discover that the outside world is a far more horrific place than he could ever have imagined. He must find a way to work with the strange and distant Hagan, to save the world from the worst environmental disaster the planet has ever known.

FINAL ILLUSION

Gerald and the group of people from the 20th/21st century continue to expand their community but are hampered in their efforts by a small number of visitors from the far distant planet of Thaulus, who bring both the hope of restoring the Earth and the threat of complete devastation. The truth about Hagan's plan is finally revealed, and not even Gerald can stop him.

SAVING GRACE

War changes everything. Grace and Greta are two sisters hoping to get married and start a family. Instead, World War II breaks out and the men are sent to fight, changing the course of the girls' lives in ways they could not have imagined. They must struggle with infidelity, pregnancy and infertility as well as bombs and rationing before the war comes to an end and they can find happiness.

THE PRETZEL AFFAIR

When Petra meets Kurt, she realises he is her true love, her soulmate, but before she can get to know him, he disappears from her life.

Asked to help with the publicity for a local orchestra, she travels to Dusseldorf and is surprised to find that Kurt is organising things in Germany. They grow close, but her hopes are dashed when she discovers he is engaged to the beautiful Anna.

She has known Richard since school. He would make a good husband: they have always been friends and they have a lot in common, but she cannot forget Kurt. Can he ever feel the same way about her?

Printed in Great Britain
by Amazon